# AT WILLOWS EDGE

## A NOVEL BY

## MEREDITH KENNON

This book is a work of fiction. Names, characters, places, and incidents either are products of the author's imagination or are used fictitiously.

Any resemblance to actual events or locales or persons, living or dead, is entirely coincidental.

© Copyright 2010 by Meredith Kennon

All rights reserved, including the right of reproduction in whole or in part in any form.

For additional information regarding the author, including future works,

please visit the author's facebook page and meredithkennon.blogspot.com.

ISBN-10: 1-4414-2197-1

ISBN-13: 978-1-4414-2197-5

*Also by Meredith Kennon:*

*Under the Same Umbrella*

*Tattered Letters*

*Almost Enough*—First of the Greystone Series

This book, *At Willows Edge,* is the second in the series.

Watch for *Return to Greystone* in 2011

## Acknowledgements

I would like to thank those who helped with the writing of this book, among whom included Marian Odland of Kathleen, Georgia; Diane Peterson of Springfield, Illinois; Ruth Wiedrich of Aberdeen, South Dakota; and Katy Williams of Bennington, Nebraska. Their help included proofreading and guidance in achieving historical and cultural accuracy.

I greatly appreciate Henry and Joni Wiedrich of Blair, Nebraska, for their willingness to give legal assistance and their time for creating and maintaining my blog at meredithkennon.blogspot.com and my facebook page. I extend special thanks to my husband, Henry, for his help and support, which was constant and invaluable.

I thank Create Space for their fine standards in publishing and Mark Jenkinson of Margate, United Kingdom, for providing the art for the cover.

*For my husband,*

*Henry,*

*the love of my life*

# AT WILLOWS EDGE

## Chapter One

At the sagging clothesline, pegging out their bed sheets to dry and whiten in the hot afternoon sun, Gilda inhaled the sweet aroma of crushed grass underfoot and sighed contentedly. When the last of the pillow slips waved in the gentle breeze, she stooped to appreciate the fragrant, pink blossoms of her treasured rose bush and gave it a drink from the watering can, conveniently at hand. Alert to her feelings of absolute fulfillment, Gilda sought a place to sit and ponder her good luck and marvel that she had endured her dull and disappointing life, before Thomas had magically entered it.

Finding some protection from the harsh sun in the cluster of willow trees, she plopped down on the lush grass and secured her skirt under her legs. Leaning back on her extended arms, she watched the planes take off, circle around, and come back in again at nearby Lindley Field, a training airfield for the Royal Air Force.

It was the twenty-sixth of August, 1944, and although the seemingly-endless war was not yet over, Gilda's happiness could not be contained. When working at the manor, she now made a concerted effort to act sober and grave when in the company of the many airmen to whom they fed their daily breakfast. The men certainly did not act at all downhearted and were always cheerful and optimistic, but Gilda feared her obvious and continuous bliss gave her the appearance of shallowness. She certainly did not want to appear to be unaware of the tragic situation that existed throughout the war-torn world.

Mrs. Wood and her help, Sam and Dotty Cooper, were alert to her recent pretense of gravity and had teased her for it. Glad that they were aware of her ruse, Gilda could, at least, be her newly-defined, elated self around them.

Sam had said, "Smile on, Gilda. Our greatest weapon in this war has been our determination to press on and be cheerful, in spite of the chaos going on around us."

In reply, Gilda had said, "I can't smile all day long, anyway. I've found that my face actually aches if I don't give it an occasional rest."

Yesterday's news that Paris had been liberated from the Germans had given cause for great rejoicing all over England. To Gilda, it meant that she could wear her smile with abandon, and everyone's morale would soar until something dreadful happened to end the celebrating. This was inevitable in wartime and had proven true in the last five years, but Gilda hoped it might be different this time.

## At Willows Edge

The Allies were pushing the Germans back, and everyone thought that surely the war would end soon.

Gilda loved the hours that she and Thomas spent cleaning their thatched-roof cottage and overgrown garden, as together they strived to make it livable and welcoming. They had married three weeks before and had taken a five-day honeymoon on the coast, where, although they couldn't entirely forget the war, they had done a reasonably fair job of it.

Sitting in the shade, Gilda realized that she had not written in her diary since the day before the wedding, so she ran into the cottage to get it. Situated once again under the dappled canopy of willow trees, for which their cottage was named, she tucked her thick, dark-brown hair behind her ears and began to write.

*August 26, 1944*
*Dear Diary,*

*I am no longer Miss Gilda Morris, but the new Mrs. Thomas Gardner. We are working very hard to clean up our garden and cottage, known locally as Willows Edge. Our official address is Number 4, Gypsy Row, which I think has a certain amount of charm to it, too, but it has been a long-standing tradition in the village to give names to the grandest and humblest of homes. Ours is of the latter group.*

*Gypsy Row is located in the southeastern part of Englewood, just north of Lindley Field, and our cottage is the southernmost one, giving us a fairly unobstructed view in three directions. To the north, the closest cottage can barely be seen through the stand of willow trees and the low hedge which divides us. Our landlord says it is owned by an elderly couple with whom no one seems to be acquainted. Having lived in Englewood for many years, I've known of most of its inhabitants, but there have been some newcomers since the beginning of the war, and I haven't kept up with it. Unless we seek out our considerate neighbours on Gypsy Row, we rarely see them, giving us a situation that is blissfully private.*

*Sitting in our garden on the most beautiful day of the year, I am so deliriously happy, I feel a bit guilty about it. Our wedding, three weeks ago, was perfectly wonderful and our honeymoon magical.*

*I first met Thomas in January, when he arrived at RAF Lindley Airfield, named for nearby Lindley Hall Farm. He was to train pilots, and because he had been recently wounded, he was billeted on the ground floor of Greystone Manor. He needed comfortable accommodations and a little help taking care of himself, at first. I was assigned to be that help, which I reluctantly agreed to, having had no previous nursing experience whatsoever.*

*Mrs. Wood had just arranged for me to be called up as a cook's assistant at the manor. She had been ill and shorthanded, and it had been no small task, considering my physical handicaps, for her to convince her London contact that I could do the job.*

*I had been working there but a few days when Thomas arrived. He was still in pain, intensified by the jolting jeep ride from his home in Surrey. His broken wrist and ankle were the result of an emergency landing on the coast of Suffolk after a failed mission over Berlin. Soon after being released from a London hospital, he had insisted on being transported to his voluntary training assignment long before he really should have been, and that is how we met. Besides meeting his needs as his nurse, I became his secretary for a few blissful weeks, doing all of his writing and obliged to pen his love letters to his then-fiancée, Candace Gates. Before long, he was billeted at the airfield itself, where he conducted training of the new flight crews, and soon after, he went back to flying missions in the war.*

*He has since been wounded again, this time in*

*France, on D-day, and decorated for his valour. He has also been recently promoted to Wing Commander. Thomas's superiors say it is likely he will remain here for the remainder of the war, which is the best news of all, and his dear mother Priscilla agrees with me.*

Gilda paused to listen to the energetic singing of some larks in the tree above her. They had become accustomed to the roar of the airfield and often could be heard heartily competing with it. Smiling, Gilda returned to her writing, in earnest.

She wrote on, *Thomas's mum, Priscilla, who became a widow during the London Blitz, and David, whose wife died before the war, surprised us all by announcing at our wedding that they would be married quietly, while we were honeymooning. We have not seen them since, but we hope to, soon. Her David is Dr. Armstrong, Thomas's orthopedist, who we first met last winter when he came to Greystone to put on Thomas's walking cast. Concerned by my dreadful limp, which was all I'd ever known, it was Thomas and David, who conspired to get me an elevated shoe. Thomas involved his mother in the project, which is how she and the doctor met. They have since provided me with two pairs of wonderful shoes, and I walk as normal as anyone now.*

*At Willows Edge*
*I met Priscilla last spring, and she has since included me in an exciting business venture, Gowns by Gardner, which we will open in London after the war.*

Smiling at the happy words on the page, Gilda was slightly startled when a figure suddenly blocked the sunlight above her. She looked up to see her mother, Agnes Morris, looming there with her two foster children in tow. Lucas Smith, the eldest at fourteen, was grinning from freckle to freckle, and his little sister Matty was smiling, too, while swinging the arm of her foster mother back and forth, wildly. The contrast of Matty's vigorous arm-swinging and Agnes's stern face made Gilda want to laugh, but she refrained. She would wisely save that juxtaposition for her diary.

She exclaimed, "What a pleasure to see you! What brings you my way?" She jumped up from her spot, carefully closing her diary and tucking it under her arm.

"Well," said Agnes, "the children wanted to help you a bit in the garden today. Since I got off a little earlier than usual from the bakery, I decided to come along. Lucas wants to pull some weeds, he says." She turned and scanned the garden critically, a look Gilda remembered well from her childhood.

Lucas explained, "Thomas told me he had more weeds and rubbish than he will ever have time to clear away, so I told him I'd help out."

"Why, thank you, Lucas. All we've done, so far, I'm afraid, is clear this section and plant our rosebush," said Gilda, pointing to the area around the clothesline.

"Will your landlord not help clean it up?" asked Agnes with a frown.

"He hasn't been able to, due to his demanding war work in Nuneaton, and we got reduced rent if we did the cleanup ourselves. Because we liked its location, so convenient to both the airfield and the manor, we would have taken it under any terms. However, we will certainly be glad to get the rubbish cleared out and the weeds under control. Hopefully, we'll accomplish it before the trees start dropping their leaves."

Proudly, Lucas said, "Leave the rubbish to me. I'll get rid of anything that can't be burned and make a pile for burning. I'll use our wagon and get it done in a few days. Simon and I have our garden in fine shape."

"That is very good of you, Lucas. Thomas will be so pleased. Will you remind me to send our leftover whitewash home with you today in return for your kindness? I assume you still wish to paint the cottage sitting room?"

Grinning again, Lucas answered, "Simon certainly does, so I suppose I do, too."

Looking around the unkempt garden, Gilda said, "Thomas and I have had little time to do much of anything out here, and we are still trying to make the inside livable. Come in. I'll show you our progress."

Gilda led the way through the freshly painted front door and deposited her diary and pen on the table in the diminutive foyer. She said, "We know that once winter sets in, we can work inside, exclusively. But, as I'm sure you remember, the house was so dreadful, it could not be procrastinated."

"What's *prochastidated* mean?" asked Matty, who still clung to Agnes's hand.

Lucas answered soberly, "I learnt in school that it means you should be getting at it, but haven't, like your messy bedroom." He looked around the sparsely furnished sitting room, with little more than its large stone fireplace to recommend it, and said, "It looks jolly nice in here, I'd say, Gilda."

He spoke with such sincerity that Gilda almost laughed aloud, but instead, she said, "Thank you, Lucas. We are getting a start in here, but let me show you what we've really been working on. Although the bath took days to clean thoroughly, it still looks horrid, so I won't show you that, but the kitchen is shaping up nicely. It was a nightmare to clean, too, what with so many nooks and crannies, but do come see. It's become quite cheerful."

Agnes eyed her daughter, as she walked gracefully ahead of them into the quasi-primitive kitchen that she was so proud of. Thomas and Gilda had white-washed the plastered interior walls and the stone exterior ones, as well, and in spite of the limited light from two smallish windows, the room was now bright and welcoming.

Lucas and Mattie looked around briefly, but soon lost interest, leaving mother and daughter alone.

A rickety gate-leg table with two mismatched chairs sat against the stone wall under the high, east window. Gilda had covered the table with a lovely cloth of yellow and white check, and on it, for a centerpiece, she had placed a collection of wild flowers in a clear-glass milk pitcher. At the windows were white muslin curtains, which Gilda had made herself, and Agnes noted that the narrow border at their hemline was of the same gingham material as the tablecloth. Gilda knew her mother was noticing the handsome details of her efforts but did not expect her to comment or compliment. That would have been asking too much.

"I see you are using a sewing machine. Did you go out and buy one?" asked Agnes in a tone that triggered alarm bells in Gilda's head.

Knowing her mum was critical of throwing money around, she answered patiently, "No Mum, Mrs. Gardner brought me one of hers when they came up for the wedding."

Not acknowledging Gilda's answer, Agnes asked critically, "Doesn't Thomas have the money to buy a sturdier table?"

Gilda marveled that her mother could be so contradictory. Critical that they may have purchased a sewing machine, her mum was, in the same breath, equally disparaging that they hadn't yet bought a table. She replied, "We are trying to live strictly on our military income right now, Mum. We've had no opportunity to look for furniture, and knowing we'll be going to London after the war, we feel it will be much easier if we have nothing large to take with us."

"I suppose that is a wise course to take," agreed Agnes reluctantly, as she stoically took in the rest of the fresh-smelling kitchen.

A monstrous, black cooker stood against the north

stone wall, taking up most of the space there, and on a nearby shelf, Gilda had organized her pots and pans. On the west wall, the only other window looked out over the front garden, through the rustic gate, and to the field beyond. Below it, sat a low chest of drawers and a single shelf on top of which Gilda had stored their modest supply of food. The drawers held the linens that were every bride's pride and joy and an especially coveted commodity in wartime. From her exquisite stash, Gilda's mother-in-law had given them to the couple.

On an ancient deal dresser, which was positioned against the interior wall adjoining the sitting room was a motley collection of fine china and white stoneware, which Gilda appreciated to the fullest. Seeing her mother eye the contents of the cupboard, Gilda commented, "These are the remnants of generations of chinaware from the manor. We found them in the storeroom one day, and Mrs. Wood said we could have them."

Agnes reached for a tea cup and examined it with care. In a gentle tone, she said, "I'd treat this little beauty with care. It's quite old."

Encouraged by her mother's softened demeanor, Gilda asked eagerly, "Have you seen something similar?"

"My mother had a single cup and saucer with the

same markings, and she claimed that they were ancient," said Agnes wistfully. "She gave them to me years ago. I wonder what became of them."

Taking new courage, Gilda said cheerfully, "Now, that is a story I would very much like to hear in full. Could I make you some tea while you tell me?"

"I've had my tea and should get the children out to the garden. They'll need supervision," answered her mother in her ordinary gruff tone. Realizing that Lucas and Matty had become bored with the details of Gilda's kitchen and were thus wandering around the cottage, Agnes summoned them.

"How are the children doing?" asked Gilda quickly, before they were within earshot.

"In general, English children are an amazing lot, having been sent away from their families and not even seeing them for years on end. But, what with having their mum die so recently and knowing nothing of the whereabouts of their no-good father, these two are top drawer," said Agnes proudly, thrusting forward her large bosom. Gilda's reaction to that was an involuntary jump, which she concealed by waving away an imaginary fly.

Agnes said, "You wouldn't have pests in here if you didn't leave every door and window gaping open all day."

"A few pests are more tolerable than the stale air that was in this cottage, all closed up like it was for two years," answered Gilda defensively. Checking herself, she asked in a more pleasant tone, "It's fresher now, don't you agree?"

The conversation ended quickly when Lucas and Matty joined them. Gilda said, "I wish I had some sweets for the two of you, but I'm afraid we will have to wait until the war is over for such treats."

"The good news from Paris makes me desperate for peacetime," said Agnes wearily.

"What's peacetime like, Aggie?" asked Matty, who had no memory of life before the war.

"I'll tell you all about it when I put you to bed tonight, Poppet," answered Agnes, ruffling the child's strawberry-blonde curls affectionately.

Feelings of pure jealousy overtook Gilda, and fearing the emotion was written all over her face, she turned away.

Agnes hurriedly ushered the children outside to the garden, saying, "Lucas, let's first decide where to deposit all these weeds, once we've finished pulling them."

They quickly determined a good burning spot, and then Agnes and the children chose a particularly overgrown corner of the garden to work on. Agnes patiently taught the children what to pull and what to let be, and Gilda joined them with a trug of ancient gardening tools and the leftover whitewash for them to take home with them.

They worked companionably while Lucas and Matty chattered excitedly about the recent holiday that they had taken to the coast. They had been invited by Lucas's former foster parents, Alvin and Betty Leventhall. The party had gone by train and stayed at a cottage in Cornwall, which had been arranged for them by some old friends of the Leventhalls.

The children had many seaside tales to relate, in spite of the beaches having been cordoned off with entangled barbed wire to protect the coast from invasion. There, they had celebrated Lucas's birthday, and Matty had begun her collection of seashells.

Matty was looking forward to going back to school soon, but Lucas was undecided about going to school at all. He said, "I'm fourteen now, Gilda. I don't have to go to school anymore, unless I want to."

Before Gilda could comment, Agnes proudly asserted that Lucas was a bright lad and would be going to school full-time again this year. Gilda remembered having to leave school at twelve, when at the top of her class, but said nothing.

When they finished, Gilda took off her gloves and put them back into the wooden trug. Then, painstakingly, she folded the crisp sheets from the clothesline with Mattie's dubious help, while Lucas and Agnes put the weeds on the burn pile and put the tools away.

Gilda appreciated the work accomplished by her helpers and thanked them profusely before they trekked for home. She waved them off from her front door and went inside to put the fresh-smelling sheets on their bed in the small room at the back of the cottage. Then, seeing the time and expecting Thomas at any moment, she began preparations for their evening meal.

He arrived on his standard-issue bicycle and entered the cottage with a burst of energy. He eagerly told Gilda about his day and the elevated morale at the airfield since yesterday's news of the liberation of Paris. As he helped her set the table, Thomas noticed that she was more subdued than usual and asked, "Did you have a satisfactory day, darling?"

"Certainly, you know I love being here on my own. I washed our sheets and let the wind iron them for me," she answered, smiling sheepishly.

Remembering that she had ironed hundreds of

aprons for her mother's workplace before coming to work at the manor, Thomas laughed aloud and kissed his lovely bride. "Well, I thought you seemed a bit downhearted."

"Well, this afternoon, Mum brought the children over to work in the garden, and they were very helpful."

"That was very good of them. What happened?" he probed gently.

"Although my mum is probably as nice to me as I've ever hoped her to be, she has so much affection for Matty, I can't help feeling jealous. I know my reaction is childish, but I can't stop myself from asking why she couldn't have found it in herself to love me like that. "

Looking into her beautiful, but troubled, brown eyes, Thomas said gently, "I know, darling. I don't understand it, either."

"Well, I do know why, don't I? I mean, having a daughter with birth defects such as mine was a blow to my parents on top of all my dad's problems from the war." Gilda held up her left hand on which she proudly wore her lovely diamond ring and, for the first time in several weeks, really minded that her hand was missing the thumb and index finger.

Looking down at her shoes, she added, "And now that I have my elevated shoe, thanks to this war, and don't walk around with that dreadful limp anymore, I think my mum sees it as an accusation."

"She should, actually. They failed you, Gilda, but things are getting better. You know your dad doesn't act like her. And, to be completely honest, I think your mum is really trying to understand her own behavior and is a bit jealous of you."

"That is hardly believable," said Gilda, putting their plates of tinned ham on toast on the table.

"She would love to be happy, Gilda, but she can't quite figure it out. We, on the other hand, are very happy and have the absolute privilege of knowing it," said Thomas genuinely, his blue eyes sparkling.

Gilda loved how he always said exactly the right thing, sometimes even gently chastising her, to get her back on the right track.

He took her heart-shaped face in his hands and gave her a passionate kiss, which she heartily reciprocated.

"Let's eat," said Gilda finally. Then, with a playful gleam, she added provocatively, "Before we do anything else."

Thomas laughed aloud, and they sat down together to their wartime fare.

## Chapter Two

Eleanor Wood, the mistress of Greystone Manor, was glad to get off the train. At last she'd arrived in Nuneaton, and could make her way home. She wished, for the first time ever, that the railroad builders had laid the tracks all the way into Englewood, so she could simply walk the quarter mile home. That seemed less tiring and far preferable to going through the exercise of hunting down a hired ride from the bustling station.

Lugging her case and scanning the crowded area for a taxi, she was pleasantly surprised to see an acquaintance eagerly waving at her. Mrs. Adair had spotted Eleanor, and still waving, jumped from her car and called out to offer to take her friend north to the manor.

After carefully making her way across the congested street, Mrs. Wood resisted weakly, saying, "It's terribly out of your way, Camilla."

"It is, just a little, but please allow me to take you home. Ever since I decided to take the car out this afternoon, I've been burdened with patriotic guilt. Giving you a lift home will appease it. My daughter Fiona, could have easily gotten a ride to the station some other way, but I wanted to steal a few more minutes with her."

"Then I accept. It's been a very long day."

Eleanor heaved her bag into the open boot with a considerable effort and got into the comfortable, old Daimler with a sigh of relief. As the sun was beginning to sink into the west, the women made their way through the busy streets towards Greystone Manor, which was four miles north of the Nuneaton.

When asked about her journey, Eleanor explained that she had spent an entire week in Herefordshire with friends. She would have loved to have had the freedom to say that she had spent time with her grandson, Willy, and her son's fiancée, Jane Davies, but that was not a possibility, just yet.

Willy, now nearly two years old, had never met his father, William Wood. In Singapore, he and Jane were to have been married quietly and quickly, soon after she discovered she was pregnant. But, on the fifteenth of February, 1942, Singapore fell to the Japanese, and even a rushed wedding became impossible in the chaos. Jane and her mother escaped with their lives, sent off by William and Mr. Davies, who they had not seen or heard from since.

There still had been no word of Jane's father, but Eleanor had finally received a short missive from her son three months ago. In the one hundred words allotted,

William wrote simply that he was in a POW Camp and had been a prisoner of the Japanese since the Fall of Singapore. Trusting that his fiancée and her mother had returned safely to England, he informed his mother of their engagement. He asked her to let Jane know that he was still alive, and that he would send future letters to her. He did not, however, include the information that Jane had been pregnant when he had put her on the boat.

Upon receiving the news, Eleanor had made a brief visit to Trubury, Herefordshire, and had learned of Willy's existence and Jane's reluctance to contact her, not knowing how she would be received.

Since Jane's mother Ruth had planned to be gone for a week, it had been arranged that Eleanor would go to Trubury, and in her mind, it had been a perfect visit. Little Willy had inherited his mother's coloring and facial features, but after spending wonderful hours with him, Eleanor detected many of his father's mannerisms and expressions. Happy memories of William and Andrew's childhood had flooded back, and Eleanor had exhausted herself both physically and emotionally in the process.

Eleanor thought very highly of Jane and was grateful for the chance to know her better. She was bursting to tell her cook, her gardener, and Gilda all about her visit with her grandson. The three members of her staff and her grown daughter Edith were the only ones privy to the whole story. However, the news that William Wood was still alive had become common knowledge throughout the community.

Realizing that Mrs. Adair was talking to her, Eleanor pulled herself back to the present and conversed companionably on the short drive home. She asked, "Is Fiona on her way back to London, then?"

"Yes, she was eager to go. I think there's a boyfriend. Did you hear that Paris was liberated by the Allies yesterday?"

"Yes, indeed," said Eleanor. "Nothing else was talked of on the train coming home, and I heard it on the wireless myself yesterday."

They drove up to the front of the large house, and as Camilla wanted to get home before dark and the mandatory blackout, Eleanor thanked her and went inside. She was more than grateful that Dotty and Sam had taken her little black terrier, Spanky, home with them to their comfortable accommodations above the carriage house. As much as she'd missed the endearing character, she wasn't up to his demanding affections after her exhausting day.

After dropping her bag in her room, Eleanor went

into the kitchen, hoping that Dotty and Sam had managed all right that day, seeing as Gilda had been off duty all day, too.

Too tired to do anything productive, Eleanor had a sandwich and listened to the wireless situated in the corner of the kitchen. Having unwound sufficiently to sleep, she retired to her bedroom, located across the hall and down a few feet from the door to the kitchen. It had once been her husband's office and was now the only room in the manor that she could truly call her own.

As she performed her ablutions in the small bathroom next to her bedroom, she heard some airmen, her wartime lodgers, coming into the manor. They came and went at all hours, and since the manor never slept, it was rarely locked at night. Eleanor had even become accustomed to the early morning flights that took off in the darkness and returned at first light. She thought about the terminology she'd heard so often in the breakfast lines, such as "circuits and bumps" and flight destinations such as "Prestwick in Ayr" and "Nutts Corner in Belfast." Eleanor smiled at the thought of all the things she had learned and all she had come to accept since the beginning of the war.

To the bathroom mirror, she said, "Wilbur could never have imagined that all of this would come to pass when he first saw this place in 1927."

Greystone Manor was a very old, many-gabled, stone house that, although it had impressive stature and symmetry, was far more forbidding than inviting. Eleanor and her husband, Wilbur, had bought it upon retiring home to England after many years in Singapore.

When he died ten years later, she'd had the brief notion of selling it, but once the war started, Eleanor was happy for her home to become part of the war effort. Like other larger homes in the area, it had provided shelter to the child evacuees from the cities, the homeless of Nuneaton after the bombing raids of 1941, convalescents for a time after that, and finally, airmen stationed at the newly-constructed Lindley Field.

Presently, two of three rotating shifts slept on the upper floors and had their breakfasts at Greystone Manor. The third shift took their turn in the many Nissen huts at the airfield and happily returned to the house a few days later. Once the second breakfast was served at two o'clock each afternoon, Eleanor and her small staff were done for the day and could prepare for the next.

Except for the kitchen, and Eleanor's bedroom and loo opposite the adjoining hall, the house provided common areas for the airmen, but they rarely used them.

## At Willows Edge

They came and went quietly by the front door, through the manor's great entrance hall, used now as an enormous dining hall. Through the serving area, which was the original dining room, and behind a closed door next to the library, they accessed the upper floors.

The library was for their leisure, as was the large drawing room, but there was a consensus that it was best for Mrs. Wood if they recreated elsewhere. Only during winter storms, when they were literally grounded, did the grateful airmen hover around the roaring fires that Mrs. Wood provided. A massive stone fireplace in the great hall, which was the first thing one saw upon entering the manor, was open to both the serving and eating areas and was the most appreciated feature of the house, except, of course, for the excellent breakfasts served there.

The airmen loved their shifts at the big house, because the cook, Dotty Cooper, made their breakfasts memorable. She added real eggs to the powdered ones and served up other treats, like bottled applesauce. Her husband Sam kept the chickens and gardens, and with the help of Gilda, no other permanent help had been needed at the manor since earlier in the war.

As Eleanor sat at her dressing table that evening, she removed the many hair grips to free her long, gray hair and began to brush it with slow, even strokes. Her exhausted, blue eyes looked back accusingly at her from the looking glass, so she directed her gaze to the framed photographs on her chest of drawers. She paused at the pictures of her three children.

Andrew, the younger of the two sons, had been lost in Singapore, and it had been months before she had known he was missing and even longer to learn he was confirmed dead. Of the three children, he had inherited the most from her, from his light hair and blue eyes to his temperament and interests. Her eyes lingered on her lost son remembering his childhood like it was yesterday.

Looking next at William's picture, she marveled that, after all this time, he was still alive in a Japanese prisoner-of-war camp. His coloring was dark, and he had always looked much like his father and also his sister, Edith. Eleanor studied William's face, comparing it to that of his own young son, and wondered what William would look like when, at last, she saw him again.

The photograph of her daughter, Edith, portrayed her truthfully as the independent creature she had always been. Her straight, dark hair and eyes, inherited from her father, gave her almost a gypsy-like mysteriousness, and an enigma she certainly was. Eleanor wished she knew what plans Edith was making with her American soldier. Part of the Women's Land Army, Edith had written that she had been very busy at Banks Farm—too busy, in fact, to come home for some time. Eleanor wisely recognized that such busyness didn't necessarily mean that her daughter hadn't found the time to meet up with Larry Bradford from Colorado.

After laying a workday frock over a wooden chair, Eleanor wearily climbed into bed and eyed her diary with the notion of writing in it, but instead, determinedly turned off the bedside lamp. There would be time and energy enough tomorrow to record the thoughts of her heart.

❧❧❧❧

The following morning was a reunion of sorts when Spanky came in with Dotty to discover that his mistress had come home. There was so much barking and carrying on that Sam finally removed Spanky from the house altogether.

That evening, after listening to the news on the wireless in her kitchen sitting corner, as she called it, Eleanor went to bed early to write in her journal. She wrote, *My trip to Trubury was lovely, not only for the chance to get to know Willy better, but also to get closer to*

*Jane. She is a quiet girl, and I'm afraid that even my reserved personality overwhelms her, at times. She still fears that I hold some resentment for her not sharing Willy's existence with me earlier, but I really don't, and I've tried to assure her of that.*

*The first night I was there, an animated Jane let me help her tuck Willy in his bed. However, when we went downstairs to the sitting room, without Willy in our midst, Jane became quite shy, much like the day of our very first meeting. She was nervous, it turned out, because she had taken a step toward contacting William without telling me. She told me that she had written the short letter at the very moment she had learnt from the Red Cross that they would accept a few words (twenty-five, she said) and try to get them delivered to William. She was embarrassed that she had claimed to be his wife and next of kin. I assured her that I was thrilled that she had acted on her first opportunity. She shared her letter's content, and it read as follows: Dearest William, Safe at home. Son Willy healthy, beautiful. Our mums and your sister well. My father missing. Andrew lost. So sorry. Love, Jane*

*I had hoped she would show me the letter she had received from William weeks ago, but when she didn't offer, I decided not to ask.*

*Jane said that the Red Cross could not begin to promise the letter would actually be delivered. But, some letters do get through, apparently, and what a wonderful feeling I get when I think of the possibility of William's learning that his son and fiancée are well and waiting for his return. It might be just what he needs to continue bravely on to the end. God bless him.*

❧✥❧✥

The following Tuesday morning, Officer Thomas Gardner heard the news that the Germans had surrendered Marseilles, France. That alone was cause for celebration, but soon after, the report came to the airfield that in the first daylight attack over Berlin in three years, they had not lost a single plane. Emotions ran high for Thomas and another officer at Lindley, who had been through so much in the war. They agreed that, since it may prove difficult to concentrate, if distracted, they would focus on their duties and do their celebrating after hours.

It seemed like the good news would never end when Thomas learned the following day that the efforts to deflect the buzz bombs, or doodlebugs as some called them, had become extremely successful. Of ninety-four recently launched, only four of the Germans unmanned flying bombs had gotten through.

Perhaps the surge of good news was an emotional trigger, because early the next morning, Thomas awoke screaming, startling Gilda and himself. When he calmed down, he was embarrassed and apologetic about awakening his bride. They got up and made tea, sleep far from their minds. At the kitchen table, Thomas said that it made no sense to be having nightmares at this stage of the war, when things were going so well. Gilda was surprised and troubled, too, that Thomas had had the episode.

She asked him to share it, if it would help, but he decided not to describe it. It was silly to mar the present good news with the reminders of tragedies from the past, he said. They retired to bed to make love and watch the sunrise together. When Thomas went off on his bicycle, Gilda prayed that the nightmare would not be repeated.

She arrived at work promptly at eight o'clock that morning, having thoroughly enjoyed her walk there in the sunshine. Since Gilda's marriage, her workday had been shortened from ten hours to eight. It had been arranged that Dotty and Eleanor would handle the early breakfast, and Gilda would do the washing up and assist Dotty in preparing for the second. Following that, Gilda and Eleanor did the cleanup, and Dotty went home to Sam. Under this arrangement, Eleanor got a break during the day, Gilda did not have to walk so early in the morning, and she was still home ahead of Thomas by a couple of hours, allowing her time to do her own housekeeping and cooking.

Entering the manor by the kitchen's north door, Gilda was alarmed to see Dotty and Mrs. Wood sitting at the kitchen table without so much as a cup of tea in front of either of them. They looked up at her entrance, and she asked nervously, "What is it? What's happened now?"

Dotty answered for Mrs. Wood, who was pale and shaken. She said, "Mrs. Wood got a telephone call this morning from Jane. In looking over the letter from William that Jane received last summer, she realized, for the first time, that it had not been written by William at all. She couldn't see now how she could have missed it before, but she now believes that it was written by a fellow inmate. That has led us to worry that William was too sick to write at the time."

"Oh, Mrs. Wood, are you all right?" asked Gilda, tossing her bag on a hook and rushing to her side.

"I will be. It was a bit of a shock, though. When I was in Trubury, I wanted to ask to see the letter, but when Jane didn't offer it to me, I refrained. She told me this morning that she regretted not showing it to me. She said I probably would have been wise enough to notice that it was not William's handwriting."

"She meant well, Mrs. Wood," said Dotty.

"Oh, I know she did. It was such a sweet, romantic letter, almost poetic, she said, that she felt that it had been for her eyes only."

"Couldn't there be another explanation other than illness?" asked Gilda. "Mightn't William have been away at some work site, so his friend took it upon himself to write it, not wanting William to miss an opportunity to send a letter home?"

Eleanor said wisely, "Any number of things could have been the reason, none of them very comforting."

"I told her not to read too much into it," interjected Dotty.

"And the letter wouldn't have gotten out of the camp if he'd shared any real details," added Gilda.

"All of which is true," said Eleanor, sighing heavily.

Gilda asked, "Would you allow me to do your duties today? Perhaps you would like to go for a walk or enjoy your rose garden. It's going to be a lovely day."

"I do not want to be left alone to think," answered Eleanor determinedly. "This may sound silly to you, but both times we've heard from William, I've been very aware that it is all such terribly old news. It's weeks old, months old, in fact. How can I begin to imagine what has happened in the meantime? Has he gotten well? Has he gotten worse? In the case of bad news, such as this, I can't help thinking that he has gotten entirely well, by now, and that worrying at this late date is time misspent."

"You are an inspiration to us all, Mrs. Wood," exclaimed Dotty.

"So you have given yourself the gift of a happy outlook, if I may repeat your own words," added Gilda, smiling encouragingly.

"I have, indeed," said Eleanor. "It was the unexpectedness of it that knocked me off balance. We've had such good news of late, too."

When Dotty got up, Gilda said she should get to the washing up. Eleanor asked her to stay sitting with her a few moments longer, so Gilda took the opportunity to talk about Thomas's nightmare earlier that morning.

Eleanor said, "I think it was caused by all the good news coming at once. First there was Paris, and then, Marseilles. Even Hitler's flying bombs seem to have stopped, thank God. I wonder if all sorts of underlying trauma may be lying in waiting to expose itself when it is safe to do so."

"What do you mean?" asked Gilda.

"Well, haven't you ever noticed that in the thick of something difficult or tragic, people have such strength, only to collapse when it's over?"

"I have experienced so little. Do you mean that Thomas may yet have to face, in full, the tragic events of the last five years?"

"He may accomplish it all in his dreams, which may prove beneficial. Dreams may very well be the body's own mechanism for coping."

"He has much to cope with. When his father and brother died in 1940, I'm sure he never really had the chance to grieve their violent deaths."

Eleanor added, "Not to mention two crash landings, a skirmish with the Germans in France, and any number of other dreadful experiences."

"I hope he can deal with it all. He's lost many crewmen he was close to, as well."

"Thomas has you to lean on, Gilda. He would have been in a terrible spot if he'd married that Candace Gates woman."

"I thought of her just the other day and wondered what she might be doing now. Thomas predicts she'll marry right away, if only to prove a point."

"She can do as she wishes, so long as I don't have to watch her do it."

"Did you ever meet her, or even see her?"

"No, but I may never forgive her for the way she insulted you that evening in Surrey."

"She can't hurt me anymore, Mrs. Wood, but thank you for caring so much," said Gilda, glancing at the clock and getting up. "I've got to get to work, or we may not have a second breakfast today. What would the airmen think then?"

Gilda reached to cover Eleanor's hand with her own and said, "I truly believe that William is all right."

"I'll share my worries with my diary tonight and get on with it. How does that sound?"

"And I shall do the same," said Gilda, smiling at her brave mentor and friend.

❦❦

As Gilda was preparing to leave for home that Friday afternoon, Eleanor took her aside and presented her with a simple necklace for her coming birthday. From the chain, hung a golden pendant in the shape of a bird in flight.

## Meredith Kennon

When Gilda had left home in January and had moved into the manor, to save herself the arduous walk to and from her parent's cottage in the dark each day, Eleanor had written in her diary that Gilda had gotten her wings. It was then that she had ordered the lovely pendant.

When she presented it to Gilda, she said, "I know your birthday is Sunday, but I may not see you before then. I am so happy for the way things have turned out for you. I'm incredibly proud of you and think of you as a daughter."

When Gilda heard Eleanor's voice crack with emotion, she was touched to her very core. She knew what the pendant was intended to signify and said tearfully, "If not for you, I'd still be pressing aprons at Cottage on the Lane."

"I'm so glad you're on to better things," said Eleanor tearfully.

"Oh Mrs. Wood, I just know that William will come back alive. I hope you aren't too worried."

"I worry, but not excessively," said Eleanor in her normal, cheerful voice. "No one around here seems to let me."

Gilda heartily embraced Eleanor, who said, "Go on home, now. Away with you."

## At Willows Edge

Thomas had already declared that Gilda would have to choose her own birthday gift this year. He assured her it was not because he had no ideas, because he fully intended to give her a token gift of flowers or something else readily available, but he wanted her to think about what she most wanted. He wanted her to do the choosing, something she'd had little experience with. She had agreed but made him promise not to be too persistent about buying it before the war ended. She implied that her options would be greater after the war, but, in truth, Gilda was trying diligently to stretch their money. She was determined to live on their incomes, solely, and not delve into any of Thomas's savings or his family's wealth.

Gilda's parents invited them for dinner on her birthday. Lucas and Mattie had presents for her, which she received graciously. Lucas had made her candle-holders from sticks, and Matty had painted a picture of Willows Edge, which Gilda declared would be framed and hung in a prominent place.

That evening, after the children were sent to bed, the four adults listened to a program on the wireless, after which, Thomas and Gilda prepared to make their leave.

Before being allowed to go, Gilda was given a few eggs from her father, and her mother presented her with the old teacup and saucer that matched the ones in her cottage kitchen. Agnes had found them in a trunk after a long search, Simon attested. Gilda was truly touched and hugged her parents at the door.

They walked home by the light of their dim torches, carefully carrying her many gifts and talking about the meaningful gesture of the cup and saucer. Thomas had noticed how well Gilda's dad seemed and said, "Simon seemed especially outgoing tonight. Maybe he's finally put the Great War behind him."

"If he can get through this winter without being sick, I shall credit the coming of the children, which, as you know, was Mrs. Wood's idea."

"What an exceptional lady!" exclaimed Thomas.

Already thinking about what she would write in her journal the following morning, Gilda just nodded wistfully.

*September 4, 1944*
*Dear Diary,*

*I am twenty-two years old. I had the best birthday of my life yesterday, receiving many kindnesses, and even gifts, from my friends and family. The children gave me their thoughtful offerings, and my parents made a real effort, too. I'm touched that my mum searched out the old teacup and saucer from her own belongings. She gave me something that I know she treasures, which means much to me. She even hugged me at the door when Thomas and I left the cottage last night.*

*On Friday, Mrs. Wood gave me a lovely pendant necklace of a bird in flight, which symbolizes my leaving home to work at the manor last January. I have her to thank for my new life and agree with Thomas that she is an exceptional lady.*

*Thomas's birthday is on the twenty-third of December. His mother once told me that she almost named him, Noel. I'm glad she did not, because I still have nightmares about a boy at school by that name. I think it's funny how someone can ruin a name for you. (Candace, for instance) Now, why did I mention her name?*

*Back to the subject of my birthday, Thomas gave me some fresh wildflowers that he'd picked on his way home from the airfield and some sweets he'd bought off an American. Furthermore, he has promised me whatever my heart desires when things become more available again. I already have so much. I wouldn't want to be greedy, would I?*

## Chapter Three

On September eleventh, very early in the morning, Thomas had another nightmare. This time, it took Gilda longer to wake him, and he was truly shaken. Gilda stroked his thick blonde hair and soothed him with declarations of her love. Once he was fully awake, he slowly unfolded to her the content of his nightmares.

"I was on a mission to drop a barrel bomb on a dam in France. Did you ever hear anything about them?"

"Barrel bombs? I don't believe so," she answered quietly.

"Well, they were a brilliant invention, which enabled us to hit dams near the coast. The bombs were in the shape of barrels, and as they fell from the planes in a reverse spin, they rather skipped across the water, giving us the best chance to hit the dams at the base, their weakest point."

"Did you go on such a mission?"

"No," answered Thomas, "I knew of the operation, because I trained with some of their crews on the Lancasters. All decent chaps."

"And your dream was about the barrel bombs?" asked Gilda gently.

"In both nightmares, it was the same. I approached the target and released the bomb. As I flew low over the dam, I saw many little children playing there. They even looked up to wave to me, just before the bomb hit and blew them all to bits."

"Oh Thomas," cried Gilda, "How horrible! Why is this happening?"

"As hard as I have tried to keep such thoughts very much in the background, I think it means that I have killed many innocent civilians in my war career as a bomber pilot. And now, it appears that I am being forced to come to grips with what I've done."

"But you're a war hero!"

"I'm not suggesting I would change anything, even if I could. I did the job that was required of me, forced on me by that devil Hitler. And now, it seems I have to deal with the reality of it."

"What can I do to help?"

"You are here by my side; that's all I need. I'll be all right in time, and the nightmares will surely pass. Please, darling, don't worry."

"I'll try." Gilda paused before asking tentatively, "Would it help to think of something else?"

Rising up on one elbow and feigning cheerfulness,

Thomas asked, "Sure, darling, have you got a project for me to get a start on this weekend?"

"No, I have a project that we've already started, which I will have to finish on my own."

"You are most mysterious, Mrs. Gardner. Do explain."

"I think I'm pregnant, Thomas. I haven't had a monthly cycle, since we married. I think we may be having a honeymoon baby."

Jumping from the bed, Thomas dove into his trousers and stood looking out the east window, unable to speak.

Worried by his silence, Gilda approached him from behind and put her arms around his waist. When he began to chuckle quietly, she heaved a huge sigh of relief. "I'm glad you're pleased," she said. "I was worried it was too soon and might add to your worries."

"No, not at all. We've done nothing to prevent it. Besides, I believe children should come in their own time."

At their simple breakfast of toast and coffee, Gilda said, "Now, don't go telling anyone. I'm not absolutely positive, but I hope we'll see your mother and David soon. He will tell me who to see and when."

"We should get the telephone turned on, in case you

need it. We should have done it weeks ago."

"Perhaps, later. I'm at the manor most of the time and rarely here alone. If I'm not to worry about you, you can't fuss about me, either."

"I'll give it my best effort. Don't work too hard, then," said Thomas, getting up to go to the airfield. He bent over and kissed his bride tenderly before hurrying out the door. Gilda sat quietly for a few moments in utter happiness, before she, too, got ready and left for work.

When she entered the kitchen at the manor, an animated conversation between Dotty and Eleanor stopped abruptly, alarming her. This time, they did have tea cups in front of them, which was somewhat comforting, she thought, so she leisurely hung her pale-gray cardigan and bag on a coat hook, before approaching the table to hear what she feared might be more bad news.

Eleanor knew they had alarmed her, so she hurriedly spoke of something she and Dotty had talked of earlier that morning. "We have just heard that the blackout is being relaxed and that a dim-out is beginning. Won't that be splendid, Gilda? We won't have pedestrians running into trees in the dark or people driving into creeks and drowning. And there will be no more checking the bloody blackout curtains to make sure no chink of light escapes!"

Dotty nodded her approval for Mrs. Wood's quick thinking and got up to get a cup of tea for Gilda.

Gilda said, "That is great news. I've only got blackout curtains in the bedroom, so far. We can't put on a light anywhere else in the cottage, once the sun goes down. I was just thinking I'd better get to work dressing the rest of our windows in the dreary things, before the days get too short. Now, I may not have to, after all."

After a brief pause, she asked, "Is that all, then? The blackout? No other news? I thought you were keeping something from me."

At that moment, for the first time since suspecting she was pregnant, Gilda felt suddenly strange. She excused herself and went to the loo to splash her face with cool water.

When she returned to the kitchen, she sat down, and noting with curiosity the self-satisfied expression on Dotty's face, waited for an explanation.

Dotty confessed, "We were actually talking about you when you arrived this morning. We thought you were keeping something from us. You are, aren't you?"

"How did you guess?" exclaimed Gilda. "I just told Thomas my suspicions this morning, and he'd not noticed anything at all to give him a clue."

*At Willows Edge*

"Women pay more attention to things than men. It's as simple as that," said Dotty with sincerity.

Eleanor added, "We couldn't help noticing the beginnings of tiny dark circles under your eyes and other clues that only a woman would notice. Have you had your pregnancy confirmed by a doctor?"

"No, I just began suspecting it myself a few days ago. I was going to talk to David when I saw him next. I felt a bit off for the first time, just now, so I really don't need a laboratory test to tell me what I already know."

"Since we're on the subject, Marva had her baby girl on Saturday," said Eleanor. "Edith rang me with the news last night."

"Did she? How wonderful! I must write to Marva," said Gilda excitedly.

"They are naming her Victoria," said Dotty, shaking her head. "I'll never know how people can put such big names on such little mites. It should be illegal."

Gilda and Eleanor laughed at her but soon realized she wasn't joking. Encouragingly, Gilda said, "They'll probably shorten it to Tory or Vicki."

"Then why not name her Tory or Vicki in the first place?" argued Dotty.

Eleanor asked, "Isn't your real name Dorothy?

Isn't Sam actually Samuel?"

"Absolutely not," answered Dotty defiantly.

Eleanor thought it would be interesting to see their birth records but let the subject drop.

They reminisced of hosting Marva's wedding in May, upon learning that her parents had just lost a son in Italy. Eleanor had generously taken on the wedding preparations at the manor, having just heard that her own William was still alive. As Marva was pregnant, it had been a relief for the bride's family to have the couple married, before Marva's soldier went to the continent on D-day.

Gilda smiled at the memory and asked, "Is Jack doing all right on the continent, then?"

Eleanor nodded, and the conversation was ended by Sam coming in for his morning tea with Spanky at his feet.

Looking at the time, Gilda stood up to begin her work, when a wave of nausea hit her. She ducked quickly out of the kitchen again. This time, cool water on her face did not prevent her having a violent episode, which left her pale and weak. When she reappeared in the hallway, Eleanor was there with some peppermint tea. She escorted Gilda into her own bedroom and told her to rest until she felt better.

Left on her own in Eleanor's quiet bedroom, Gilda

gratefully sipped the hot tea, hoping fervently that she'd experienced the first and the last of her morning sickness. She caught a glimpse of herself in the dressing table's mirror and thought her face was as white as the pillow she was resting on. She then closed her eyes and allowed herself the first nap she had taken in years.

An hour later and much refreshed, Gilda bent over the deep kitchen sink and washed the breakfast plates at a record pace to make up for her sick time.

☙❧☙❧

The following afternoon, a letter came to Greystone Manor from Thomas's mother, Priscilla. It was addressed to Mrs. Wood, but Gilda saw it first, so she took it to Eleanor, who was in the kitchen, and asked if she'd like time to read it in private.

"I wonder why it's for me. I can't imagine that there is any secret from you enclosed. Let's read it together. Her letters are always such fun to receive."

*Tate Gardner Place, Lawton, Surrey*
*September 9th*
*My dear Mrs. Wood,*

*I don't mean to alarm you, but David has convinced*

*me to write to you and ask if he and I might come and stay with you for awhile. Any ideas we have had for a relaxing honeymoon period have been squashed. If you are full-up at the manor, as you have been in the past, we'll go elsewhere, but David was hoping that, as he is part of the war effort, we might prevail upon the RAF for a corner of their quarters. We would be welcome, no doubt, at Thomas and Gilda's cottage, but it is very small. We would so hate to trouble them right now and disrupt their new life together.*

*Strangely, it appears that my nerves have failed me, at last. Indeed, we have been delighted with the current news of France and the relaxing of the blackout, which are events that we have long dreamt of. Fear of buzz bombs seems to be a thing of the past, too, now that so many are deflected, but I must confess that I need to get out of here for awhile. David has made me resign from my various committees. Since he treats patients all over England, he insists he can actually base himself out of Warwickshire more conveniently than Surrey, as it is so centrally located.*

*However, just yesterday, a terrible explosion rocked a neighbourhood in southeastern London. Perhaps, you have not yet heard the report. It wasn't a buzz bomb. The authorities are trying to discover the source of the blast, but so far, their best guess is a gas pipe explosion. The crater left by the explosion is some forty feet across and almost twenty feet deep in places. What gas line explosion has ever caused so much damage, I ask you? They have occurred all over London for years now, but nothing with such extreme results. This is apparently the last straw for my emotional constitution, and David insists we go somewhere safer for awhile.*

*Now, Mrs. Wood, please carefully consider if you can really have us. If you cannot, we have a couple of other options, besides Thomas and Gilda's tiny cottage. David has a sister whom I have yet to meet, but he has postponed my meeting her for a reason, he assures me. He describes her as overbearing, but he is sure she could have us in Birmingham, if you cannot. We could possibly settle at a country inn, but we haven't yet explored that option.*

*I wanted to write my request, so as not to put you in an awkward position on the telephone. I'm giving you time to think it all the way through. We may just show up at your door, and you can tell us then whether or not to go to Birmingham. We must leave here immediately. I cannot say more at this time, but expect to see us in a few days. David will check on his patients' bones, as we make our way north.*

*Meredith Kennon*

*I have to trust that you will send us on if you cannot accommodate us. I've never thrown myself on anyone like this before, but we are quite desperate to leave. I must pack now, because David wants to see his patients in this area before we leave, and he insists that I go with him everywhere. There is much to do.*

*I have enclosed a cutting from the newspaper that will especially interest Gilda and Thomas. Candace Gates is engaged to be married, and the grand event begins with an enormous house party on the eighteenth to make it official. It appears to me that she is merely announcing her upcoming announcement, which is par for her, the strange girl that she is. She wants the word out, no doubt, so that photographers will know to be on the scene.*

*Her fiancé is no war hero, but it looks like she's found someone who will be able to pay the bills. I recognised his surname as that of a wealthy merchant in London, which is the reason the newspapers will want to cover the event. Well, Candace is always good for a laugh, and we're ever in need of that. I apologize for the suddenness of this request and my methods. My goodness, I'm behaving as oddly as Candace!*

Sincerely,

Priscilla Armstrong

When Eleanor looked up from the letter in her hand, she saw that Dotty and Sam had joined them. She could tell by the focused expressions on their sincere faces that they were already trying to find a solution for housing the couple at the manor.

The Armstrongs were held in high esteem for all they had done for Gilda. They had conspired to get her two pairs of specially-made shoes, so that she could walk normally and without pain, which was how the Armstrongs had met each other and Gilda in the first place. And secondly, Priscilla had recently involved Gilda in her prospective business venture, Gowns by Gardner. She was teaching her to design and sew dresses and had offered her a bright, post-war future in London, even before Thomas had realized he was in love with her.

To her staff, Eleanor asked, "Since we appear to be having a meeting, what do you think?"

Gilda spoke up first, saying, "Well, for one thing, I'll have them at the cottage before I send them to David's sister. If Priscilla is having trouble coping, a domineering sister-in-law can't be a possible solution."

"We have far fewer airmen than we used to," said Eleanor, "and there are some empty rooms upstairs, but…"

Uncharacteristically, Sam interrupted, saying,

"We'd have to partition a section off, or we'd be breaking military rules. And it would be nice if there were a bathroom for their private use, or else they would have to trek all the way down here."

"Let me talk to the quartermaster this afternoon and see if I can get permission to have them, or better yet, get part of my house back for my own use," said Eleanor smiling. "I would love to have Priscilla and David here. I'm honored that they asked me, first, I really am."

Dotty added, "I'm sure they will have their ration cards, so feeding them shouldn't be a problem."

Everyone agreed with distracted murmurs.

With great concentration, Sam said, "We'll have to open the stairway off the back hall again, Mrs. Wood, unless it would disturb the quiet in your room. The airmen could still use their stairs off the dining room, and the Armstrongs could go up and down the back ones. If a wall separated their quarters from the airmen's, and they had their own stairway, I don't see how the RAF could refuse you."

"I agree, unless they are reluctant to relinquish some space," said Eleanor. "I think I'll ring right now to see if the quartermaster has time to see me today."

With Eleanor's permission, later that afternoon,

## At Willows Edge

Gilda took Priscilla's letter home to share with Thomas. When she left the manor, Mrs. Wood and the quartermaster were still ironing out the details, but it appeared that Sam's plan would ultimately be approved with less red tape than expected. Part of the upper floor would be returned to Mrs. Wood for her own use, and the stairs off the hall next to the kitchen would be reopened. The quartermaster felt this idea was an easier option than the RAF housing the couple in an all-male environment.

Gilda couldn't wait to see what Thomas might read into his mother's letter. It was not only mysterious, she thought, but also a little alarming. And, although she hadn't known her mother-in-law for very long, Gilda suspected that there was much more to the story than Priscilla had divulged in her letter.

Upon reading the letter, Thomas, still so jubilant about becoming a father, saw only the advantage of Dr. Armstrong's coming to advise Gilda on her pregnancy. He failed to be disturbed by his mother's nervous condition, so Gilda chastised herself for reading too much into the letter and tried to take upon herself his optimistic viewpoint, for his sake as well as for her own.

"Gilda, if David and Mum do stay here until you are due, I want him to deliver the baby. He was a country doctor before specializing, he once told me."

"That is all months and months away, yet, but there is no one I trust more."

"Does Sam need any help preparing for them?" asked Thomas.

"I'll find out tomorrow," answered Gilda. "Can it really be possible that the request may be approved without having to go through four offices?"

"Possibly, at this stage in the war. It might take a couple of telephone calls, that's all."

"What do you think about Candace's announcement?"

"I think she's just as self-centered as ever, but I'm glad she's found someone. I pity him, though."

"She'll marry him before he has a chance to change his mind," said Gilda smiling.

"I'm glad you married me, before you changed your mind," said Thomas playfully.

"Well, that's very gratifying. Now, tell me about your day."

*Chapter Four*

Preparations for their accommodation were well under way when David and Priscilla arrived at the manor three days later. Eleanor watched from the front door as the couple considerately parked their car some distance away from the driveway that was used primarily by the RAF. As they made their way to the door, the doctor's hat nearly blew away in the chilly breeze, and Priscilla pulled her jacket tightly around her portly figure. Eleanor thought they looked like a well-suited couple who had been together for decades rather than the newlyweds that they were.

Eleanor had known for some time that David's first wife had died of cancer before the war and that Priscilla's husband, John, had tragically died in the Blitz. As she graciously greeted Dr. and Mrs. Armstrong and welcomed them into her home, she thought, "Things have a way of working out."

David and Priscilla had, of course, left their bags in the car, not knowing whether or not they would indeed be staying on at the manor. However, when they saw Eleanor's joyful countenance at the door and heard the sound of hammering coming from the upper regions of the house, they were quite assured of their welcome.

As Eleanor directed them to the kitchen for tea, she explained that on the first floor, a temporary wall was being built at the west end of the rear hallway. All the airmen had been moved to the east and north wings, and the west wing, no longer needed by the Royal Air Force, was now designated for civilian use. David and Priscilla would have a large area, including a bathroom, for their own private use, and Eleanor expressed that she was pleased to have some bedrooms freed up for any other guests she might have in the future.

After tea, David presented their ration cards and insisted on discussing a fair rent and sharing the workload before bringing in their belongings. The new lodgers took the first day settling in, and Thomas and Gilda came to the manor that evening only long enough to greet them.

Gilda insisted on having Priscilla and David at Willows Edge for an early dinner the following evening, and she had the day off in order to prepare for them. She conferred with Dotty, and they came up with a good meal of new potatoes and carrots from Sam's garden, buns, and very small portions of beef. As for the pudding, Gilda made her first rhubarb pie, of which she was quite proud.

Thomas helped her move the rickety table into the sitting room before he left for the airfield that morning, and that afternoon, Gilda dressed it with a lovely tablecloth that Priscilla had given them. She set the table with the mismatched dishes from her collection, and, for decoration, placed berries and dry leaves next to each place setting.

Gilda laughed when she recognized that all but the meat and buns had come from the harvest at the manor. They had, however, not been so easily acquired, because, early that morning, she'd had to wait longer than usual in queues at both the Englewood butcher and bakery.

Candles lit their dinner that evening in the little cottage sitting room, and the meal was thoroughly enjoyed by all. Gilda's efforts were complimented, and abundant praise was given for the work that had been accomplished on the cottage and in the garden. When Thomas walked their guests back to the manor, Gilda recorded the event in her diary.

*September 16, 1944*
*Dear Diary,*

*Priscilla and David have come to stay at the manor. How long they will be here is difficult to say, and David offered nothing on that subject at dinner. I believe they will stay until the end of the war and hope they do.*

*I noticed dark circles under Priscilla's eyes, as only*

*a woman will do, according to Dotty and Mrs. Wood, and there were lines of stress and worry on her brow. Thomas must have decided not to mention my pregnancy until later, for which I was glad. It didn't seem like the right time to announce it. I will tell the others at the manor to keep quiet about it for now.*

*As lengthy as her letter had been, my mother-in-law was extremely quiet tonight. There was some talk of the London explosion, which was to have been the reason for their flight, but I had the strong sense that something else was bothering her. I hope neither of them is ill.*

*Speaking of which, (illness, that is) I cooked for them this evening, dividing a portion of meat among us that, years ago, would have been considered a single serving. It bothered me to smell the beef cooking, so I ate but a little of it. Otherwise, I enjoyed the meal as much as anyone. I have not felt really sick, since the morning I was ill at the manor. My first rhubarb pie was a marginal success. If I could have used more sugar, it would have been much more palatable.*

*In spite of their present mood, Priscilla and David remembered my birthday and gave me a length of light-green fabric. It was, of course, from Priscilla's stash at home, since buying anything is so arduous right now, but I like it very much. They also told me the sewing machine was mine to keep, which I thought was too much, but they insisted.*

Eleanor, too, wrote in her journal that evening. She began, *Our good friends, David and Priscilla Armstrong, have come to live with me at the manor. Something alarming has happened to Priscilla, for I know that it takes more than a distant explosion to make her jumpy. There is definitely something else wrong. David is wonderful to her, so I don't mean to imply that there are problems between them. I hope she will confide in me if needs be. Perhaps, I'm just jumping to false conclusions, since we are all war-weary, by now. I know I am.*

*It occurs to me that I should share with her the existence of Willy and Jane in my life. It will be a difficult secret to keep from them, anyway, what with them living right here in the manor. Perhaps if I confide in her, she will let me help her sort out what is bothering her.*

*Priscilla brought very few personal belongings, but instead, a sewing machine and the notions and materials for her trade. I gave her an extra room upstairs for a workroom. I hope she and Gilda will have plenty of time to spend working together on their gowns. It will be a good thing for both, a testament to the belief that the war will soon end and other ventures can begin.*

*My reliable intuition tells me that Thomas and Gilda did not announce their pregnancy tonight, so I'll tell Dotty and Sam to be mum on the subject until their announcement is made. Gilda will talk to David soon enough.*

*Upstairs, the new arrangement has worked out perfectly, and Priscilla seemed very pleased. The spacious dressing room, which connects to the main bedroom, is large enough to accommodate the bed, so David and Priscilla can use the larger room as a sitting room, as such. Priscilla seemed like her old self when she teased me that I should be so fortunate to have a sitting room of my own. I told her that my corner in the kitchen with my two shabby chairs and my wireless sufficed me. And mention of that reminds me that I should find a wireless for their sitting room. I must remember to call on Mrs. Adair. Without going so far as to use the black market, she can get her hands on almost anything.*

*Lucas Smith came over and willingly painted both rooms a pale grey. The paint had been in my garden shed for years and looked thick and unusable at first, but Lucas thinned it with mineral spirits and made it work. I like the expression "fresh as paint," because nothing could be truer; the rooms look very fresh, indeed. I have once again noticed that new paint always lifts the spirits; I must remember that.*

*Their sitting room looks very inviting, now that it has a worn Persian rug, two over-stuffed chairs that are comfortable (if not beautiful), some ladder-back chairs, a tea table, another smaller table, a table lamp, and a standing lamp. Sam and Dotty helped me pull these items from storage, and I have to say, it is wonderful having some of my old things in these rooms again.*

*I want my guests to be very comfortable, for I sense they will be with me for some time. Their bathroom needs work, but it is, at least, in working order and is located between their living space and the room that has been designated as the sewing workroom. The Armstrongs were very pleased with the arrangement and have offered to pay rent, as well as prepare the nightly meal that they will share with me. I shall feel quite pampered being cooked for each evening.*

*I consider myself most lucky that the military did not tear down walls and make large dormitory rooms on that floor. They did so in the attic, but I don't care about that. They have been good to me, indeed, and I think they believe that I have been good to them, too.*

*I've had a letter from Wilbur's niece, Sophie. She has been invited to Scotland for Christmas, which has inspired me to think about my own plans. I must write back to her soon. She's been good to me when I've needed a break from the war. Now that I have more space, I can invite her to visit here sometime next summer.*

*If the war is over by Christmas, and perhaps, even if it is not, I am going to invite Jane, Willy, and of course, Jane's mother Ruth, to come to Greystone. We'll make quite a party if Edith comes home with her American, and the Gardners and Armstrongs, too, are in attendance. Gilda may want to include her parents, their foster children, and the Leventhalls (the children's former foster parents from Shrewsbury), which will be more than fine with me. What is Christmas without children? Without a doubt, it loses some of its magic.*

*I wonder if Jane would come, though, if she knew there would be a crowd. She's not as eager as I am to tell people that Willy is William's son and my grandson. Well, I wouldn't tell but a chosen few, but I'm sure Jane has suffered enough on that score.*

*My next project will be to put Edith's old bedroom to rights. She will be happy to have her room back. I want to paint it blue again, if I can find the leftover paint. Perhaps, I could add the remaining grey to make it stretch. Lucas will know what to do.*

*This feels much like when Wilbur and I first bought the manor and fixed it up to make it our own. It has been a privilege serving my country, and the RAF has been kind and fair to me. However, it is terribly exciting to call my home my own again—at least part of it, anyway. I'm getting writer's cramp, so goodnight.*

ಊಊಊಊ

On the following Tuesday, in Nuneaton, Dr. David Armstrong called upon two of his patients, who were recovering from war injuries. He wondered, at times, if he was just fixing them up to go out and get wounded again, but that was his job, which he did, in spite of his natural abhorrence of war.

His first patient was a young man, who appeared and acted like a mere teen and couldn't wait to heal and return to the fight. The second patient was somewhat older than the other, but appeared a decade older, having fought for England from Dunkirk to D-day.

Having done what he could for his patients and heading back to the manor in a heavy rain, David remembered that Priscilla was dying to read a newspaper. No one at the house subscribed to a paper, because Mrs. Wood thought it was more patriotic to hear one's news from the wireless, saving all natural resources for the cause. Although he thought Mrs. Wood a bit extreme on this issue, David agreed it had been nice to take a short break from the news, even beneficial.

Stopping at a street corner in the urban center, David bought the daily paper from a grinning lad, who seemed impervious to the chilling downpour. David tipped the lad generously, truly grateful that he had not had to get out of his car. Instead of going home directly, he decided to read the paper himself and found a place to park the car at the well-known Riversley Park. He had once read that it was the pride of whole community, and the doctor sensed how much it must have grieved the people to give up its handsome iron fences for the war effort.

Except for the drumming of large rain drops on the car, the park was quiet. The weather had turned back any prospective visitors, so David lit a cigarette, a rare indulgence, and opened the paper to enjoy in absolute solitude. Under headlines of local heroes and the commencing of the dim-out, his eyes landed on a London article entitled, "Gates Home Demolished During

Engagement Party – Many Killed."

He read on, "Local beauty, Candace Gates, and her fiancé, James Kenderly, were among the many killed at her parents' home in Brockley in the Borough of Lewisham, when a huge explosion rocked the area. Four large homes were severely damaged on Adelaide Road, and there were many injured, but the destruction of the home of Laurence Gates, a local entrepreneur, was complete. It took a direct hit, and no survivors are reported. At least thirty people were in attendance there, where the engagement of their daughter was to be announced that evening. It was just before seven o'clock when the explosion occurred, and officials have yet to determine its cause. Ironically, Mrs. Gates escaped, as she was with her driver at the time, collecting her elderly mother, who lives in a nearby village. The known dead includes…"

Stunned by the story, David was loath to pass on the terrible news but knew that Priscilla would need to be told and preferably by him. Realizing that the rain had abated, he immediately started his car, tossed his unfinished cigarette out the window, and drove back to the manor carefully, trying to avoid any deep puddles in the narrow country roads. At last, finding himself at the side door of the manor, he sought out Mrs. Wood.

Expressing to her that he feared his wife could handle no more stress, he handed her the newspaper, pointing to the article describing the tragedy. Once she located her reading glasses in her pocket and gave the article a quick perusal, Eleanor offered to be present when he told his wife, hoping it might make it easier.

As they climbed the narrow servants' stairs off the back hall to the Armstrong's quarters above, Eleanor asked, "Other than Candace, did your wife know the family well?"

"No, she had met them, but once," answered David, following her up the steep steps.

Stopping and turning, Eleanor said, "Of course, she knew Candace very well."

"Oh yes, well enough to know what a selfish girl she was and totally unsuitable for Thomas. I just fear that this may be too much for her at this particular time."

"I understand. So this is not a personal loss, but you fear what such news might do to Priscilla's fragile peace of mind."

As they continued up the creaking stairs, turning at the landing and making the final climb, David replied, "That is a very good way of putting it."

Before entering the sitting room, David whispered, "Priscilla is not the type to emote openly or embrace hysterics, but I do hate to report this. We'll break it to her, gently, shall we?"

Eleanor nodded, and knocking lightly, David opened the door. Priscilla was standing by the west window, looking out over the land. She turned and greeted them warmly.

"Come in, Mrs. Wood," she exclaimed, "I've been watching the dark clouds disintegrate, and I believe we might have a bit of sun yet today. Maybe Spanky would let me take him for a walk."

"Spanky will be delighted. You'll need your wellingtons, though. We got a good bit of rain in a very short time. What was it like in Nuneaton, Doctor?"

"It rained heavily there. I was glad I took my umbrella," said David nervously.

When Eleanor saw the blood drain from Priscilla's face, she knew that David had been wrong about breaking the news gently. Knowing a mother's feelings and active imagination, she said abruptly, "Nothing has happened that concerns you or yours, Priscilla. There has been another explosion in London, though, and Candace Gates and her fiancé were among those killed. I think we have alarmed you in our attempt to spare you bad news. I mean, it is dreadful news, but not to you personally, I think."

With a sigh of relief, Priscilla said, "Dear God, yes, you did alarm me. I'm sorry for the family, and this is, no doubt, wrong to admit, but I feel a safe distance between us and the tragedy. It's like watching a friend open the dreaded telegram, whilst at the same time thanking providence that the news was not for you. Selfish, perhaps, but a normal reaction, I hope."

"Absolutely normal," assured Eleanor.

Priscilla looked lovingly at her silent husband and said, "David, I am going to be fine. I suggest you go help Dotty and let me have a conversation with Mrs. Wood. I think I need to tell her what has caused such a commotion in our lives. I know she suspects something is wrong. Having just been scared to death by the possibility of more dreadful news, I think it only fair that I tell her what has been going on. The reality of it cannot be any worse than what she may have imagined, by now."

"Fine idea, Priscilla. You two stay right here. I'll bring up sandwiches and tea, and I'll even help serve the second breakfast when the time comes. Later, I'll take Spanky for a walk and tell Thomas and Gilda the sad news when they are together this afternoon at the cottage. No need to tell Gilda, just yet."

Expressing profound relief, David nodded his

thanks to Eleanor as he left the room. He closed the door quietly behind him, and the ladies listened in silence to the quiet creaking of the distant stairs beneath his weight, as he descended to the main floor to prepare their lunch.

When a plane flew overhead, disturbing the quiet, Eleanor said, "I knew what you must have been thinking when David and I approached you so carefully. I knew then that we'd made a terrible mistake. We might have given you a stroke or a heart attack!"

"I've a strong constitution, Mrs. Wood, so it has been no event of the war that has gotten me in this shape. If I may, I'll relate it to you. David and I have told no one, and I think the telling would do me good."

"For heaven's sake," exclaimed Eleanor. "Why are you two suddenly calling me Mrs. Wood, instead of Eleanor?"

"Out of respect for our landlady, I suppose," said Priscilla genuinely.

"Well, stop it. I wish to be called Eleanor. I have something I would like to share with you, too, but you go first. I have been worried about you and have believed the source of your distress to be more than you have indicated in your letter. Now, tell me what has brought you here."

## Chapter Five

Sitting quietly, with her hands folded calmly on her lap, Priscilla began to pour out her feelings of grief, shame, and somewhat-reconciled anger. She said, "As you know, my husband John was killed in 1940, in the Blitz. It was such a terrible time, for within days, our Jeremy was killed in the Battle of Britain. He went down in his Spitfire somewhere over the Channel. When Thomas declared his intentions of joining the RAF, if accepted, I had to reach deep within myself to support him in his decision. Like everyone else, I had no choice. I had to learn to be strong and selfless in the face of what was at stake."

"When you first wrote last spring, you shared some of those terrible events," said Eleanor quietly.

"Yes, all of those things happened four years ago, and I think I have coped quite well. But, it appears something else happened four years ago, about which I did not know, until recently. Last summer, whilst cleaning my kitchen, I came upon a note from a woman named Charlotte. On stationery with an address on Grosvenor Square, she wrote that she believed London to be a safe enough place to be, in spite of the dire warnings. It was a love note to my husband John, stating that she needed desperately to be with him."

"Oh Priscilla, I'm so sorry!"

"Knowing what I do now, had my husband's body not been positively identified near the hotel where he had always stayed, I'd have strong suspicions that he might be alive today and had used the raid as an excuse to disappear."

"How terrible! Does Thomas know any of this?"

"He knew of his father's affair, because it was he who found the note in his father's coat pocket. He hid it in a drawer in the kitchen, until such time he could confront his father with it. Well, I found the note shortly before he returned from France last summer. When I suddenly offered him my diamond for his future bride, he sensed that I knew about John's infidelity. When he checked the drawer and found the note gone, his fears were confirmed. Of course, John died before any confrontation took place, and Thomas eventually forgot about the note he'd hidden in the drawer."

Eleanor remained silent, nodding her head understandingly from time to time. Knowing that the story had not yet been told in full, she patiently waited for what would come next.

Priscilla got up from where she was seated near her

guest and walked to the window and gazed out, reminding Eleanor of her stance when they had first entered the room.

Looking out over the rose garden to the hilly meadow beyond, Priscilla finally said, "I had never suspected that John was unfaithful, but with David's help, I came to grips with it in a short time. I was already falling in love with David, and I told him everything."

"Has something happened very recently, then, since Thomas and Gilda's wedding?"

"Yes, about three weeks ago I received an urgent letter from a man in a hospital in Cambridgeshire. He urged me to come alone to speak with him about a delicate matter. I shared the letter with David, so he drove me up to Rothgate Hospital in Thornton. There, I met an old man, who had procrastinated, until his dying breath, something important that he had promised to do for his daughter. He has since died, which information David was able to seek out for me."

Eleanor struggled to hear Priscilla's words, because her voice had become more and more subdued. Turning and realizing this, Priscilla quickly returned to her chair to finish her tale.

Eleanor asked, "Had you never met this man before?"

"No, I had never even heard of him, but his last name, Bennington, sounded familiar, although I could not place it right away. Late in life, he and his wife had had a baby girl. His daughter, who would have now been in her late twenties and still unmarried, was hit and killed by a car in the blackout more than a year ago. She had a child, now age three, who lived with Mr. Bennington and his sister. I should explain that as his wife had died years before, he and his daughter, Charlotte, had been living with his aging sister since long before the war began."

Priscilla and Eleanor heard the creaking of the steps, indicating David's return. He entered and set the heavy, silver lunch tray on the oval, oak tea table. He asked how they were getting along and was told kindly by his wife that he was not needed. Without argument or comment, he slipped out quietly, closing the door behind him.

"That man certainly loves you, doesn't he?" asked Eleanor.

"I have never felt so loved. He has been my strength throughout all of this. When he drove me to Cambridgeshire, he waited for me outside the hospital room. When I reappeared, I was extremely shaken, and he has been doting on me ever since."

Priscilla paused before asking, "Have you not guessed the message that the man delivered to me?"

"I'm sorry, but no. I haven't the slightest idea."

"Harry Bennington was the father of Charlotte Bennington, none other than my husband's mistress. My husband was the father of her child, but apparently never knew it, according to Mr. Bennington. He believes John was killed before she'd had a chance to give him the news."

Eleanor's sharp intake of breath was her only response as she listened to Priscilla's heartrending story.

Priscilla continued, "She was never of Grosvenor Square, her father said, when I asked him, but she knew that John would not have checked on that. As he was so intent on secrecy, I was told, they never met at her private residence. She was nothing more than a brilliant con artist, playing the part of an elegant lady, making herself noticed at the best hotels and restaurants, whenever she could get to London. And those are my words, not his."

Priscilla looked up long enough to see Eleanor's sympathetic nod and continued. "Apparently, she did some kind of war work that required her to be in London much of the time. Her father implied that she was intent on finding a rich husband. She preyed upon wealthy men, including my husband, communicating with him, I suspect, through his hotel. I'm not excusing my husband for a moment, Eleanor. He was no victim, as I see it, but when he was killed, her plan backfired. Back in Cambridgeshire, Charlotte lived quietly with her father and aunt. Her father said that she had grown more mature under the forced consequences of her choices and had subsequently done a fine job of mothering her fatherless child."

Eleanor asked, "So, what did he want from you? Why did he summon you to Cambridgeshire and tell you all of this now?"

"His daughter left a will, leaving her daughter to my custody, whenever her father and his sister deemed it necessary. It's unbelievable, I know, but she wanted more for her child and knew enough about me, I suppose, to believe it was a wager worth taking. The poor old man had left his shameful duty of telling me until he was on his deathbed, when he could no longer put it off. His sister is far too old to care for the child alone for very long, and there is no one else to step in."

Leaning forward in her chair, Eleanor asked, "My dear woman, what have you done since?"

"I left the hospital room in shock, telling him to inform his sister that something would be arranged before Christmas. I have come here, not to hide, really, but to try to figure out what to do."

"And what a toll it has taken on you," inserted Eleanor.

"It has been too much, I confess. My shame is that I don't want to meet the child. I don't even want to know her name. To be truthful, I have left no forwarding address, and for all appearances, it seems I'm running away."

"Thomas knew of your husband's infidelity, but I assume he knows nothing of this."

Priscilla nodded and said, "I cannot bear to take on the child, and yet I must do something. I have always loved children and believed it would have been wonderful having many, but this, I am not prepared for. This is an impossible request."

"I see no shame in your not wanting your husband's love child. Your feelings are perfectly normal. It's just that…"

"That there is a little unwanted girl who will be tossed into an orphanage, never to be thought of again, unless I act. This child is Thomas's half-sister. He would be so ashamed of me to learn how I have behaved."

"You have been merely reacting, Priscilla. No one would deny you the time you need to do that. The child is in no imminent danger, and no quick thinking is required.

I'm honored that you have told me all of this. Perhaps there is someone I know who can help you sort it out."

"You mean a vicar?"

"No, I hadn't thought of that, but I have contacts who have worked in the temporary distributing of the children from the cities. Is that something you might consider?"

"I just don't know. I'd hate to think of her always being in a temporary situation. I don't think David is very proud of the way I'm handling this. He has been very supportive, but he has made little comments like, 'every child deserves to be loved.'"

"He's right in the sense that John's little girl is not the guilty party. She is a victim, Priscilla. We'll find a solution that everyone can live with."

"I believe we shall. I'm glad I told you, because it's done me good to say it all aloud."

"Of course," said Eleanor. "Our tea is probably cold. Let's have a bit of sandwich, while I tell you briefly about a situation of my own."

The ladies moved to the table, where the tea cozy had kept the tea a reasonable temperature. They quietly ate for a few minutes, before Eleanor shared her own story.

She began, "Wilbur and I came home from

Singapore in 1927 and, on a whim, we bought this house. We had no one but ourselves to consider because, except for a niece of my husband's, who I still visit occasionally, we have no other family here in the country. Edith was young, of course, and came home with us, but her older brothers stayed in the east. They visited only once in all that time, but we always had letters to connect us until the war put a stop to it."

Eleanor paused to remember her sons' faces, the last time she'd seen them. With tears in her eyes, she cleared her throat and continued. "When Singapore fell, we had no way of knowing what had happened to them. Finally, a British soldier got the news back home that he had witnessed the killing of many Englishmen, including my Andrew. Then, last May, about the same time we first heard from you, I received a letter from my oldest son, William. He has been a prisoner of the Japanese all of this time. You have, no doubt, heard most of this."

Priscilla nodded and said, "Gilda told me about the letter you received from him after so long. If I'd been in your shoes, I'd have nearly given up hope by then."

"I think I had given up hope, but when I got the telegram saying that Andrew was indeed gone, I realized that it was very wrong of me to believe William lost, also. I determined it was cowardly, and I was terribly ashamed. After a terrible time, only pure determination helped me get well and recover from an overwhelming depression."

"Oh Eleanor, I cannot imagine you in that condition. You are such a tower of strength."

Shaking her head sadly, Eleanor said, "I was no tower of strength then."

"I thought I heard someone mention that you've heard from him again," said Priscilla.

"Well, yes, his fiancée has, but it turns out that the second letter was penned by someone else, giving rise to another whole myriad of worries."

"His fiancée? Oh Eleanor, you've been through so much."

"We both have, Priscilla, but there is more. To me, though, this is good news, not bad. I was quite shocked when, in his letter, William requested that I contact his fiancée, Jane Davies, from Herefordshire, who I doubted was still single after such a long period of time. I marveled at his faith in her constancy, but when I visited her and her mother, I discovered why. They had barely gotten out of Singapore alive, and, because of the suddenness of the attack, there had not been time for my son and Jane to marry. William trusted she was waiting for him, because she was pregnant when she escaped Singapore. She has a little boy, Priscilla. I suddenly have a grandchild, and I just recently returned from a visit with them."

"Oh, how very wonderful! What marvelous news!"

"I think it is, too, Priscilla, but remember, he is illegitimate. Very few know of my grandson because of that. The people in Jane's village have had time to get used to the idea, I suppose, but I hate to have gossip spoil her reputation elsewhere, and William's, too. She did not have the courage to contact me, so you see, if I had not heard from William, I might never have known I was a grandmother."

Priscilla suggested, "Your William was wise to write first to you. It took the responsibility off of Jane for having to contact you."

"That is true. I still marvel at William's faith in her. He's had no way of knowing for certain that Jane even made it to England, or if she delivered a healthy child, and yet he continued to believe. Just recently, Jane sent a message to him through the Red Cross, which may or may not ever get to him."

"What an amazing story," exclaimed Priscilla.

"Edith, Gilda and the Coopers know, and no one else. You may, of course, share this with David, as I'm sure

Gilda has told Thomas. I've been thinking about inviting Jane and her mother to bring my grandson here for Christmas, but that will be for them to decide. I will have to understand if they just can't handle the situation. Jane may fear she won't be accepted."

"News of this child is certainly more acceptable than my sordid situation."

Eleanor took a sip of her tepid tea, and looking up, responded, "Jane adores the lad completely, but I'm sure that she and her mother thought the situation hardly desirable at the time."

Priscilla and Eleanor met eyes and, for the first time, they laughed. They didn't know exactly what had struck them funny, but their conversation had been a bizarre one, and some comic relief was certainly welcome.

Eleanor said, "Priscilla, only in wartime could these kinds of scenarios play out."

"I agree with you wholeheartedly. What is your grandson's name?" asked Priscilla, as she stacked their cups and plates on the large silver tray.

"Jane named him William, after his father, and we call him Willy."

Priscilla shook her head and folded her hands quietly in her lap, as before. Looking down, she said shamefully, "As I said earlier, I do not know the name of John's little girl. I couldn't bear to look at the papers that I'd been given. Aren't I awful?"

"No, Priscilla, you are not awful. Now listen, the sun is shining. Would you like to join me for a walk into Englewood?"

Gathering their plates, Priscilla cheerfully responded, "I would enjoy that very much. Thank you, Eleanor. Thank you very much."

"None needed. Let's see if we can get out of here without Spanky at our heels. I do hope he's somewhere bothering Sam or David and completely oblivious to our leaving. His antics are too much for me some days. And, Priscilla, this is not the time of life for you to be taking on the care of a small child. Something else will have to be done, something wise, something you have not yet thought of. Would you trust me to talk discreetly with people I trust about this situation?"

Priscilla nodded and gave Eleanor a quick embrace, saying tearfully, "Thank you for understanding and sharing your own story. I will keep your William in my prayers."

ঌ৽ঌ৽

David waited until he knew that both Gilda and

Thomas were at home that afternoon. He and Spanky came through the rickety, wooden gate to Willows Edge and found them in the garden, leaning on their rakes, while burning a pile of dead weeds and leaves. Without fanfare, he handed Thomas the article he'd clipped from the paper.

Stunned by the news, Gilda invited David in for tea. He refused, saying that he should probably go on back to the manor and help Priscilla with dinner. He said that although it had been quite a shock to him when he'd first read of the tragedy, he was ready now to not only quit talking about it, but to quit thinking about it, as well. He confessed his big concern had been for Priscilla, with whom he had already shared the news.

Thomas asked, "How did Mum take it? Is she all right?"

"The worst part was when she realized that Mrs. Wood and I had come to tell her something. She feared momentarily that something happened to one of you. When Mrs. Wood saw Pris's distress, she told her the news quickly. As Gilda may have mentioned, your mother and Mrs. Wood spent a long time in our sitting room upstairs this afternoon. I'm glad that Pris has someone like Mrs. Wood to talk to. She is a very grounded and inspirational lady."

"That is indeed so," said Gilda, putting her arm around Thomas's waist in a way that suggested to David that her reaction to the news was either protective or possessive, either one being acceptable to him.

"Well, I'm off. I just wanted to let you know about the Gates family. The war isn't over yet, in case anyone was thinking that it might be."

"Thanks for letting us know about the tragedy, Doctor," said Thomas, shaking his hand.

Calling to the terrier, which had disappeared into a thicket, David headed out the gate and into the setting sun toward Greystone. Spanky caught up with him, and they disappeared from sight.

Gilda asked, "Thomas, are you all right?"

"Poor Candace; I never loved her. I thought I did at one point, and this is terrible news, but it isn't about me. I feel disconnected from the event. I'm very troubled, though, about the unknown source of the blast."

"What do you mean?"

"I suppose I'm just agreeing with David. The war isn't over, by a long shot, and there are threats to us, still," said Thomas gravely. Disturbed by what ominous truth might be behind the unexplained blast, Thomas propped their rakes against the nearest tree and led his bride into the cottage.

❦❦

Gilda was not surprised when Thomas had another nightmare early the next morning. She was getting truly concerned now and thought that David should be told. At breakfast, Thomas scolded her when she brought it up. He said, "I will not tell David any such thing until you have talked to him about your pregnancy."

"I suppose I should. Let's invite your mum and David here on Saturday afternoon. We'll show them around the garden and tell them what is going on with us. I wonder if your mum will trust us with her troubles."

"Do you really think she's having a hard time?" asked Thomas innocently.

Remembering Dotty's observance that men were not at all perceptive to subtle things, Gilda asked sharply, "Do you not?"

"You are beautiful when you get cross," said Thomas teasingly. "Now don't worry; it's not good for you. Of course, I've noticed she's not herself, but let's trust her to tell us when she's ready."

"And will you tell me if there is something

troubling you? I'll understand completely if you are disturbed by Candace's death and feel you should do something about it."

"Like what, send flowers?"

"I don't know. I just wanted you to know that I won't be jealous if you are struggling with her death, and I'm willing to listen if you want to talk about it."

"I love you, Gilda. Have I told you that today?"

"No, but it's early."

"Well, I love you."

"And I love you."

Thomas grabbed his jacket from the hook, and at the kitchen door, he turned and said, "Now, don't worry about anything. Everything is going to be fine."

## Chapter Six

Before leaving the manor on Friday afternoon, Gilda sought out Mrs. Wood to tell her that she would see her again on Monday, unless needed before then. Eleanor took that opportunity to sit down with Gilda, briefly, to tell her that if she hadn't already told Thomas about the existence of her grandson, Willy, she would like her to do so now.

"I didn't think it was my secret to tell, although I've had to stop myself from unthinkingly referring to the situation," admitted Gilda.

"Well, I've decided to have a Christmas celebration this year, and I didn't want to lure Jane and Willy over here, where lots of people would be curious about them and my connection to them. It's best if people know ahead of time. I'm planning to invite them to come, including her mother, of course. I suppose I should approach her about how she wants to be introduced. Willy calls me Grandmother, so pretending he's not mine, seems silly. I'll just have to see how she feels about it."

"Thomas will be so happy for you when he hears."

"I told Priscilla this week, because we had the unexpected occasion to have an intimate conversation. I'm sure she has told David about Willy by now."

"So you know what's bothering them?"

"I do know, but you'll have to wait for them to explain. There is nothing to worry about. Things have a way of working out."

"Have you ever told Dotty and Sam the whole story about Willy?"

"I don't remember telling them, but they know. Somehow, they know."

"Well, I didn't tell them. Perhaps, Edith?"

"I doubt it, but Dotty is observant, by her own admission."

"If we all know already, why would there have to be any explanatory introductions at Christmas?"

"That's a good point, but I was thinking about inviting your parents and the Leventhalls to join us, as well."

"I think they might be having Christmas in Shropshire. The Leventhalls invited them as early as August."

"I could tell Jane, then, that she would meet no one who didn't know and accept her situation. I've never done much socializing here, so I can't imagine, after all these years at war, the neighborhood would suddenly be interested in my most personal affairs. We are all worn out, and the only news we really want is that of Hitler's surrender."

"A wise lady once told me that gossip and idle talk, although hurtful, only truly threaten those who fear their status is endangered. You've said yourself that you have never sought status here, so if Jane can handle the situation, live by your own words."

"I said all that?" asked Eleanor skeptically.

"You told me that once when the girls at school were tormenting me. You know, Mrs. Wood, until now, I've resented my parents pulling me from school when I was doing so well, but the education I received from you was vastly superior to what I would have gotten in school. I will never be able to thank you enough."

"Run along home, now. Tell Thomas to come and see me soon. I've hardly seen him, lately."

"Thomas has invited his mum and David to come to the cottage tomorrow afternoon for tea. We hope to work in the garden all morning. The leaves are falling, and we've been raking and burning. Why don't you come along? We are going to tell them about the baby."

"How wonderful! You look radiant, lately. Are you feeling as well as you appear?"

"I've felt quite well, lately, thank goodness. Will you try to come tomorrow?" asked Gilda.

"I'm afraid I cannot. The Girl Guides are coming to do their bit of cleaning, and I need to be here. Thank you, though."

ೊೋೊೋ

David and Priscilla came through the gate at about four o'clock, and finding Thomas and Gilda in the back, offered to help with the raking. Thomas waved off their offer to work and, instead, showed them the garden, giving Lucas credit for all the rubbish he'd hauled away. Then he took them to the neat rose bed he'd dug near the clothesline for Gilda's personal enjoyment.

Thomas asked his mother about how to care for the rose before winter. She willingly showed him how far to cut back the stems and how to mulch and protect the partially exposed, and therefore, vulnerable, root ball from a harsh winter. As he listened carefully, Gilda and David wandered off to appreciate the drooping, leafless branches of the elegant willow trees.

Just before catching up with the others, Thomas said to his mum, "I think that Gilda and I have done enough for one day. A few remaining leaves don't discourage us at all." Pointing to some leaves already drifting toward the ground, he added, "Besides, they're an honest mess, and there will be more."

Meeting his eyes intently, Priscilla quietly asked, "An honest mess, did you say?"

By her tone, Thomas knew that his mother was ready to talk, so he said simply, "Let's go in. Gilda made biscuits this morning, and I'm primed for tea." He called to the others, and they all went inside together.

The kitchen table was still in the sitting room, where Thomas had moved it the week before. They had decided that since they had so little furniture anyway, the table might as well stay where it was, ready for visitors at any time, and the couple had found the view from the sitting room window far superior to the cold, stone wall of the kitchen.

David praised the autumnal arrangement of leaves, branches, and berries that Gilda had strewn along the full length of the roughly-planed, wooden mantel above the ancient, stone fireplace. Gilda thanked him over her shoulder, as she and Thomas went into the kitchen.

Priscilla sat down on one of the wooden chairs by the table in front of the window. The bright sunshine behind her, from the window's southern exposure, put her in silhouette and highlighted the strands of silver hair now mingled with the chestnut brown hair that she had always worn short and curled. She faced David, who had seated himself in a chair on the opposite side of the table. Thomas brought a plate of biscuits from the kitchen, as Gilda called out cheerfully, "I'll be there in just a moment. I'm starting the water for tea."

She joined the others at the table, and when they were all seated, Priscilla asked, "Thomas, have you ever told Gilda about your father's problems before his death?"

Stunned by the unexpected question, he answered, "No, it wasn't my place to tell anyone."

"Not even Gilda?" asked his surprised mother.

"I rather wanted to forget it, Mum," said Thomas honestly.

"Before I tell you what has recently transpired, would you, David, please tell Gilda about John."

"I will take it on, my dear, to spare you," said David sincerely. A lock of his silvery hair came down over part of his worried brow, and taking a deep breath, David began. "Shortly before John was killed, Thomas discovered a note from John's mistress in his father's coat pocket. Before he could do anything about it, his father died, and the note stayed hidden in the drawer, where Thomas had put it.

Priscilla found it days before Thomas returned from France last summer. She had a hard time dealing with John's betrayal at first, but she confided in me and with Thomas's support, she put it behind her, until now."

"Oh Priscilla," said Gilda sympathetically.

Concerned about her well-being, David asked Priscilla if she wanted him to go on. She said, "Let's wait for the tea, and then I'll tell the rest of the story."

Just then, noise from the kitchen indicated that the water was boiling, so Thomas and Gilda went to put the tea and cups on a tray. When they returned, Gilda poured out, and they all sat down and dealt with their tea. All but Priscilla sipped cautiously from their cups and waited patiently for her to share her ordeal.

"I want you to know that I share no shame in what John did those many years ago. It was his sin and his problem. He had been gone many years, and I was already very fond of David. I didn't let his infidelity ruin my life. I was stronger than that. What has happened most recently is entirely different, and I do feel ashamed of myself for the way I'm dealing with it. I'm behaving like a coward."

"I can't imagine that, Mum," said Thomas lovingly.

"It is actually you, Thomas, who I'm afraid will be the most disappointed in me."

"An honest mess, of some kind?" asked Thomas, smiling sympathetically.

Gilda and David sat quietly, not understanding the exchange.

Priscilla answered, "It has become my mess and my shame, and I'll tell you why."

She painfully told them about the arrival of the mysterious letter and her visit to Cambridgeshire. She described the stressful drive there and her strange conversation with the dying man in the dismal hospital room. When she came to the part of discovering that John had had a child by this woman, she stared at the tea she had yet to touch.

Stunned to silence, Thomas and Gilda waited. Priscilla went on, "I promised the dying man that I would somehow relieve his elderly sister by Christmas, arranging some kind of situation for the child by then. He wanted it sorted out much sooner, but knowing I was reeling with the news, he nodded his agreement. That was almost four weeks ago."

Looking directly at her son, she said, "Thomas, you have a half-sister in Cambridgeshire. I do not know her name, and I don't seem to want to know it. I've not contacted the man's sister, and I know that I must, because

## At Willows Edge

David has since learned that the poor old man has indeed died. All the paperwork is in place, so all we have to do is collect her. If the old lady should suddenly die before we fetch the child, it could get very complicated."

"I wish you would have told me all of this sooner, Mum. I could have helped," said Thomas genuinely. "I could have taken the responsibility from your shoulders. Why should you have to deal with this?"

Priscilla's voice became uncharacteristically shrill as she answered, "Because, Thomas, I don't want you to deal with this, either. I fervently wish I could make the whole thing go away and pretend it never happened. How are we to deal with this? You and Gilda cannot take the child! I couldn't bear it. For my sake, you can't!"

Now weeping quietly, Priscilla turned toward the window and said no more. David looked from Gilda to Thomas, and no one spoke for a few moments.

Gilda finally said, "Priscilla, John has put you in a terrible position, an untenable one, in fact, and I would like to offer some of my own feelings, if I may."

Thomas took Gilda's hand, David nodded at her reassuringly, and Priscilla turned to face the others again. Gilda began, "I don't think that anyone in this room should take on the responsibilities of mothering the little girl. It would be completely unfair to you, Priscilla. John has done you enough harm. However, that isn't my only reason for feeling so. Children are tremendously sensitive. A situation like this would make the child forever wonder what was wrong with her, or if she had made a mistake, no matter how kind we were and how hard we tried to hide the truth from her. I know better than anyone that every child needs to be loved. Every child needs, for a time, to believe that he or she is the center of an adult's universe. Babies can die from simply not being held. Isn't that true, David?"

When the doctor nodded gravely, Gilda concluded, "When youngsters sense something is wrong, they can't help believing that something must be wrong with them—that they are the problem. It can damage their very essence. For that reason, I think the little girl should be collected as soon as possible, and a loving family found to adopt her, but not us, Priscilla, nor you and David."

"And I agree," added Thomas soberly.

Priscilla smiled weakly. She had so feared Thomas's reproach, and her fears had been unfounded.

Thomas went on, "This is the perfect time to tell you that we are quite certain that we're having a child of our own."

"Oh, what wonderful news," exclaimed Priscilla.

*At Willows Edge*

After first making sure of his wife's consent, Thomas said, "Gilda has been wishing to speak to you, David."

"Would you like to talk to me now?" asked the kindly doctor.

"I would, indeed," replied Gilda, beaming radiantly.

Gilda and David left the others for a few minutes, so that he could ask Gilda a few questions in the privacy of the bedroom. All of her symptoms pointed in only one direction. Gilda was indeed having a honeymoon baby.

Given a due date of May third, Gilda was elated when they returned to Thomas and his mother in the sitting room. They were sitting together on the wooden settee, Thomas had given his mum a fresh cup of hot tea, and she was enjoying her first biscuit.

Cheerfully, Priscilla asked, "Did Eleanor tell you about her hopes to get Willy here for Christmas?"

"Who is Willy?" exclaimed Thomas.

"Oh, I'm sorry. Eleanor assumed you knew," said Priscilla, now embarrassed.

Gilda said, "No problem, Priscilla, Mrs. Wood thought I'd told him by now."

To Thomas, Gilda said, "Eleanor gave me permission, just yesterday, mind you, to tell you about her grandson. When she heard from her son William last spring, she went to visit his fiancée, Jane Davies, now living in Herefordshire. She got there to learn that Jane had delivered a son a few months after returning to England. He's about two, now. That is who Eleanor spent a week with last month."

"I can't believe you didn't tell me," said Thomas, playfully accusing.

"It seems you had a few secrets of your own," accused Gilda teasingly. "And, knowing that gives me a better understanding of your nightmares, lately."

"Nightmares?" asked David and Priscilla together.

Thomas proceeded to tell them about the recurring dream, and David suggested someone for Thomas to talk to, if the nightmares persisted.

With all things out in the open, they lingered over their tea for another hour and chatted comfortably. They mulled over the information now revealed, sometimes laughing at the strangeness of it all and at other times, very soberly wondering how it would all work out.

Finally, David and Priscilla congratulated Thomas and Gilda again on the exciting news of her pregnancy and left for home on their own in the near-dark.

Thomas took Gilda in his arms and told her that her

common sense had saved the day. He said, "Until you said what you did, Mum had it in her head that if she were a better Christian, she would raise the child herself. She was angry at my father, but it was her self-loathing that was eating her up. Thank you for your wisdom."

"Any wisdom I have was learned from Mrs. Wood, and I wonder what she would think of what I've said today."

"Mum told me privately that Mrs. Wood had believed, too, that she should not be expected to mother Dad's love child."

"But, your mum thought we would expect that, didn't she? Or, she thought we would want to take the child ourselves."

"I don't know, but I think her biggest worry was what we would think of her, and also, what we would require of her. I'm sure we can find a wonderful home for the little girl. Until that is arranged, though, we still don't have a place for her, and I believe she must be collected immediately."

"Mrs. Wood is helping them find a temporary situation, and you will make arrangements to pick her up?" asked Gilda, making sure she understood the arrangements correctly.

"Yes, they will leave all the legal papers here for me to go through, and David will get them again in a couple of days. Then, he'll work on the legal side of things, and I'll work out the financial details. We'll take David's car to fetch her. I assume you'll go with me?"

Gilda answered him by throwing herself into his arms and telling him she loved him more each day. His response was picking her up in his strong arms and carrying her to the bedroom.

## Chapter Seven

The following day, from the telephone in the library at Greystone, Thomas rang the old woman in Cambridgeshire. She was a spinster by the name of Amelia Bennington. She was very relieved to hear that someone was fetching the girl, because she desired to share a home with an old school friend of hers in Yorkshire. She had already given her notice on her rented house and had counted on the girl being gone long before Christmas. As Thomas hung up, he thought about Gilda's remarks, and wondered if the little girl's essence had already been materially damaged.

He had made arrangements to pick up the child, whose name turned out to be Emma, on the following Saturday afternoon, the last day of September. If he suddenly learned that he was to work that day, David had agreed to go in his stead, taking Gilda with him.

David used the following week to find a solicitor to look over the documents and determine if anything else needed to be done before the child was collected. Thomas talked to his banker in London to begin making financial provision for his half-sister.

Eleanor worked feverishly trying to find a good

temporary home for the child and to begin the search for a permanent situation. She had embraced this assignment and had determined to find a quick solution, for everyone's sake.

All that week, after the second breakfast was served, Eleanor made her telephone calls discreetly from the library off the dining room. She began by ringing Mrs. Gladys Templeton, who had been so helpful getting Lucas and Matty billeted under the same roof. Although it had been Mrs. Wood's idea entirely, Mrs. Templeton had made all the arrangements, giving Gilda's parents no option, explaining that keeping child evacuees was compulsory. Mrs. Templeton had assured Mrs. Wood that she could put Emma into a temporary situation rather easily, but she had also given her a list of people, who might be helpful in finding a permanent situation.

Mrs. Wood kept her tablet with her at all times, so that when someone returned her calls, she had all the information right in front of her. She accepted calls in the kitchen at any hour, interrupting whatever she was doing willingly, because time was of the essence.

She should not have been surprised, then, but was, when on Thursday afternoon, after Gilda had gone home, Dotty asked, "Mrs. Wood, might I speak to you privately?"

*At Willows Edge*

Looking around the kitchen and finding that they were completely alone, Eleanor answered, "There's no one here, Dotty. What could be more private than this?"

"We might be alone right this moment, but you know as well as I do, that as soon as we start to talk, the blower will start ringing or someone will barge in needing something."

Eleanor sensed the seriousness of Dotty's mood and suddenly had the sinking feeling that Dotty and Sam were leaving her to go to another post. She closed her food accounts book and immediately got up from the table and went to the north-facing window. Looking out, she couldn't see Sam, but Lucas was there. He was working to earn money for buying Christmas presents and had been raking and burning leaves and preparing the gardens for winter. Opening the heavy, kitchen door, Eleanor called to him to come in.

When he entered, she pointed to some bread and biscuits and told him to help himself to some tea. When he agreed to answer the telephone and deal with whatever came up, Eleanor beckoned Dotty to the library, where she closed and locked the door. They sat down together on the two old leather chairs, and when they were comfortable, Eleanor said, "We will not be disturbed, Dotty. Tell me what's on your mind."

"Thank you for taking the time to hear me out, Mrs. Wood," said Dotty. "I just wondered how old you thought Sam and me might be."

Taken completely by surprise by the unexpected question, Eleanor said she'd never really thought about their ages. She said, "I'm aware when you have birthdays, but you know I've never asked you how old you are. Why are you asking me this now?"

"Well, Mrs. Wood, Sam is older than me by quite a few years. He robbed the cradle, you might even say. When you came here, we'd been married, but two years. He was almost thirty, but I was a mere nineteen."

Intrigued, Eleanor said, "I apologize for thinking you were both ageless. I'm sorry. Has something happened to upset you both?"

"Well, yes it has, Mrs. Wood. I'm now just thirty-six years old. And although Sam looks much older than he really is, because of his bone problems, he's only forty-seven."

"Well, since we're on the subject, I'm in my sixties. What are you trying to tell me?" asked Eleanor, now exasperated.

"I know you're in your sixties, Mrs. Wood. What

kind of servant would I be if I didn't know that?"

"I don't like the word 'servant' at my house, Dotty. Now what have I done to upset you and your good husband so?"

Up until that point, Dotty had been indignant, but now, when it came right down to it, she was losing her nerve. She looked at the rows and rows of books on the shelves, believing Mrs. Wood to have read all of them, and suddenly felt terribly inferior.

"What did you want to speak to me about, Dotty?" insisted her kind employer.

"Sam and I don't have what you have or know what you know, Mrs. Wood, but we are hardworking folks with steady employment and a fine place to live."

"I'm glad you think so," said Eleanor, appearing as confused as she felt.

"Well, we couldn't help being aware of all the goings on here, and it occurred to us that you should have at least considered us," said Dotty petulantly.

"Considered you for what?" asked Eleanor. She raised her hands, palms up, imploring Dotty to get to the point.

"It wasn't our choice that no babies came our way, Mrs. Wood. That was God's doing, and we've had to live with it. We've not been so foolish as to shake our fists at heaven, and we're thankful for all we've got, but we've had our trials like anyone else. And there is no worse trial, I can tell you, than being childless in a world full of children. Well, I'll come right out with it, then."

Eleanor nearly laughed aloud, because she had been waiting for exactly that—for Dotty to come out with it, which she still had not.

Eyeing the usually-wise Mrs. Wood and wondering how she could be so dim-witted in this situation, Dotty waited. Their eyes met and locked. Eleanor searched hopelessly and frantically for a glimmer of insight and wondered why Dotty couldn't just say what was on her mind and spare her the suspense. Dotty waited and prayed for the lights, finally, to go on in Mrs. Wood's brain, a brain for which she'd always had the highest praise until this very moment. Providence intervened, at last, when suddenly Eleanor leaped from her chair like a youngster, crying, "Do you and Sam want the little girl?"

"Well, of course, we want the little girl, and her name is Emma. I happened to see that on some papers that Dr. Armstrong was carrying. She has a name, and I wish I knew why no one uses it. I'm sure we'll get over it, Mrs. Wood, but Sam and I can't understand why you and Mr.

and Mrs. Armstrong didn't at least think of us."

Sitting again, Eleanor said, "I am so sorry. I honestly don't know why we didn't think of you, and it wasn't right. I truly apologize, Dotty, and I would appreciate it if you would pass that on to Sam. Just between us, I did think Sam was older than he is, and I apologize for that, too. You needn't tell him that, though," said Eleanor sheepishly. "But, Dotty, who told you all of this? Do you know the entire situation?"

"I work with you all day, Mrs. Wood, and I know you better than anyone. You've been on the telephone a lot, and you and Gilda have dropped a few hints here and there. I'd have to be an idiot not to know the story by now. I'm sorry for Mrs. Armstrong, I really am. This is a great tragedy for her, but my greatest concern is for a little girl, whose own kin can't even bring themselves to use her name."

"Well, Dotty, little Emma doesn't really have any kin. I mean, Thomas is her half-brother, but in deference to his mother's pain, I suspect she will never know their connection."

"If me and Sam have our way, she will have kin. That's what I wanted to tell you, and I thank you for listening."

Dotty stood up and the two women left the library together. Eleanor said, "I'll talk to Priscilla and David about this, probably tonight. It's up to them, of course, and they may be pursuing other avenues, but I know for certain that they will be thrilled at your coming forth and offering. They, too, will be embarrassed for not thinking of you. Remember, though, it is a huge thing to ask of anyone, and perhaps they didn't want you to feel pressured by such a request."

"That's all right, Mrs. Wood, you don't have to make excuses for them. They never gave us a thought, either, but if they will now, all will be forgiven. And before you say it, let me. I won't hold you responsible if they don't see us as adequate parents and turn us down, for some reason or another. Sam and I have prepared ourselves for disappointment. We've had plenty of practice."

"Oh Dotty, I do love you so," said Eleanor impulsively. "What would I do without you?"

"I hope neither of us ever has to find out," said Dotty matter-of-factly, as she removed her apron, grabbed and donned her ratty, brown cardigan, and headed for the door. She couldn't wait to tell Sam she had confronted Mrs. Wood and had done a fine job of it, too.

*At Willows Edge*

At dinner that evening, Eleanor asked the Armstrongs if she might visit them upstairs in their sitting room, just as she soon as she had the kitchen in order. She said there were some things she'd like them to know but wanted it to be a private conversation, where they would not be interrupted. As if to make her point, at that moment, they were interrupted by a telephone call from the quartermaster. Eleanor took the call, gesturing to Priscilla and David to continue eating without her.

When the washing up was accomplished, and she had all things in preparation for Dotty's arrival the next morning, Eleanor climbed the steep stairs. She knocked lightly on the Armstrong's door and was welcomed in.

When they were seated comfortably in the pleasant room, Eleanor said, "Well, there has been an interesting development today. I've been anxious to tell you, ever since I heard, but I knew it was best to save the discussion until this evening. Of course, I don't know how you will feel about this, but I can't imagine that your thinking can be too far from my own. I'm not sure how to begin, though."

Eleanor suddenly felt uneasy, knowing how important this conversation was to Dotty's happiness. Wringing her hands, she said, "I'm unexpectedly nervous."

"My dear woman," said David leaning toward her,

"I hope we aren't making you anxious. You must know we trust your judgment completely."

Eleanor said, "Well, I suppose I'll just relay to you what happened this afternoon after Gilda left for home and allow you to draw your own conclusions."

David and Priscilla nodded encouragingly.

"Dotty asked me for a private conversation and was dead serious about it. We called Lucas inside to answer the telephone, if it rang, and we secluded ourselves in the library. To tell you the truth, from the look on Dotty's face, I was afraid that she and Sam were leaving my employ, but I was wrong. Dotty was very indignant, though, and these are her words exactly. She said, 'I just wondered how old you thought Sam and me might be.'"

"She took you to the library to ask you that in private?" asked Priscilla surprised.

"Well, she wanted me to know that, although Sam is eleven years older, she is just thirty-six. She told me that she and Sam had never blamed God for their not being blessed with children, but they had always longed for them."

Eleanor looked up when she heard Priscilla gasp.

Priscilla reached for David's hand and exclaimed, "Oh, Mrs. Wood, do Dotty and Sam want the child?"

Relieved beyond measure and nodding excitedly, Eleanor said, "Well, you are far quicker on the uptake than I was, I assure you, much to Dotty's dismay."

"I wonder why we didn't think of it," said Priscilla.

"That's exactly what Dotty asked me, and it wasn't at all easy to appease her. And to make things worse, I kept saying, 'the child this and the child that,' until she told me defiantly that the child had a name and that it should be used. When I think of all the telephoning I did! Dotty and Sam were right here all the time, just waiting for us to consider them. I'm embarrassed, I truly am."

"I should have thought of it," said David shamefully.

Priscilla said, "I can think none more worthy. I'll admit that Sam looks much older than forty-seven, and that, I believe, will be the excuse I'll use when I talk to Dotty about our failure to recognize them as the perfect solution. Sam needn't ever know our thoughts on that subject, surely."

Wisely, David added, "Sam won't mind being your excuse. He just wants Dotty to be happy."

Eleanor said cautiously, "Perhaps, his age should be a consideration, though, Priscilla. If I died suddenly and the estate was sold, I suppose it is reasonable to believe that the new owners might let the Coopers go and bring in someone else or do without extra help. They may not always be financially secure, but they will be as long as I live."

"Mrs. Wood, let me put your mind at ease on that score," said David. "Thomas is arranging for a trust to provide for the little girl all of her life. That is the easy part."

Priscilla agreed, "That is indeed the easy part. That I can handle. I didn't want to raise John's love child, but more than that, I didn't want to be accusing myself daily for not loving her adequately. I can cope with almost anything, but guilt."

"Well, Dotty made it clear that they want her desperately. I don't know what they will think of the trust. They will want full responsibility."

"We'll arrange it in whatever way Sam and Dotty want it, but I doubt they would object to her receiving a legacy of some type when she comes of age."

"Yes, they would agree to something like that, I'm sure. And when you talk to them, you must remember not to refer to her as 'the child.' Dotty was more indignant about that than she was at not their being considered. She used her amazing detective skills and apparently read the child's name from some papers you were carrying, David."

"Well, I'll be," said the doctor, chuckling.

"We'll remember," said Priscilla, sighing with relief. And then shaking her head, she said, "I suppose that means that David will have to inform me of the child's name."

David nodded kindly at Priscilla, who suddenly realized something and asked, "But Mrs. Wood, is this arrangement all right with you? Are you in favor of this? Surely, it will complicate your life, the very thing I've been running from."

"The greatest part of my life has been being a parent. I could not deny the Coopers that, and I trust that they know what they're taking on. I feel very certain of this, really. In all these years, Dotty and Sam have never done anything to warrant my concern. They deserve my absolute confidence, nothing else." Eleanor's voice broke with emotion, and, embarrassed, she dug in her pocket for a handkerchief.

Priscilla looked at her husband and said, "I believe this will work out, David. What a relief it will be to have it all settled."

David said, "If this is what you want, Pris, then I'll sit down with the solicitor and make it all legal and proper, ready for you to sign. As long as Mrs. Wood is comfortable with it, I think it is a wonderful solution. When Thomas brings her here, she'll go right into her new family, which will be far better than a temporary situation."

Leaning forward, Eleanor cautioned, "But Priscilla, you need to think about whether it will be difficult having her here while you're still in residence."

Priscilla answered, "If I find it too hard, I'm the one who can leave. No, I wouldn't dream of letting that influence my decision or delay her coming."

Eleanor asked, "Do you wish me to speak to them?"

David replied, "I would like the honor, if you two ladies would give it to me. They will not get indignant when I ask questions about living space and the child's care during work hours. I'm a doctor, and they will think it is all part of the process and not take anything personal, as they might if either of you take it on. Mrs. Wood, I thank you for all you have done for us."

Rising to leave, Eleanor said, "To those in my employ, I'm necessarily called Mrs. Wood by long-standing tradition that even a war cannot reverse, but not you. Let me parrot Dotty and say this—I have a name. It is Eleanor, and I'd like you to use it."

David laughed and said, "As you wish, Eleanor."

## Chapter Eight

Early the next day, when told that the Coopers wanted to adopt Emma, Gilda, like everyone else, was embarrassed for not having thought of them as an option. She knew that Thomas would want to know right away, so she telephoned the airfield hoping he could take the call.

Thomas was pleased that a solution had been found and thought it was a good one, as long as his mother didn't object to the child's connection to Greystone. He said, "I think it is wonderful, really, but our association with the manor is, I would say, a permanent one. If Mum doesn't want me to have any contact with the child, this would definitely complicate things."

Gilda replied, "I asked that question, myself, and Mrs. Wood told me that apparently it's a risk your mother is willing to take. She is greatly relieved that the situation is not only permanent, but also, excellent. Your mum already feels the lifting of the burden of responsibility and has said that if things become too difficult for her here, she and David will just go home."

"Well, then," said Thomas, "it looks like we've found our solution. I must run, but I look forward to seeing you in a few hours, darling. Give my best to everyone."

Going home from work that afternoon, Gilda was tired, but not because of her workload or the effects of her pregnancy. She was tired from watching Dotty's nervous energy all day, as she and Eleanor made a dozen trips from the manor to the carriage house. With amusement, she thought their excitement and anxiety about the child's coming was downright exhausting and was glad that David had taken Priscilla with him all day. Her presence would have added another element of anxiety to the mix.

Walking along, Gilda did some deep soul-searching. She accused herself, "I claim to have been Dotty's friend all these years, and yet, I have never asked her about her deepest desires. I should know as much about her as she does me, and yet I do not."

Going home by way of the main village road and heading north and east across a field that had been already harvested, Gilda could walk home from the manor in less than a quarter hour, and she relished every minute of it.

Sensing the delicious properties of autumn, which was her favorite season, Gilda decided to forgive herself for her selfish attitude and determine to be a better friend to Dotty in the future. Like everyone else, she found comfort in the excuse that Sam looked years beyond his age.

On this late-September afternoon, there was a clear quality to the air, even though the smell of burning leaves could be identified within it. Taking caution to avoid holes that might turn an ankle, Gilda directed her thoughts to more pleasant things.

She decided to think of just the right words for describing this perfect autumnal day in her journal. Words like crisp, chill, mist, golden, swirling, harvest, bounty, and death came to mind. Then she concentrated on phrases, coming up with "chilling gale," "mournful trees stretching their bare arms towards the cold sky," "cloaks of swirling gilded leaves," and "silhouetted trees, reminiscent of carelessly tatted lace or even skeletal omens of winter's power." Gilda laughed at her vivid and morbid thoughts and quickened her pace toward home.

As she neared the cottage, the sky became suddenly overcast, and Gilda felt an eerie darkness enfold her as a chill went up her spine. She chuckled nervously, thinking, "That's what I get for thinking that skeletons and death are synonymous with glorious autumn."

As she came through the gate, a slight movement caught her eye in the drooping tendrils of the willow trees to her left. She was sure that, for a fleeting moment, she had seen a figure in the trees behind the hedge. "Is anyone there?" she called out.

Shakily, she produced her key and hurriedly approached the front door. Once inside, she locked the door again. Not turning on any lights, she raced toward the tiny lean-to attached to the back of the cottage, where she did her washing each week. From the only north-facing window in the cottage, Gilda desperately scanned the willow trees for what she believed she had just seen. Peering through the dirty window, she could see nothing. Whatever she had sensed to have been there in the trees was gone now.

When Thomas arrived home an hour later, Gilda had washed her favorite outfit for their day trip on Saturday and had nearly forgotten her fright.

For going into to the village, she still wore the tan-colored trousers, now shortened, that had once belonged to one of Mrs. Wood's sons. And she still wore the man's white shirt that Mrs. Wood had given her. Sometimes, she wore it tucked into the trousers and belted, and at other times, for a different look, she wore it long, over the trousers, fastening the belt on top. She was glad she had not altered the waistline of the pants, because she knew that soon she would be growing out of her clothes. Once again, her white shirt would be versatile and comely, for she could wear it unbelted throughout her entire pregnancy.

When Thomas found her ironing his uniforms in the room behind their bedroom, both his excitement and anxiety about the trip were evident on his face.

They ate their evening meal by candlelight and went to bed early. The plan was for David to pick them up at seven o'clock in the morning. They would drop him off again at Greystone, before heading south and then east to Cambridgeshire. David had driven that stretch recently and said it always took longer than expected.

ॐॐॐॐ

Once the decision to place Emma with the Coopers had been made, everything else was effortless, it seemed. David made sure of the legality of what they were doing, and Priscilla signed all necessary forms to begin the adoption process.

At Sam's invitation, David visited the Cooper's carriage house and found it perfectly adequate to handle the addition of a child. The Coopers had emptied their box room, and a small bed and a chest of drawers had been moved in. The walls had been whitewashed, and the bed was made up with a pink counterpane. A well-washed rag rug lay by the bed, and a picture of a pony had been hung above it.

Although a small room, a low, white-curtained window looked out over the manor drive, expanding its visual space, and the doctor could imagine the little girl enjoying its lovely view. He also noticed that the blackout curtains had already been removed. No doubt, the adults in England minded the blackout more than its younger residents, who knew nothing else, but this gesture of kindness was another testimony of the Cooper's thoughtfulness for the child's well-being. When David mentioned that he hoped the dangerous full blackout would not be instituted again, Sam said simply, "Amen."

David was touched when Sam showed him the mirror that he'd hung for Emma on the wall behind the open door. It was positioned near to the floor, in consideration for a child's height, and for the same reason, a newly-painted step stool was positioned by the bed.

Sam had asked for Mrs. Wood's help acquiring some children's books. She did not have to call on the resourceful Mrs. Adair this time, for Eleanor had saved all of Edith's favorite childhood books. A quick search of the library was all it took for her to locate them, and from the stack, she selected a few age-appropriate stories.

## At Willows Edge

Dotty was so excited about the child's imminent arrival that she burned herself, taking bread from the oven, and broke two glasses in a single morning. Eleanor shared in her excitement and tried to calm her devoted cook as best she could.

Sam seemed to take everything in stride, worrying about accomplishing the necessary tasks and letting Dotty deal with the emotional side of things. He was terribly happy, though, that fate had been so kind to his young Dotty, who he had loved since she was fifteen. He had been satisfied enough with their childless life, but he had always known that Dotty had suffered from the deprivation.

❦❦

Thomas drove the doctor's black Austin through Northamptonshire, Bedfordshire, and into the southern part of Cambridgeshire. Gilda was enthusiastic about everything she saw. Thomas watched her closely, and as he had done before, appreciated her excitement as they drove through the countryside. He sometimes forgot that, in all the years since her family had moved from London, she had been only to Surrey twice and to the coast for their honeymoon. It also occurred to him that her parents had probably gone nowhere in all that time and wondered if that explained some of her mother's previous behavior.

Gilda's interest in the passing scenery was contagious, and Thomas eagerly answered her questions to the best of his ability. Teasingly, he said, "I'm not an atlas, darling. Perhaps you'd like one for Christmas."

She countered with, "Greystone has half a dozen atlases. I've just never opened one, unless given a specific assignment by Mrs. Wood. Maybe I shall, now that I know I have hope of seeing a little of the world."

As she spoke, she turned her head toward Thomas quickly, and one lock of thick, dark-brown hair fell down over one of her eyes, reminding Thomas of the day he had first met her and the heavy fringe that once hid her beautiful, dark eyes.

"I do love you, Mrs. Gardner," he said.

"Now, that is a subject I would love to delve into further. It's more interesting than geography, I think."

"Indeed," answered her husband, smiling devilishly.

⸻

Upon nearing their destination, Gilda pulled a pair of white gloves from the pocket of her light jacket. Then, pulling some fabric remnants from her other pocket, she carefully filled the thumb and index finger of the left glove.

## At Willows Edge

Seeing her pre-meditated efforts to conceal her birth defect, Thomas said, "I've never seen you do anything like this before."

"This is the first time in my entire life that I have gone to such lengths to conceal my hand, but I don't want my missing fingers to be an issue when we fetch a child and drag her from the only home she has ever known."

"Matty and Lucas are young, too, and they were much in the same situation when they arrived. You went to no such efforts then."

"My dad had time to warn them, which I'm sure he did. Just trust me, Thomas; it's better this way. She's not even four years old. Don't worry; I'm not sinking into old patterns of inferiority. In fact, it distresses me to cover my diamond ring with its lovely, miniature rose leaves, but today is different. I don't want it to be about me." With that said, she reached into the backseat, retrieving her best hat, and placed it on her head at a jaunty angle that said that she would brook no further argument on the matter.

"I'll trust your judgment, then," said Thomas affectionately as they arrived in the village of Houghton, near Colchester.

They pulled up in front of the address given them, and without small talk, tea, or even introductions, Emma was handed over to the Gardners with one suitcase and a tote bag of her favorite things. Thomas carried the suitcase to the car, and Gilda walked with Emma, who did not take Gilda's offered hand. Her only apparent concern was not parting with her bag of belongings, which she carried with her shoulder raised high to keep it from touching the ground. She did not even turn around to wave to her great aunt, and upon looking back herself, Gilda saw no one at the door for Emma to wave to, anyway.

On the quiet drive home, Gilda and Thomas were dying to discuss the cold way in which old Miss Bennington had sent the child away. With Emma in the backseat, they could hardly discuss their impressions of the little girl or her wicked Aunt Amelia, so they took in the scenery around them, whenever a break in the hedgerows gave them the chance.

The first words that came from Emma were, "Where are we going?"

Turning toward the backseat, Gilda asked, "Didn't your aunt tell you?"

"No, she didn't have time, said Emma clearly.

Surprised at the revelation and also how articulate the little girl was, Gilda looked at Thomas with a look that said, "The old crone had time; she just wouldn't take time."

Returning her glance, Thomas's grim expression told her that he felt as she did.

From the backseat came, "Grandpapa died, and I can't see him anymore. Aunt Melia is going far away, where I can't go. They don't like little girls far away."

"We are going to a place where little girls are liked very much. Would you like to tell us about your grandpapa?" asked Gilda kindly.

"No, I don't know you yet," answered Emma frankly. She diverted her attentions to the contents of the canvas bag, drawing from it, a stuffed kitten and a naked baby doll. From the bottom of the bag, came a tattered grayish blanket that, Gilda deduced, had long ago probably been a lovely blue. Unaware that Gilda was intently watching her, Emma carefully wrapped the doll in the blanket and rocked it back and forth for a full hour. She did not make eye contact with Gilda again.

Gilda's first impression of the little girl was unclear, and she was of two minds about her. She was either quite damaged and insecure, thought Gilda, or she was alarmingly independent. It was hard to get a really good look at her face, because the child did not look up and her sandy-colored hair was in disarray, coming down over half of it. Gilda made herself quit staring at the child and looked out the window, taking in the dying foliage of the high hedgerow within her reach.

When a vista finally opened before them, she asked Thomas, "Isn't it interesting how different the same landscape appears when you are coming from the opposite direction?"

Thomas nodded at her affectionately and took her gloved hand in his for a moment, until he had to gear down for the approaching curve in the road and the village ahead.

Once they had fueled up, Thomas suggested they find a spot to eat the sandwiches that Gilda had prepared for their journey home. Obliging foliage gave some cover for their use as a loo, for which the dancing Emma was in dire need of, and still wearing her gloves, which Thomas found amusing, Gilda gave everyone a sandwich and a cup of water. Emma ate hungrily. Gilda found that disturbing and thought, "Had the old woman not fed the child anything before sending her away?"

Now satisfied and sleepy, Emma stretched out on the backseat and fell asleep surrounded by her prized possessions. Rather than talk, Thomas and Gilda enjoyed the warm sunshine of the autumn day and communicated only with their eyes.

Fidgeting with her hat in her lap, Gilda remembered

*At Willow's Edge*

her walk home the night before and the figure she thought she'd seen in the willow trees. Now it seemed unlikely that anyone had been there, and she was glad she'd not mentioned it to Thomas.

༺❦༻

In order to make Emma as at ease as possible, it had been decided that Dotty alone would be in the manor kitchen when they arrived. Dotty had noticed that Emma was still referred to as "the child," by the Armstrongs occasionally, but as happy as she was, she couldn't pass judgment on anyone, least of all the dear Mrs. Armstrong.

Thomas and Gilda arrived with Emma by teatime. The second breakfast had been served and put away, and there were no airmen at the manor to intimidate the newcomer. Thomas carried Emma's suitcase, and, once again, Emma carried her own tote bag.

As the three of them entered the manor, they could smell the aroma of baking biscuits coming from the kitchen, so they went there directly. Thomas set down the suitcase by the kitchen door and crossed the floor to speak quietly to Dotty.

Dotty greeted them all casually, and although difficult, did not give particular attention to Emma standing in the doorway. To Dotty, Thomas said quietly, "She slept most of the way back and wasn't inclined to talk to us, so I have yet to tell her what comes next. All she really understands, so far, is that little girls are welcome here at the manor. How would you like to handle it?"

"Let's not force anything. I'll just see if she wants a biscuit, and we'll go from there," said Dotty thoughtfully.

"I'll follow your lead, then," said Thomas, relieved. "Where are the others?"

"Making a point not to be here. No one wanted to overwhelm the little mite. Now, let me get you and Gilda some tea."

"I thank you, Dotty, but if she doesn't make a fuss, it might be better for us to leave you two alone."

Gilda had convinced Emma to put her bag on top of her suitcase, so she could take off her warm jumper. She placed the folded jumper on top of the other things, allowing Emma to take in her surroundings for a few moments before ushering her to the loo.

When they returned to the kitchen, Dotty said to Emma cheerfully, "Come on in. Would you like a biscuit and something to drink after your long drive?"

Emma nodded eagerly and climbed up on one of the kitchen chairs. Thomas and Gilda hung back, allowing

Dotty to do all the talking.

Setting a plate of biscuits and cup of milk on the table in front of Emma, Dotty asked, "When you are through having biscuits, do you think you might help me finish baking the rest of these?"

"I can help?" asked Emma, pushing her wispy, windblown hair away from her face.

"You can if you want to—if you aren't too tired," said Dotty.

"I'm not tired," said Emma, taking a long drink of the cool milk that Dotty had saved back for her. Remembering that Thomas and Gilda were still there, Emma turned to them and said simply, "I want to stay here."

"Is it all right then, Emma, if we go to our own little house and come back later to check on you?" asked Thomas cautiously.

"Don't take my things," said Emma abruptly.

"We'll leave all your things right here by the door. We'll come back after awhile, then," said Gilda backing into the hall.

Emma looked at them stoically and said, "Goodbye."

"Goodbye," said Thomas and Gilda together.

When they were gone, Dotty sat down at the table with a cup of tea and silently ate biscuits with Emma. She knew she must follow where Emma led her, so she said very little.

"These are good," said Emma, keeping her eyes on her treat.

"Why, thank you. I can make them even better than this, but I need the right kind of flour and more sugar. I'll have to wait for that awhile longer."

"Can I wait with you?" asked Emma sweetly.

"I'd really like that," said Dotty with tears in her eyes.

"These are better than the ones Aunt Melia makes," said the child, holding up a biscuit.

She smiled at Dotty, and Dotty smiled back, asking, "Would it be all right if you stayed here tonight? My husband is hoping to meet you, too."

"All right, but does he like little girls?" asked Emma in her high-pitched voice.

"He does," said Dotty. "We all love little girls here."

"Aunt Melia is going where no one likes them."

"That's lucky for us, then," said Dotty cheerfully.

"Where will I sleep?" asked Emma.

"Well," began Dotty cautiously, "Mrs. Wood has lots of beds here at the big house, but I have the best house because it is small and snug. I have a nice bedroom that's just right for a little girl."

"I'll take that one," said Emma, pleased that she was being given choices to make on her own.

"That would make us very happy," said Dotty. "I think we'll get along fine."

When the biscuits were baked and put away in the tins, Dotty helped Emma put on her warm jumper again, and they went out the kitchen door to find Sam. When they finally found him in the garden shed, he brushed the dirt off his hands and then reached overhead where an old tricycle was hanging from a hook. He brought it down, saying, "I should get this fixed up for you. Have you ever ridden one of these, Emma?"

"No, not yet," she answered eagerly. Emma hadn't dared hope this new place would be such a good one but was thoroughly delighted that it was.

Dotty watched as the countenance of the once-unwanted child changed in the face of such good luck. Her sandy-blonde hair, badly blunt-cut just under her chin, was blowing around her thin face, but peeking behind it, blue eyes sparkled with excitement. Dotty was pleased that the child's hair was the same color as her own, and she made it her solemn vow that one day the child's face would be as plump and rosy as her own, too.

Dotty asked Emma if they should send a message to Thomas and Gilda that they need not come back right away.

Emma answered, "I think they're tired. They should just go to bed."

Grinning broadly at Sam, Dotty said, "I think they would like that idea very much."

Sam's response was a hearty laugh, followed by a coughing fit.

"Is he all right?" asked Emma.

"Oh yes," said Dotty, "I shouldn't have made him laugh so unexpectedly."

"Oh," said Emma thoughtfully.

When Sam recovered from coughing, on Dotty's request, he found David, and asked him to run up to Willows Edge with the message to come a different day. David agreed to the errand gladly.

Dotty led her little charge across the paved courtyard, where they went up the outside steps to the carriage house above. Emma loved it up there and ran from one window to the next, looking out over the garden. When

Dotty showed her into her room, she could only be persuaded to leave it to have a quick dinner in the tiny kitchen. She was then pleased to be put in her bed, where Sam told her a story. Together Dotty and Sam tucked her up beneath the pink counterpane and left her for her first night in her new home.

As they were leaving her room, Dotty said, "Night night, Emma." Carefully closing the door, making sure to leave a crack, so they would hear her if she cried, Dotty added, "If you need us, Emma, we are in the next room."

"I know," was the child's simple response. She rolled on her side with her kitten pulled close and fell asleep immediately.

Dotty had a more difficult time falling asleep and made sure that Sam couldn't do so, either. She chattered on and on, and Sam didn't attempt to stop her until it was past midnight. Then, all he said was, "Tomorrow is another day, my dear. What do you say we get some sleep and take this up again in the morning?"

Dotty kissed her man and quit talking, but her thoughts went on and on into the night. They had been given Sunday off entirely to get to know Emma, so Dotty allowed herself to wallow on in her happiness into the wee hours of the morning. She knew that she would have all the energy she needed for tomorrow, because she was running on excitement, and that, she knew, would keep her going strong, for a day or two anyway.

## Chapter Nine

David had gotten little information about the child out of Sam when he was asked to go to Willows Edge to tell Thomas and Gilda not to return that night, so all he could tell them was that things seemed to be going fine. Likewise, he got little or nothing from Gilda and Thomas, who were visibly exhausted from their day, so he had nothing to report to Priscilla upon his return. That was not an issue, though, because Priscilla did not ask a single detail about the child's arrival, temperament, appearance, or even her well-being. David was disappointed in her lack of interest but reminded himself that he was not in her shoes and must not judge. He couldn't help thinking, though, that her own well-being was jeopardized by her apathetic approach to the situation.

༺❦༻❦༻

Thomas spent Sunday alone at the cottage, doing chores, both inside and out, because Gilda necessarily had to work to cover Dotty's absence at the manor. She had been more than willing to come in before six, but David and Priscilla had offered to help Eleanor with the early breakfast, as well as Dotty's other duties. That seemed little to ask in light of what had been accomplished on their behalf that week.

At Gilda's normal time, she left the cottage and headed across the field, which had become her regular route since the harvest. To her surprise, she met an elderly gentleman. They greeted each other in passing, not stopping to chat. Crossing the main Englewood road and making her way across the manor lawn to the kitchen door, Gilda thought about the hatless gentleman and wondered who he was. Entering the manor, she put him out of her mind, as she greeted Spanky with the obligatory enthusiasm before getting to work.

There were always fewer airmen to feed on Sundays, and during the occasional lull in her workload that day, Gilda thought about the man she had met in the field and speculated about with whom in the village he might be connected. She even wondered if it was he who she had seen two days before in the willow trees. She decided he was not. The other figure had seemed furtive and menacing, quite unlike this comely gentleman with his relaxed gait and gentle countenance.

As Gilda, Eleanor, and the Armstrongs worked side by side in the old kitchen that day, there was no talk of Emma, the subject most on their minds. Besides Dotty and

Sam, only Thomas and Gilda had met Emma, and she was foremost in all their thoughts. Priscilla was somewhat curious, in spite of herself, as were David and Eleanor, but since Priscilla had made such a point of not wishing to know the child, she thought it best not to inquire for details now. And since she was quiet on the subject, it seemed inconsiderate for anyone else to pump Gilda for details.

As for Gilda, having not been asked to share anything, she concluded that the subject of Emma was best left alone, although it hung in the air like a bad kitchen odor. Their stilted conversations touched only on the safe subjects of the airmen, the weather, and the work at hand. Gilda thought it was amusing and couldn't wait to see Thomas and tell him about the unusual atmosphere in the kitchen that day.

ஃ∙ஒ∙ஃ∙ஒ

Sam and Dotty had decided to take Emma to Englewood for their first day together. After a leisurely breakfast, they walked to Englewood, past Gilda's childhood home, Cottage on the Lane. There, from the shed behind the house, Simon and Agnes Morris saw them and waved. They knew nothing of the adoption, so they were only marginally curious about the little girl walking into town with the Coopers and their picnic basket.

Matty and Lucas could be seen busily tending to the pig and chickens in the pens beyond and didn't see the Coopers stroll past. Dotty was pleased that they had not had to stop and talk to anyone. She and Sam just wanted Emma to themselves for a day, before they had to share her with everyone. They needed to explain the permanent nature of their arrangement to her, and they needed to know how she felt about it. The Coopers knew Emma's feelings on the matter would not change anything, really, but they felt strongly that she must at least feel like she was consulted, and that her feelings and opinions mattered.

They first took Emma to the eleven o'clock church service, although they had not attended a single meeting in more than three years. They wanted to rear her properly and knew that her religious education should begin at once. Dotty was adamant that the church sanctuary was the ideal place for children to learn to sit quietly, the beginnings of self-control, so Sam had agreed to go. When the service was over, the Coopers stopped long enough in the foyer to help Emma with her coat and collect their basket. They were greeted by villagers, who, although they were curious about the little girl, were too polite to inquire, and Dotty and Sam offered no information on the subject, smugly going on their way.

They next took her to the small Englewood Park, where they consumed their picnic lunch. Knowing they were making an outing that day, Eleanor had made up the basket for them early and had set it at the bottom of the steps that rose to the flat above the carriage house. Dotty and Sam had been touched by the thoughtfulness of the basket, and Emma had made a full inventory of its contents before starting out.

Although it was a sunny day, it was cool and the park was empty. Sam pushed Emma in a swing for awhile, and then they started a collection of fallen leaves, in which Emma became totally engrossed.

Finally, Dotty thought the time was right to have the necessary conversation with Emma to explain to her the permanent plans that had been made for her. The Coopers had dreaded this, actually, because, although Emma was happy with the situation at present, they feared she might not want it long-term.

Although Sam had been capable of identifying leaves and pushing the swing, Dotty felt that talking to Emma should be her responsibility. Finding a warm bench in a sunny spot, they sat down, placing Emma between them.

Dotty asked, "What's your full name, Emma, do you know it?"

"My name is Emma May, but Aunt Melia only calls me that when she is angry with me, so I don't like it much."

"That's understandable," said Dotty. "Do you know your last name?"

"It's *Beneton*," said Emma with little confidence. "I think," she quickly added.

"We are the Coopers, Emma. My name is Dotty and this is Sam. We would like to talk to you about something important."

"What?" asked Emma, as she looked longingly at her surroundings. Watching her, Dotty knew that Emma was already losing interest in all this talking, and before she could think of what to say next, Emma asked, "Could we play some more? I love it here."

"Yes, we'll play some more, but since you love it here, how would you like to stay with us at our house?" asked Dotty.

"Well, you said I could stay until you got more sugar," said Emma accusingly.

Remembering their exchange in the kitchen the day before, Dotty smiled, but could think of nothing at all to say. Emma turned her body around on her stomach, and when she felt her feet touch the ground, she pushed herself away from the bench. "I can stay," said Emma without emotion, her blue eyes betraying nothing. "Aunt Melia won't care."

Dotty was glad that Emma wanted to stay, but the purpose of their conversation had not been fully achieved. She opened her mouth to respond, but wanting this so much, tears sprang to her eyes, and she could not think how to proceed.

Sam said, "Come here, Emma." He had thought he should leave this chat to Dotty, but in the face of possible rejection, it appeared her courage had failed her.

He picked up Emma and gently placed her on his knee. He said, "We've never had a child before and were wondering if you would like to be our little girl. Your new name would be Emma May Cooper, and we would be your mama and papa forever. If you say yes, then that is what you'll call us, and we'll get back to playing. What do you say to that?"

Emma nodded energetically.

"Well then," asked Sam, "Can you say Emma May Cooper?"

Emma jumped off his knee, crying happily, "Emma May Cooper, Emma May Cooper, Emma May Cooper."

She took Sam's hand and said, "Come on, then."

With a wink to Dotty, indicating victory for which he wanted full credit, Sam took Emma to the far side of the park, while Dotty intermittently wept and mopped her face with her crumpled handkerchief.

They returned home in the late afternoon, attended to the chickens' needs, and together climbed the steps to the carriage house. They had no intentions of stopping in at the manor. They had been promised a day alone, and they were taking it.

With fresh eyes, Emma explored again every corner of her new home and laid personal claim to everything in her own room. After an early meal and a quick bath, Emma went to bed as willingly as she had done the night before. Once again, Sam told a story at Emma's bedside, and together, Dotty and Sam tucked her in. The only thing that differed from the night before was when Emma said, "Night, night, Mama and Papa."

It had been an emotionally draining day, and Dotty, who had gotten little sleep the night before, fell asleep long before her husband.

Sam had found that he was as thrilled to be a parent as was Dotty, and he marveled at the goodness of God in giving them this miracle in the midst of war and chaos.

*At Willows Edge*

Sam was glad that Dotty was sleeping soundly, because it saved him embarrassment when tears of joy coursed down his face and unto his pillow.

༄⋆༄⋆

When Gilda returned home that afternoon, Thomas had cleaned the cottage and prepared her a dinner of tinned ham and potatoes. He listened with interest as Gilda washed her hands at the sink and described the strange atmosphere that pervaded the normally-relaxed manor kitchen.

Thomas carried the tray laden with their filled plates, utensils and glasses, and Gilda brought the jug of water and two lovely, white serviettes from her valued chest of linens. Sitting down together at the table in the sitting room, Gilda finished telling him about her day at the manor.

"Now, tell me about your day," she said, nodding her approval of their modest dinner.

"Well, I had the pleasure of meeting our nearest neighbor."

"I passed a man in the field, on my way to work this morning," exclaimed Gilda.

"When I spoke of you, he mentioned meeting

someone in the field, and I told him it must have been you. Since you have tomorrow off, I took the liberty of inviting him for dinner." Thomas looked up from his plate and cringed, knowing what was coming.

"Whatever shall we eat, for heaven's sake?" asked Gilda with horror.

Laughing, Thomas replied, "We were so enjoying each other's company in the garden this morning, he said he'd love to have us over for dinner to continue our conversation. When he stopped by to see his brother-in-law, near Birmingham, on his way here yesterday, he was offered a couple of pheasants, which he said he'd love to share with us. He hesitated to make the invitation, he said, because his house isn't yet fit for company. So, I asked him to come here, and he said he'd bring the meat cooked at about seven thirty. Does that solve the problem, darling?"

"Well, it's a strange arrangement for a first invitation, but it does make all the difference," said Gilda visibly relieved. "I'll make another pie, apple, this time, and I'll think of something else to go with the pheasant, probably potatoes and a vegetable."

"Excellent," said Thomas beaming.

Pushing her food around her plate, Gilda asked, "What's his name?"

*At Willows Edge*

"Richard Fitzgerald. He and his wife bought their cottage some years ago," explained Thomas.

"And Mrs. Fitzgerald isn't here yet?"

"She died in America. He's alone now and has been for some time, I think. When I asked him questions about himself, he said it was a long story and would tell us both tomorrow. I think he's had an interesting war, which can be said of everyone, I suppose."

"What did you talk about?" asked Gilda.

"Oh, the progress of the war in the European Theatre, as well as the Pacific. We talked about the explosions lately around London and possible explanations."

"Like the explosion that killed the Gates family?"

"Yes, he said his widowed brother-in-law showed him the information he'd started collecting of some unexplained explosions that have been reported in the newspapers and even some unreported blasts he's heard of near and around London and on the continent. He was making a study of it. Mr. Fitzgerald said he had accused his brother-in-law, the clergyman, of making a hobby of it."

"Whatever will we talk about when the war is over?" asked Gilda wearily.

Gilda suddenly thought of the figure that had

frightened her in the trees two days before, and she was about to mention it, when it occurred to her that she could ask Mr. Fitzgerald if he'd had anyone open the house recently for his return. That would explain everything, she thought, and there would be no need to worry Thomas unnecessarily.

The following evening, after an enjoyable meal, the men did the washing up, continuing their friendly conversation. Thomas then walked Mr. Fitzgerald back to his cottage in the dark. With the help of their torches, they made their way the short distance up the narrow lane.

Thomas asked, "Do you have a car, Mr. Fitzgerald?"

"I do, but the vicar has had use of it during the war, and I can see no reason to change the arrangement, just yet, since he was kind enough to drive me and my things up here in it."

Thomas nodded and making small talk, asked, "Did you know that all these little cottages have names?"

"My address for the post is Gypsy Row," answered Richard. "The folks that lived here before us had a name for it, too, I think, but I can't recall what it was."

"I wonder if Gypsy Row was so named for a transient gypsy population that may have camped here at one time," speculated Thomas.

"That would be an interesting subject to look into."

As they approached the door, Thomas asked tentatively, "I heard you tell Gilda that you'd not hired anyone to open your house for you. I saw someone in the willow trees early yesterday morning. I wasn't even dressed yet. I happened to peer in your direction from the lean-to window and saw someone, just standing there. I wondered if you knew of anyone who might have had any business on the property that lies between us."

"No, Thomas, I can't think of any reason for someone to be here on my account. I let no one at all know that I was returning."

"Well, I didn't want to alarm Gilda. Anywhere else in town, I would think nothing of it, but out here, well, it bothered me. Maybe, these feelings are due to the war, you know, thinking everyone is a spy or something."

"That seems natural enough."

Thomas chuckled at himself, and Richard thanked him for the evening and went inside.

Deep in thought, Thomas walked home.

ॐ∽ॐ∽

Since the men had insisted on doing the washing up,

Gilda, exhausted as usual these days, retired to her room, reached for her diary, and began to write.

*October 2, 1944*
*Dear Diary,*

*I really enjoyed getting to know Mr. Richard Fitzgerald tonight. He is such a kind and charming man. I would guess he's about sixty-five years old. He has longish, steel-gray hair, hazel-coloured eyes, and a very pleasant face. He's a tall and gangly man and had to duck his head, going from room to room in our cottage. When I cautioned him about the low beams in the sitting room, he laughed and said he had already learnt that lesson the hard way in his own cottage, which is similar to ours.*

*He told us he'd had a career in art, running a London art gallery for many years. I laughed when he told us he was a frustrated artist, his desire exceeding his talent. I thought his appearance fit the part of an artist, though, remembering his loose, relaxed gait as he crossed the field towards me yesterday. I remember thinking he looked rather out of place here. I realise now that I had put him in a bohemian light, considering him the type of person who might get bored with our provincial traditions. First impressions are lasting and often foolish, I think. He*

*At Willows Edge*

*belongs here as much as anyone.*

*Mr. Fitzgerald is so open and friendly, I feel like I've known him for a long time. I must, or I could have hardly allowed him to do the washing up on his first dinner invitation.*

*He has just returned from America, coming home on the USS Wakefield. He had great difficulty getting passage and a friend of his had to pull strings and call in favors in order to get him on an American military ship.*

*He explained that he and his wife had purchased their cottage when they retired from London, early in 1939. They wanted a small, affordable place in the country, so they could follow their dream and travel. Mr. Fitzgerald wanted to paint scenery, and his wife wanted to see the world. He told us how his wife's first priority was to get to America, though, where their daughter had just had her third child. They had never seen any of the children, so they went for what was to be a short stay.*

*Mr. Fitzgerald said they should have left New York much sooner, but he couldn't pull his wife away from the grandchildren. When they did try to book passage, England had just declared war, and his wife was terrified that their ship might be sunk. He had felt early on that it was still safe enough to journey home, but then, of course, it became impossible.*

*His wife died two years ago, and he had been trying to get home since. He has a son, who is or was involved in the war, but Mr. Fitzgerald doesn't know what has happened to him and fears he is dead. He said it has been awful wondering what has become of him. The navy has traced him to Singapore. I told him that he must meet Mrs. Wood, because she has had similar experiences.*

*I thought it was very healthy for Thomas to tell Mr. Fitzgerald about his war experiences. He told it all very matter-of-factly, but Mr. Fitzgerald had no trouble understanding the depth of what Thomas has been through. I think that with Mr. Fitzgerald's friendship, Thomas may have the help he needs to put his nightmares to rest. He hasn't had one since his father's infidelity was made known to me, however, so perhaps, that was part of it, too.*

*I remembered to ask Mr. Fitzgerald if he had hired someone to open the house for him, and he said he had not. Although my mystery is not solved, I'm determined to forget about it. I don't want to give Thomas anything else to worry about.*

*Emma's arrival has been interesting, but that story will have to wait. I hear Thomas coming back in, so I'll finish up. I'll just add that Mr. Fitzgerald cooked the pheasant himself, and it was delicious. My pie was fair, but Mr. Fitzgerald went on and on about it. Oh, and one last note, he didn't seem to notice my deformities. Thomas must have told him ahead of time to make it easier for me. I have a wonderful husband. I still have to pinch myself at times to believe my great luck.*

৵৶৵৶

To put his own mind at ease, the next day at the airfield, Thomas placed telephone calls to the local inns within two miles of Englewood. There were two that qualified as decent places to stay and another, which was merely a boarding house. He asked the managers of each if there had been any new or unusual guests staying there the last few days and got the same answer from the desks of the boarding house and the inn nearest Nuneaton. Their guests were primarily permanent ones, having been residents since the beginning of the war. The other innkeeper, at Codgett's Country Inn, said that there had been few strangers in their midst, except for the occasional patronage of those wealthy enough to escape the city from time to time.

The man said, "My residents are gentle folks. If you are looking for criminals, you should look elsewhere. And, before you ask, I do not divulge the names of my guests, unless officially required to."

Thomas thanked the man and said, "I understand completely. I'm looking for a different type of person anyway."

When Thomas finished making his calls, he was confident that the lone person he had seen was neither a spy, nor a gypsy. He reminded himself that people were free to walk the countryside in England without being questioned and decided he would leave well enough alone, for now.

As he walked over to speak to the maintenance crews about a particular problem they'd been having, he reasoned that he wouldn't have paid any notice to the mysterious presence, in the first place, if he hadn't sensed that the person was being sneaky, staying intentionally out of view. Thomas laughed at himself and quickened his step.

Approaching the Nissan hut, Thomas greeted the group leader cheerfully and asked, "Have you noticed how strange we've all become as a result of this war?"

"Of course, dear fellow, absolutely. Case in point, do come talk to my crew, some of the strangest chaps in all of England."

## Chapter Ten

Eleanor Wood wrote in her journal, *It is the twenty-fourth of October, and we have a situation here that I could never have imagined. Emma has already found her way into everyone's heart, but one, which is, of course, Priscilla's. I think she was curious, at first, to catch a glimpse of her husband's love child, but since then, has been cautious when on the ground floor, making sure she is never in the child's presence.*

*The rest of us at the manor, including many airmen who Sam talks to on the grounds, have been introduced to Emma over the course of the last few weeks. I thought she might be a strange, damaged child, but Dotty and Sam are doing wonders with her. She appears to be as secure and happy as any other child. She has added a new dimension to our life here at the manor, for which I'm very pleased, in spite of Priscilla's dilemma. She said herself that she would leave if it was too difficult for her. I'd really hate to see them go, but Priscilla is so unhappy.*

*Dotty has the same work schedule as before, and since the gardens have been harvested and stored, Sam can spend his days with Emma. She helps him with the chickens and goes wherever he goes. I have made friends with her,* and as I predicted, Dotty has carried on her workload as devotedly as before.

In the summer months, Sam often has breakfast here at the manor, but now that it is cooler, we see little of him, unless we summon him. So, as infrequently as we see Emma here inside the house, it is strange to me how reclusive Priscilla has become.

I have asked her if there is anything we might do to make her life more comfortable, but she insists that she is fine. She goes with David a lot, and as much as I've anticipated the announcement that they are going back to Surrey, no such announcement has come. David has been assigned many patients in this area, victims of D-day. Apparently, to go back to Surrey right now would create some confusion in his workload and would inconvenience others, which David would hate, so he and Priscilla stay on.

When I go upstairs, I sometimes hear Priscilla at her sewing machine. Gilda goes up occasionally to help her and make plans for their future business, but she has told me herself that Priscilla's heart is no longer in it.

So the arrival of Emma May Cooper, who loves the sound of her new name, and repeats it constantly, has brought great happiness to the Coopers and equal *unhappiness to another. Of course, the good doctor has made friends with Emma, but I doubt that the child has seen so much as a glimpse of Priscilla. If she has, she must have a sixth sense and knows not to pursue her. This creates somewhat of a strange atmosphere in the house now, which I find a bit nerve-wracking. There's an indomitable spirit inside Priscilla somewhere, and for the sake of all of us, as well as herself, I hope she finds it soon.*

*I hired Lucas to pick the apples, and I cannot remember ever having a more abundant crop. Wilbur would be proud. We bottled much applesauce, which was quite tart, lacking the sugar that I normally like to use. We have eaten lots of pies, also very tart.*

*I couldn't stand to waste anything, so after bottling all the applesauce we could stand, I decided to try my hand at drying apple slices. It was quite a process, and I have to admit the smell has been obnoxious, at times, but I became rather obsessed with the idea of doing it. Although, Pris has been so reclusive, David insisted that he take the apple slices upstairs, where he and Priscilla strung them up, covering the ceiling of the sewing room. They are still drying up there, and the overwhelming smell that permeated the room at first, has been replaced by a tart, but appealing, one.*

## Meredith Kennon

*Dotty and Gilda helped with the slicing, and with everyone's cooperation, I will have an enormous stash of dried apples. I think I will wrap them up and give them to any of the airmen I happen to see wandering through here at Christmastime.*

*As for the rest of us, Gilda's pregnancy has gone smoothly, and Thomas's nightmares have stopped, thanks in part, according to Gilda, to the arrival of their neighbour. He is a widower, just returned from America, after being stuck there since the beginning of the war. He has become a friend to Thomas, and Gilda thinks he might even be a kind of father figure to him. I'm happy for all of them, although maybe not for myself. I can't remember the last time I saw Thomas here.*

*The Armstrongs are invited go to the cottage often enough, so I suppose Thomas never sees a need to come to the manor. Out of respect for his mother, I'm sure that Thomas stays away from here to avoid Emma. How can one little child cause such a stir?*

*I have procrastinated making invitations for Christmas, which must be done soon or everyone will have made their plans already, and I'll end up with no one. Priscilla's melancholy is definitely a factor in my holding off, because I was hoping for her support. It is difficult making such plans knowing how she feels, but I truly believe it would provide her a necessary diversion. We all need a distraction from the war, so I'm going to move forward this week, find out exactly who will be here, and thereby determine how best to approach Jane about coming.*

*Edith writes that she is very much in love and that work at the farm has slowed since the harvest. I wonder why she hasn't come home since Gilda's wedding.*

*As for me, we are still in the dark about William's well-being, and the war drags on and on and on. In the London area, there have been occasional news reports of incredible explosions that rock entire neighbourhoods, and they have yet to be explained. Well, that is certainly a dire note to end on, but I must get to sleep. I will definitely pursue making invitations for Christmas right away.*

Two nights later, Eleanor wrote, *Today was rainy and cold. I spent the day with Gilda, who was in high spirits, and Dotty, who is predictably a ray of sunshine, of late. Sam and Emma remained absent and dry above the carriage house, and I saw nothing of Priscilla and David, except for hearing them come down the stairs and leave the estate in their Austin.*

## Meredith Kennon

*Our work was especially light today, so Dotty, Gilda, and I drank lots of hot tea and sat for hours at the kitchen table, making plans for our Christmas gathering. I was originally thinking of it as a Christmas party, but I'm now convinced, if I really expect Jane to come, the simpler, the more intimate our event is, the more likely it is that she will.*

*This afternoon, Gilda rang her father, who told her that they had promised the Leventhalls that they would take the children to Shrewsbury for Christmas. Apparently, Thomas and Gilda had been invited, too, about which we all laughed, having heard from Lucas about the tiny dimensions of the Leventhall's home.*

*Then, this evening, I made a telephone call to Banks Farm. Edith has been a Land Girl there since the beginning of the war, and Lena Banks and I are now on a first-name basis. She graciously found Edith for me, so I could ask her about her Christmas plans. I was rather broken-hearted when she told me that, if things went as planned, she and Larry were going south to meet Larry's brother, Craig, who was scheduled for his leave at Christmas. He has been serving on the continent since D-day. I mentioned to Edith how I had high hopes that Jane and Willy would be here, which I thought would make her rethink her own plans, but she simply said she would make every effort to stop through here on her way down to Kent. As much as she loves her brother, I can see that her plans will be driven by her love for Larry. That's telling. I expect an engagement announcement any day.*

*While I was at it, I rang the quartermaster and learnt that I was being given a break from feeding the airmen over Christmas. So, although we will have some men sleeping here, we will have no one to feed from the second breakfast on the twenty-third through Boxing Day.*

*All our efforts today have been productive, because I now know that the number of people coming for Christmas will be even smaller than I originally thought, which encourages me that Jane might be willing to come. I'll write her tomorrow and invite the three of them.*

಄ೋ಄ೋ

The following morning was again, rainy and chilly. Gilda came in with a wet head, in spite of her anorak, and began sneezing immediately.

Dotty exclaimed, "Good heavens, girl, don't you have the sense to bring a brolly?"

"It wasn't by the door, Dotty, and I didn't want to be late looking for it. The anorak kept me dry enough."

"Of course, and that is why you have raindrops dripping from the ends of your hair and are obviously getting a chill."

"I'm fine, really, but I'll do better going home. I promise." Inwardly, Gilda laughed at Dotty's enhanced maternal instincts since the arrival of Emma, but she loved her for it.

Over the course of the day, the skies were so dark, at times, that they had to turn on the electric lights in the kitchen to see what they were doing. The Girl Guides came, as previously arranged, to clean the common areas, and after giving them tea, Eleanor penned her letter to Jane.

*Greystone Manor, Englewood, Warwickshire*
*October 27, 1944*
*Dear Jane,*

*We are having our second miserable day in a row. The skies are so dark, we've had to turn on the electric lights to do our work in the kitchen. Our workload has been undemanding, though, so we have drunk lots of tea and made our plans for Christmas.*

*I certainly understand your hesitation to visit Greystone as the mother of my grandson, knowing full well the scrutiny that you might receive, but our group at*

*Christmas will be an intimate one. It will include Gilda and Thomas Gardner (of whom I've already told you much about), his mother and her husband (Dr. and Mrs. Armstrong, and our devoted help, the Coopers. They have recently adopted a three-year-old girl, who will be here, too. My daughter Edith has made plans with her soon-to-be fiancé (just a mother's intuitive prophecy), but she has promised to stop by at some point.*

*I would like you to consider coming, knowing that the folks attending are all basically family and in the know about your situation. There would be no awkwardness, and you would be welcomed heartily. Even the airmen will be scarce.*

*Christmas is still two months away, but we are in the process of getting some bedrooms in order. Half of the first floor is once again mine, freed up from the RAF, so we will have plenty of room. If you feel you can accept, please tell your mother and Willy that I look forward to seeing them again soon. I hope you can arrange to stay with me from the twenty-second through the New Year.*

*I know you await word from William on pins and needles, as do I, but I believe, deep in my heart, that he is surviving. It has given me so much comfort, knowing that the possibility exists that he has received your news through the Red Cross. It will give him the added courage he needs to endure the war, which I believe will end soon.*

*I look forward to hearing from you. Please ring if you hear from William.*
*Sincerely,*
*Eleanor*

❧❧❧❧

At Cottage on the Lane, Agnes had become increasingly desperate to have permanent guardianship of the Smith children. Agnes and Simon wanted to pursue legal adoption of them, and if their father was indeed dead, they believed it should be easily accomplished.

Months before, Lucas had shared with Simon that he had never known of any other relatives and confessed that he'd not even questioned his mother about it at any time. The father's name, Theodore Smith, had been on a list of the dead, which Mr. Leventhall and Lucas had seen when they had gone to London in April, upon learning that his mother had been killed in a factory accident. The list stated that the man was of Langstead, London, which meant nothing to Lucas, giving him no real reason to believe the man to be his father.

Since confirming the death the children's father

seemed the place to start, Simon had begun the process by writing a single letter at his wife's request, having no idea at all to whom he should send it. Simon summoned Dr. Armstrong to the cottage to request his help, and believing there to be a medical emergency, David arrived as quickly as possible.

Simon asked, "Didn't you help the Coopers with the adoption of their little girl?"

"I can't say that I did, really," replied the doctor, "I just carried documents from place to place. I may be able to help you connect with a solicitor in London, but I must caution you of two things. First, you must be patient. These kinds of things will be more easily sorted out after the war is over, and secondly, this could get quite costly."

Disappointed, Agnes said, "Patience is something we are tops at, Doctor, but money, now that's another thing."

Knowing he had dealt them a crushing blow, the doctor said, "Patience is the key then. Let's wait out the war. Perhaps, agencies will be created to help with these things later on, you know, at little expense. Don't lose heart."

Simon sighed and said, "No, no, we'll not do that, will we, Agnes?"

Saying nothing, Agnes got up and showed the doctor to the door. She wanted the meeting over before the children returned from school.

Lucas and Matty were both enjoying school this term and no longer gave any thought to their father's whereabouts. The man had run out on their mother years ago, and Matty had never even known him.

Lucas was popular at school and getting high marks. He had, at his own volition, taken some responsibilities off Simon's shoulders and had come to feel protective of his foster father of delicate health. Although Lucas had long known, Matty had never guessed that their foster mother had been so against their coming in the first place. Agnes and Matty had become attached in a profound and unexpected way, and even the villagers talked of the changes they had seen in Agnes Morris.

It was Agnes, who felt the need for immediate action towards adopting the children. Since hearing that Dotty and Simon had adopted Emma, she had wanted that same permanency in her relationship with Lucas and Mattie. Simon and Agnes were not privy to the knowledge that Emma was the love child of Priscilla's husband, but they had seen the great change in the Coopers and longed for the assurance that the children would not be taken from them. She would do as Dr. Armstrong suggested and wait out the war, but then, when the war was truly over, she vowed she'd do everything in her power to get the adoption accomplished.

The Morrises had accepted the invitation to go to Shrewsbury for Christmas, and since they had gone no further afield than Nuneaton in years, they were as excited as the children at the prospect. Homemade gifts were already being worked on, the family was thriving as never before, and even their daughter came to visit more often.

Since her birthday, Gilda had made a renewed effort to visit their cottage regularly. She and her mum had developed a comfortable, if not close, relationship. After one such visit, Gilda went happily home to write about her day in her journal. Arriving at the cottage at about the same time as the last sighting, Gilda was unnerved to see a figure moving along the hedge behind the willow trees. Reprimanding herself for being so jumpy, Gilda reminded herself that others, besides herself, were getting out and enjoying the day. It wasn't until the person, whose face was hidden by the jacket's hood, turned directly at her, that Gilda's heart began to pound. She raced frantically to the door, let herself in with shaking hands, and quickly locked the door.

After racing to the back window again, and seeing no one, Gilda made a fire in the huge fireplace. She got as comfortable as she could on their wooden settee, and opened her journal to write.

*October 30, 1944*
*Dear Diary,*

*I left from work a little early today to visit my parents. On the way home, I saw the same furtive figure behind the stand of willow trees as I did a month ago. Just as I was feeling ashamed of myself for being frightened of the lone, hooded person, I saw him turn directly toward me, and although I couldn't see his face, the sensation I felt was so menacing, it frightened me to my very core. I have no real sense of whether this person is a man or a woman, since I saw only the hooded coat and wellingtons.*

*Probably, I should to talk to someone about this, (maybe Mr. Fitzgerald or David) but not Thomas. He has seemed so relaxed and happy, lately. I don't want to give him something new to worry about. I have no enemies, so a lone person shouldn't have such an effect on me. Perhaps my pregnancy is causing my imagination to be overactive.*

*It has been raining for a full week, so, since today wasn't quite as gloomy, I decided to get out. I had finally decided to tell my parents about my pregnancy, and I think they were truly pleased.*

*When Dad went outside to putter around the soggy garden, Mum and I had an interesting discussion. Watching my dad from the window, my mum said he is happier now than she could ever remember. She said she felt that a large part of that happiness came from having the responsibility of the children, which made him feel useful again. She said that he was also very pleased with the way things had turned out for me.*

*And then she admitted that some of this mighty change in him may have come from his belief that he had convinced her to stop drinking. We laughed hard when my mother said, "In fact, my drinking companion, Doris, moved away to live with her brother in Cheshire. She had been the supplier of my habit, and suddenly she was gone. Alcohol, like everything else has become increasingly difficult to get."*

*I have been able to check myself as to my childish jealousy of Matty. I have never blamed the child, nor would I have taken anything away from her, but I was becoming more and more irritated by her amazing bond with Mum. Maybe, part of the change in me is that I'm pregnant. I've heard that having a child strengthens the affection and* respect one has for their own mum. I see that happening with me.

When I left their cottage, it was agreed that Thomas and I would come to dinner next Saturday night, and as for Christmas, we will exchange gifts on New Year's Eve, after their return home from Shropshire.

Thomas has not had a serious nightmare, since he started sharing his war experiences with Mr. Fitzgerald. I have encouraged their friendship, and tomorrow night, he is joining us once again for dinner. His company has been good for us. I think we were becoming a little reclusive.

Priscilla is having a hard time with the presence of Emma, but she assures me that she wouldn't change a thing. She is willing to stick it out here awhile longer, she says, and having the child in a good home is a true blessing. I always note that she never mentions Emma by name. I do believe that once Priscilla comes to grips with her anger at John for, not only his infidelity, but more so, the embarrassment and humiliation he's caused her since then, she'll find that her ill feelings toward Emma will lessen. When that happens, I believe Priscilla will become herself again.

Thomas is apparently oblivious to his mum's great trial. Dotty is so right, women do pay more attention to *things than men, and in this case, I'm glad. And that is precisely why I will not worry him with the unknown person who walks our trees at dusk. I walk the field at dusk every workday. How do I know that I don't give someone a fright from a distance? I wear a hooded anorak many days. Does that make me menacing?*

*The war drags on and on. We are all so tired of it. I'm glad we have the baby to look forward to.*

❧✧❧✧

At Greystone Manor, the post included a letter from Jane.

*Number 26, Bramble Avenue, Trubury, Herefordshire*
*November 2, 1944*
*Dear Eleanor,*

*My mother and I have talked about your invitation and will try to come. We plan to be there no later than the twenty-third and will stay through the New Year. It is awhile off yet to make firm plans, but I will let you know if anything changes. I'm sure you have said and done all the right things to your family and staff, but I can't help fearing it will still be awkward for me. I am constantly glad that I have Willy in my life and would change nothing, but meeting new people who either know all about me or know nothing of me is still a bit frightening. I will do my best to handle the situation, though, and I hope you know I appreciate your consideration.*

*It has been far too long since we have heard from William, which is my second reservation about coming. If I haven't heard anything by Christmas, I might be too distraught to come. But, I have recently been assured by my neighbour (who corresponds regularly with his informed brother in Dorset) that it is foolish to look for a letter very often. In fact, he says that the two we have already received within three months of each other, is more than most are getting. I'm trying very hard to align my expectations with reality, I really am. Thank you for inviting us.*

*Affectionately,*

*Jane*

## Chapter Eleven

Arriving for work the next day, on an especially cold morning for so early in November, Gilda joined Dotty and Eleanor at the table for tea. Gilda was now included in all the meetings and discussions, which included menus, food shortages, and even the scheduling of the Girl Guides for their twice monthly cleaning of the men's common areas.

Eleanor seemed rather pleased this morning, and Gilda soon knew why. Eleanor produced from her stack of papers, the letter from Jane. She read it to the others and looked up with a victorious expression. "Surely, we will hear from William, don't you think?" she asked pleadingly.

Simultaneously, Dotty and Gilda answered, "Of course."

Dotty couldn't help being worried about Eleanor's health. It had been just a year ago when she had come down with a cold that had progressed into pneumonia. Those had been some dire days, she remembered. She said, "Don't you go getting sick again, like you did last year, Mrs. Wood. I'm not going to stand by and watch you work and worry yourself ill again. Now, plan your Christmas in full, to your heart's content, but please leave the heavy work for me, and for heaven's sake, don't worry about anything!"

"I wouldn't dream of letting you take on extra work," exclaimed Eleanor. "Besides, it's going to be a quiet, intimate gathering. I want a tree in the hall and some decent food. That will suffice me."

"Well, good. The tree I can guarantee, but the quality of the food will be another thing, altogether."

"It will all be wonderful," said Gilda. "Tell us about Emma, Dotty. What has she been up to?"

"Oh, she is the smartest little thing! She has taken a liking to having her hair curled, so that's become a nightly ritual, and Sam always tells her a story at bedtime. She's filling out and her cheeks are getting rosy. She is a treasure to Sam and me."

"Have there been many rough spots?" asked Eleanor.

"No, there really haven't been. In the beginning, we thought there might be. It seemed natural, you know. She hasn't had an easy life. That old aunt of hers gave her very little attention, and even less affection. But, do you know what I find interesting?" asked Dotty.

"What's that?" asked Gilda, leaning forward, her elbows on the scrubbed table.

"She has never asked about the old lady, not once."

"She's happy now, Dotty," said Gilda fondly.

"That, she is," said Dotty beaming. "Sam and me want to give her something special for Christmas, but hardly know where to start. I've been fattening her up, and would you believe it? She's growing out of all her things."

Just as Eleanor was about to offer to look into finding some clothes for the child, Dotty headed her off, saying, "And don't go asking that Mrs. Adair to find Emma some clothes. Sam and me will handle it ourselves."

Eleanor nodded her assent.

"She's just a little beauty, too, you know," continued Dotty proudly. "We'll never be able to claim she looks like me or Sam, like real parents can, but we're mighty lucky she came along. I'll tell you who she looks like, though. She looks like Thomas. She's got his eyes, and that's a fact."

When the three women looked up, Priscilla was standing motionlessly in the doorway. They had not heard her come down the stairs.

Surprised by her sudden appearance, Eleanor exclaimed, "Priscilla, come join us. I thought you had gone with David, or I would have invited you down for tea."

Pale and noticeably thinner than a month ago,

Priscilla turned and walked away without saying anything.

Silence hung in the kitchen, and Dotty covered her mouth in shame. She whispered, "Oh why did I have to say those things?"

"Because you are a proud mama," said Eleanor quietly. "Now listen, Dotty, this is Priscilla's problem, and you didn't cause it. She's going to get through this, but it isn't up to you to get her there. You must enjoy this time in your life to the fullest. It isn't fair to you or Sam, or even Emma, if you guard yourself at every turn."

"I just hate to hurt someone's feelings," said Dotty, wearily getting to her feet and collecting the tea cups. "I should have been more careful. I haven't seen her for so long, it didn't occur to me that she could even be here. This has been awfully hard for her."

Gilda got up and started doing her work. As mundane as her kitchen work had been the last ten months, she had never minded it. Its simplicity allowed her mind to mull and wander in every direction, and today she thought about Priscilla and the mighty change that had come over her. Gilda didn't know what to do to help, and she really didn't want Thomas to brood about it, either. She thought, "I think Mrs. Wood is right. Priscilla has to work this out on her own."

*At Willows Edge*

Later that day, Eleanor climbed the stairs to where she knew she would find Priscilla alone. Knocking lightly first, Eleanor let herself into the Armstrong's sitting room. Priscilla was gazing out the west window, the afternoon light putting her figure in silhouette.

Eleanor asked, "Is it all right if I come in?"

Priscilla nodded and gestured for Eleanor to take a seat.

This was the time of the day that Eleanor usually rested, but she had been anxious to check on Priscilla. She asked, "Did David go far today?"

"He thought it was too cold for me to sit in the car while he did his house calls. He suggested I get to my sewing or something, because he says the days of my riding with him are about over for the winter."

"Would you like to show me what you've been working on?" asked Eleanor eagerly.

"I'm not very inspired, lately, Eleanor. I'm not very interested in my work, either."

"You know, don't you, Priscilla, that a year ago, I felt exactly as you do now?"

"You had valid reasons, though. I got through John's death, and Jeremy's death, only to discover now that I'm weak and selfish."

"That is not true," argued Eleanor.

"Why can't I get past this?"

"Give it a little more time. A person can't dictate their feelings to themselves. Feelings just are, Priscilla. Go with them for awhile longer, and I think, one day, you'll find you'll able to step away from them whole."

"I feel like you really do know how I feel."

"I do indeed. I went through it just a year ago. I had learned that Andrew was gone forever, and I had determined that William had to be dead, too. It was unbearable to imagine him a prisoner all that time, and because I couldn't handle the agony of not knowing, I determined he was gone. When I came out of my illness and my stupor, I was so ashamed of myself, I couldn't cope. But Priscilla, I had to forgive myself, eventually. I had to, because my suffering was too much. I'm not saying you have to snap out of anything right now. Just be watchful for that moment when you see that you can safely leap. When I succeeded in hiring Gilda to help here, I saw her genuine enthusiasm, and it was contagious. That was my moment to leap. When that moment comes for you, if you find the courage to do it, you will be well."

"You have been such a good friend to me," said Priscilla, noticeably struggling with her now-fragile composure.

"And you to me, too," replied Eleanor. She looked around the room, giving her friend a moment to pull herself together. She then said, encouragingly, "You'll keep going for David's sake, Priscilla, and, except for when I was at my lowest point with pneumonia, I had to keep up with certain things for the sake of the airmen. And for Dotty's sake, too, of course."

"Oh, poor Dotty," said Priscilla. "I hope she knows I'm not angry with her. I appreciate her so much."

"We knew this would be difficult, remember? Dotty knew it would be hard, too. She said so today, and she feels terrible for what she said and especially bad that you overheard it."

"It was the truth of it that struck me so hard. I've caught glimpses of her. She does look like Thomas, doesn't she?"

Eleanor nodded and said, "You are one of the strongest women I know, but your reservoir got emptied and until you get it filled again, you must just allow yourself to be."

"I'll try," said Priscilla smiling weakly. "Do you think you could tell Dotty that I'm sorry for the way I behaved?"

"There is no need. She understands."

"I suppose I should, at least, be able to make my own apologies."

"Don't worry about anything," said Eleanor getting up to leave. "I'm going back to work. What are you going to do?"

"I'm going to think," said Priscilla simply.

"A very worthy cause," said Eleanor. Then she quietly left the room.

Early the next morning, Dotty found a note on the kitchen table. It read: *Dotty, I'm ashamed of my behavior yesterday, and fear that I hurt your feelings. I'm so sorry. I don't mean to be this way, and I'm working on it. I appreciate you and Sam more than you will ever know. Sincerely, Priscilla.*

તજ્જ્જ્જ્જ

A few days later, David returned to the manor after a hard day. He had heard that one of his earlier patients, who had endured a particularly bad break of the femur, had suddenly been overcome by infection, and the young man had ultimately lost his leg. David had sent the patient back to the hospital when he'd seen the early warning signs, and he was livid that the hospital had, yet again, sent the patient back home prematurely. Driving home that day, after hearing the terrible news from a colleague, David was in a particularly bad mood.

Hitting the driving wheel with his open palm, he uttered, "I don't patch them up, just to see them lose the limb in the end. Damn, I'm sick of this bloody war!"

Driving through Nuneaton, the doctor pulled over at a corner and bought a newspaper, as was his present custom. In the final four miles of his journey, David tried to calm down. He knew the last thing Priscilla needed was him in a foul mood.

He pulled into the driveway and parked in his usual spot. Gathering his things, he made his way slowly to the side door, which had become his preferred entrance. Eleanor heard him coming in and met him in the hall.

"Hello, David," she said, "you look worn out this afternoon."

"Oh, Eleanor, we're all worn out."

"Indeed."

Opening the folded newspaper, David glanced down at the headlines and cursed. He held the front page up for Eleanor to read. She read the bold print aloud, "The V-2 Rocket Comes to Southern England. Comets That Dive From Seventy Miles."

Eleanor pulled her reading glasses from her pocket and grabbed the newspaper out of David's hand. She read out, "Churchill has authorized formal acknowledgement that recent blasts in the London area have been the result of Hitler's new vengeance bomb. Unlike the earlier unpiloted bombs, which had a particular droning sound that signified their presence and imminent explosion, there is no warning before these ballistic missiles make enormous holes in England's neighborhoods and farmlands."

Peering over the tops of her glasses, Eleanor uttered, "Dear God, what next? Priscilla knew they were hiding something from the public. She mentioned it to me more than once, and I thought it was her nerves talking, but she was right all along."

"It was the blast of one of these, I'd bet, among other things, of course, that first brought us to you, and I'm sure it was one of these bombs that killed all the people at the Gates party that evening. Priscilla is intuitive and brilliant, and there was a time when she could take almost any adversity in stride, but I think those days are long over."

"They aren't over, David. I'm sure of it."

In response, David refolded the newspaper and indicated that he was going upstairs.

*At Willows Edge*

"Allow me to make dinner tonight," offered Eleanor quietly.

David nodded his head in gratitude and slowly climbed the stairs.

That night, Eleanor wrote in her diary, *We have learnt today that the unexplainable blasts near London are the result of another of Hitler's inventions. It appears that the government has known about their existence for some time, but for whatever reason, had not told the public until today. Whatever is disclosed to the English public is also available to the Germans, so there must have been a valid reason for keeping the information from us. Since there is absolutely no warning that the bombs are coming, no one could have avoided them, anyway, even if they had known of their existence. The Gates family was destroyed by one of these, I'm certain.*

*David seems worn down, lately. He works many hours and he's not so young, either, but I think his greatest concern is Priscilla.*

*Gilda told me today that Thomas has not been to the manor, because he doesn't want to encounter Emma. He feels that distancing himself from Emma is the one thing he can do for his mother at this time. My Christmas plans include Willy and Jane (her mother also, of course)*

*Thomas and Gilda, David and Priscilla, and the Coopers. It is becoming more and more difficult to imagine the perfect scenario in my mind. It wouldn't surprise me if the Armstrongs take Gilda and Thomas somewhere else for Christmas. Who knows, they might all go down to Surrey. If Priscilla doesn't make some progress soon, I will welcome the idea of a very quiet Christmas. Jane will come with her mum and Willy, and the Coopers will be here with Emma. Two engaging children and no adult complications sounds blissful to me.*

## Chapter Twelve

One sunny afternoon late in November, Emma was playing outside, not far from where Sam was working in the chicken pens, replacing the light bulb that enabled the hens to lay eggs throughout the winter. He waved at two airmen, who were taking a stroll around the estate.

Coming upon Emma, the tallest airman asked, "Are you getting ready for Father Christmas to come?"

Emma took a step back, shaking her head.

"You had better get ready for him, then," he teased.

Emma stared at the man curiously, and said skeptically, "I don't have a Father Christmas. I have a mama and a papa."

The other airmen said, "Perhaps she knows him as Santa Claus, like the Americans staying at Arbury Hall."

"She may, indeed," said the first airman, "but I'll argue with anyone that Father Christmas is a more respectful name. If you want more presents, call him Father Christmas. You'll be glad you did."

The airmen laughed and left Emma to mull over the interesting conversation. Having had none of this vital information before that interchange, she approached Sam the next morning and asked, "Who is Father *Chrisnas*? And what about *Santer* Claus?" asked Emma, brow furrowed, intensely serious.

"Who have you been talking to?" asked her papa.

"The people," said Emma, considering that an adequate answer to his question.

"The airmen?" asked Sam, amused.

"They said I should get ready. Why?"

"Father Christmas, and Santa Claus, too, I suppose, represent the spirit of giving," said Sam, please with his sophisticated answer. He had heard Mrs. Wood say that once and was now glad that he'd paid attention.

"What?" asked Emma crossly. She put one hand on her expanding waist, her elbow jutting as high as she could manage. She reminded Sam so vividly of Dotty, he began to laugh helplessly.

"Don't laugh. It makes you cough," said Emma bossily. "Who are they?"

"All right," said Sam, realizing he's missed the mark with his previous sophisticated answer. He coughed only momentarily, before answering, "They are the same person. Some people call him Santa Claus, and others call him Father Christmas. I knew him as Father Christmas."

"You knew him?" asked Emma impressed.

"I've never actually met him, you know, but we knew each other, all right. He brought me Christmas treats in my stocking every year. I had to be good, though."

"I think I'm good," said Emma thoughtfully. She shifted her stance to a more amiable one, and put her arm down at her side.

Seeing this adjustment in attitude, Sam ruffled her hair and said, "I know you're good."

"Can I see him?" she asked.

"That wouldn't make him very happy. He tries very hard not to be seen, especially when he watches secretly to see if children are being good. When he brings the children's presents at Christmas, it ruins everything if they see him. They run the risk of him not returning the next year."

"Oh," said Emma.

Sam watched the concentrated look on Emma's face change to one of acceptance, so he said, "The chickens need to be fed. I'd better get after it."

"I want to help," said Emma, just as she did every day.

"And I need your help. You don't want to stay inside all by yourself, do you?" asked Sam, needing no answer. "Get your jumper and coat. It's cold this morning."

Now fixated on the idea of learning as much as possible about this gift-giving phenomenon and finding Dotty alone in the carriage-house kitchen that evening, Emma asked, "Do you know Father *Chrisnas*?"

"Well," answered Dotty, "he was Santa Claus to me. My American uncle promised me that Santa Claus would come, and thanks to him, there were presents for me every year. What a good man he was; God rest his soul."

"What happened to him?"

"Who, my uncle?" asked Dotty.

"No, Mama, *Santer* Claus."

"Oh, he's fine. He's a good man, too. He's fat and jolly and loves all children."

"But do you know him?" insisted Emma, losing patience.

"I just know he came to my house every Christmas. He doesn't like to be seen by children, though. It spoils his surprises for them."

"If he likes me, why can't I see him?" asked Emma persistently.

"Just be as good as you can be, and he'll see that you get something in your Christmas stocking and a present under the Christmas tree."

"I've never had one," said Emma.

"A Christmas tree or a stocking?" asked Dotty. She had grown to despise the old Aunt 'Melia.'

"I have stockings, see?" said Emma pointing to her feet.

"How about a Christmas tree in your house? Did you ever have one of those?"

"Aunt Melia kept her trees outside," answered Emma, nodding knowingly.

"We'll have one in the manor, and Santa Claus will leave something there for you, my sweet."

"He's watching me?" asked Emma skeptically.

Dotty answered, "Especially at this time of the year. He has to know who's being good and who's being bad."

"Oh," said Emma.

The following day, when Sam sent Emma to the manor with a basket of eggs, she was especially alert for any evidence that Father Christmas was watching her. She saw a stranger lurking behind the garden shed and was curious to know who it was, but when she moved in that direction, the figure disappeared from view. From what little Emma could see, though, this person didn't seem jolly and wasn't at all fat, so was ruled out as a possible candidate for Father Christmas. Once Emma had established that fact firmly in her mind, any interest she had in the furtive figure was gone.

She took the eggs around to the back door of the kitchen and knocked. Believing herself to be too little to open the heavy door, she waited patiently. Gilda opened the door and invited the child into the warm kitchen, where she offered her a bun.

The two of them had had few conversations, but Emma remembered that Gilda was the kind person who had brought her to this wonderful place, so she accepted the bun and made herself at home at the kitchen table.

Gilda asked, "You must be getting big for your papa to trust you with the eggs."

"I had to *pracsit* being careful until I could," admitted Emma.

Taking eggs from the basket, Gilda chuckled and said, "Oh, that's good, and I also see he put an extra thick layer of straw under the eggs."

Nibbling randomly on the piece of bread, Emma asked, "Do you know Father *Chrisnas*?"

"Not at all," said Gilda, honestly.

"My papa says that Father *Chrisnas* is watching me to see if I'm good," said Emma, looking around the ancient kitchen.

Picking up the oven cloth with her right hand, Gilda

replied, "I'm sure your papa is right."

Gilda stooped to take the last of the buns from the oven, forgetting the child momentarily to concentrate on the task at hand. Her left hand, still protected by an oven glove, balanced the pan, as her right lifted it out. She set down the steaming buns, noting happily that they looked unusually light.

"Is he fat?" asked Emma.

"Is who fat?" asked Gilda, turning to Emma. She looked at Thomas's eyes staring out of that little face and smiled.

"Father *Chrisnas*," said Emma crossly, raising her free hand, palm up, indicating, as Dotty would, that she was becoming exasperated.

"Oh yes, Father Christmas. I've heard that he is quite fat, but like I said, I don't know him and have never seen him. I've heard that he's real, though," said Gilda, suddenly realizing the import of this conversation to the serious little girl.

"Well, if he's fat, he's not been hanging 'round here," said Emma with conviction, once again focusing on her bun.

"Isn't that the truth!" exclaimed Gilda laughing. Emma laughed, too, revealing a deep dimple in each cheek.

When Emma left, Gilda realized that the oven glove had concealed her deformed hand from the child's view the entire time she had been in the kitchen, and Gilda was glad for it.

ঌ৽ঌ৽

That afternoon, while waiting for Thomas's return from the airfield, Gilda wrote in her journal.

*December 1, 1944*
*Dear Diary,*

*Emma and I had our first private conversation, since we brought her to the manor. I think she knows me and Mrs. Wood by name, but she is rarely in the kitchen or anywhere else in the manor. Sam keeps her well out of Priscilla's way, not that Priscilla is ever downstairs, except for the evening meal, which the Armstrongs prepare and eat with Mrs. Wood in the kitchen. David takes Priscilla's breakfast upstairs to her each morning, and they are usually gone at midday. It's not that they don't help out in other ways, because they do. Priscilla does all the ironing, and David brings in much of their personal food stores, so Eleanor doesn't have to arrange for that anymore. But, David makes sure that Priscilla is never in the company of her late husband's love child, which I believe is wise.*

*Emma is a precocious child, not the damaged little being, I first thought her to be. Her cheeks have filled out, and she actually has quite a tummy, which she juts out when she's making a point. I don't know how Dotty has fattened her up so quickly, but it's quite a transformation. I can now see that she really is a pretty little child. Her hair has become shiny, and there are roses in her cheeks. Not only that, but she has precious, deep dimples when she smiles that I'd never before noticed. How wonderful!*

*She is fascinated with the idea of Father Christmas, who she has never experienced—another indictment of her infamous Aunt Amelia. I'm sure that Dotty and Sam will make her first Christmas with them memorable. She's a lucky little girl to have come to the Coopers—very lucky indeed.*

❧❦❧❦

Emma had become increasingly obsessed with the idea that Father Christmas was watching her. She had asked almost everyone about the phenomenon, and now she was taking matters into her own hands. She had recently had a breakthrough. From the west window of the first floor of the manor, Emma had seen someone watching her. She put this possibility up against the other given facts and had hopes of learning more.

The person she had seen did not appear too thin. Fat and jolly didn't really apply, she thought, but she recalled hearing adults explaining away almost anything by saying, "There's a war on." Perhaps in war years, maybe even Father Christmas wasn't fat and jolly, she thought.

What was key to Emma, though, was that the person above stairs did not seem to want to be seen. Of that, she was instinctively certain. Having been assured by all of her sources that Father Christmas was reclusive, this new development bore looking into.

Occasionally, Emma was sent to the manor on her own, and she longed for the opportunity to occur again. She tried to think of any excuse that might offer her the remote possibility of checking out the potential Father Christmas on the first floor.

That chance came quickly, when Sam again sent her to the manor with the day's eggs. He said, "Go carefully, now, and give these to Mrs. Wood for me. Tell her the chickens are perking up a bit, and we can expect to see more eggs in the next few days."

Turning her head to the side, Emma asked skeptically, "How do you know that, Papa?"

"I think it's going to be sunny for a few days. The hens like that."

"Oh," replied Emma.

Sam laughed at her as she carefully carried the basket around the manor to the back door. She held the handle of the basket high in front of her with both hands, requiring her sturdy little legs to waddle to accommodate the bulk in front of her.

Sam loved it that she asked so many questions, and he also found it endearing that her final response was always, "Oh." When he heard the one syllable reply, he knew the line of questioning was temporarily over.

When she knocked on the kitchen door, no one answered. Not at all discouraged, Emma put the basket down on the ground, stood on her toes, and slowly and determinedly pulled the door handle towards her. To her great surprise, she managed to pull it open far enough to slide the basket and herself through, before the door's weight closed it firmly behind her. Finding herself completely alone, she carefully placed the basket of eggs on the table, and relaxed her shoulders with an exaggerated sigh, proud of her achievement. Just as she was about to call out, she realized her longed-for opportunity had come.

As quietly as humanly possible, Emma opened the

hall doorway to the steep staircase. Beginning to climb, Emma's courage almost failed her when a draught slammed the door shut behind her, but hearing no one approach, she pressed on. Up and up she went, trying not to step on the creaky places.

When she reached the upper hall, she saw that the door closest to her was closed, so she opened it easily and went in. There was no one there, so she quietly closed the door behind her and looked around for signs of occupation. She saw chairs, tables, lamps, and even some books lying about, but when she saw a framed picture of two little boys, she knew she was in the right place, for Father Christmas loved children. Emma was vastly impressed with his comfortable quarters.

She wandered into the Armstrong's bedroom, and looked around. "Father *Chrisnas* has a jolly nice place," she whispered, as she touched the soft ivory counterpane and the silky fringe that hung from the nearby lampshade.

Disappointed that she hadn't yet seen evidence of any toy-making, Emma left the lovely bedroom. She gave one last look around the comfortable sitting room, and unable to think of anything else to do, she, reached for the doorknob to leave. She watched the door start to open on its own, and frightened, she jumped back and let out a high-pitched scream.

Priscilla had been in the sewing workroom and had remembered that she had sketched a gown design the day after Eleanor had visited her. Encouraged by Eleanor's promise that her melancholy would not last forever, Priscilla had had her first artistic impression in months.

When she opened the door and heard the scream, Priscilla almost screamed herself. She refrained, though, when she saw up close, for the first time, the blue eyes that Dotty had described as looking just like Thomas's. They truly did look like his eyes, but what amazed her even more, was that the child's dimpled cheeks reminded her of her son Jeremy. He had always been proud of the fact that he had inherited his dimples from his paternal grandfather, and Priscilla would have never thought she'd see those dimples again.

Astonished by the child's sudden appearance, Pricilla brusquely asked, "My goodness, child, what are you doing up here?"

"Looking for Father *Chrisnas*," answered Emma candidly.

"Christmas is still weeks away. What made you think he was up here?" asked Priscilla. She was neither really cross nor distressed, but her mind was in confusion, trying to accept that she was having this interesting exchange with John's love child.

"Cause he watches *childrens* to see if we're being good, and I saw him up here, looking out the window."

"You probably saw me looking out the window. I do that quite a lot, lately," admitted Priscilla.

"I suppose somebody needs to keep watch when he's gone," said Emma, making use of her developing logic.

Priscilla was speechless.

Now worried about her standing with the omniscient gift-giver, Emma said repentantly, "Tell Father *Chrisnas* I'm sorry I came up. You don't want me to see you, do you?"

Before Priscilla could refute this absolute truth, Emma asked, "Are you Mother *Chrisnas,* then?"

Taken so completely off guard, Priscilla began to laugh. She walked past the precocious child and plopped down in her chair.

Emma defensively responded, "Well, I am sorry. I *s'pose* if I don't get anything in my stocking, I'll know why, won't I?"

Laughing helplessly for the first time in a very long time, Priscilla beckoned the child to come to her. She said,

"We'll pretend it never happened. Your secret is safe."

"Father *Chrisnas* won't be angry?"

"Father Christmas won't even know," said Priscilla, pulling her handkerchief from the pocket of her favorite cardigan. Dabbing at her eyes, she asked, "Emma, does your papa know where you are?"

Nodding, Emma said, "I brought eggs and opened the door all by myself."

"He might be looking for you now. You'd better run along. I'm glad you visited, though."

Turning to leave, Emma said, "Thank you, you have a nice bedroom. Not as pretty as mine, but nice."

Emma's admission that she had been in their bedroom sent Priscilla into another spell of hysteria, so Emma let herself out and went on home to Sam. She didn't tell him anything about her visit to the first floor, because, after all, her secret was safe. She reasoned, "If you can't trust Mother Christmas, who can you trust?"

Going to sleep that night, Emma whispered to her doll, "Mother *Chrisnas* is not very fat, but she's a jolly one, all right."

## Chapter Thirteen

On the fifteenth of December, Eleanor asked some airmen to take down some of the extra eating tables in the great hall to make room for a Christmas tree. They complied by taking down all but six of the long tables and arranged to have them removed from the manor.

The news that street lights were once again lighting the streets in England's cities and villages sparked in Eleanor a burst of energy. She went into a cleaning frenzy that worried both Dotty and Gilda. When asked if they could help, she told them to keep on top of their regular work, and she would take on the rest.

Eleanor rearranged the remaining tables so that they were in a more civilian arrangement, making notes on a tablet as she worked, so she wouldn't forget the festive ideas and details that came to mind. Just as her energy was waning one afternoon, the post brought a letter from Jane.

*Number 26, Bramble Avenue, Trubury, Herefordshire*
*December 11, 1944*
*Dear Eleanor,*

*Our telephone has been having problems, so rather than try to talk over the static or ring you from the*

neighbour's house, I decided to write a quick note. We are still planning to come and look forward to seeing you soon. Willy talks about you all the time, so please know you aren't forgotten. We'll be there on Friday, the 22$^{nd}$. We look forward to seeing you and visiting Greystone Manor.
With affection,
Jane

That night, Eleanor recorded, *Jane's telephone is not working properly, so I'll have to write her to ask if she would bring William's letters along with her when she comes. I'd especially like to see the most recent one for myself. I don't think she'll mind, now that I know her better, and she's already admitted she should have shown it to me, anyway. Perhaps, she'll think of it on her own, but I'll mention it anyway.*

*I'm going full-steam ahead with my Christmas plans. I have been choosing gifts (for those in our little gathering) from the many things in the storeroom. I have no intention of trying to get out and shop, for heaven's sake; I can do quite well without that frustration. No, finding little things that might give the recipient joy has been like a treasure hunt, and I'm finding great pleasure in it. As our gathering will be a small one, the planning, rather than being overwhelming, has proven to be a needed diversion from the war. I'm actually having fun.*

*The food aspect is always a little exasperating, but I'm getting help from Dotty and Gilda on that score. Not Priscilla, though. She has been even scarcer than before. I do hope she comes out of her torpor. When I walk by her room, on my way to the storeroom, I sometimes hear the sewing machine rattling, and other times, nothing at all. I haven't intruded, though. She knows where to find me.*

*I think I'll write that note to Jane now, before I forget.*

*Greystone Manor, Englewood, Warwickshire*
*December 16, 1944*
*Dear Jane,*

*I was wondering if you would consider bringing William's letters with you when you come. I would love to have a look at them myself and compare them, unless you feel you cannot share. We are all so excited about your coming.*
*See you on Friday,*
*Eleanor*

The next day brought sad news from the European

Front. Distressed and in a hurry to get outside to the dairy barn for the last milking, Edith Wood rang the manor to tell her mum to be sure to listen to the news on the wireless. Larry had telephoned her that there was bad news for the Americans. The Germans had made a surprise attack, and Edith was very worried about Larry's brother, Craig Bradford, who was on the continent. They had hoped to see him at Christmas, but that had all changed now.

Eleanor was glad it was Sunday, and that they had been given a day off feeding the men. She was suddenly tired. Subdued by the bad news at the front, she nearly forgot to put her letter to Jane in the tray for the outgoing post, and when she remembered to do it, she couldn't resurrect the elated mood she had been in just hours before, when she had written it.

That evening, alone, she sat down in her worn-out upholstered chair in the corner of the kitchen and tuned in the news. She heard the following: "The Germans have mounted a series of counter-attacks on the Western front allowing them to re-cross the borders of Luxembourg and Belgium. On the second day of what now appears to be a full-scale counter-offensive, the Germans are attacking with tanks and aircraft along a seventy-mile front guarded by American forces in the Ardennes region. The main thrust has been launched from the northern Ardennes near the town of Monschau. Two further attacks have taken place further south. German paratroopers have been dropped behind Allied lines. Allied army reports say some of them have been mopped up. Others are still at large."

When Eleanor retired that evening, she wrote in her diary, *I sometimes forget to worry constantly about the war like I used to, for two reasons. First, in spite of ongoing casualties, the Allies are winning. But, secondly, very simply, I get so incredibly sick of it. I have to admit that I have felt a little guilty for my elated mood, lately. I remember Gilda feigning graveness soon after the wedding, and I think I had better follow suit. The war is going badly, and suddenly feeling blindsided by it, I'm emotionally exhausted. I'm sure Edith will ring me when she hears more.*

*The days run together for me here at the manor, because I am the only one who never really leaves. Except for a single trip to Englewood, I haven't been off the estate since my trip to see my grandson months ago. Even Dotty and Sam get away more often, now that they have Emma. They take her to church, whenever Dotty is off on Sunday. I saw them heading up the lane toward Englewood this morning, and it occurred to me that perhaps I should go with them next week. Wilbur and I went to church on Christmas Eve, and that was our only appearance each year. As long as Wilbur made a generous contribution, no one dared to chastise us, even if the thought occurred to do so. As for Priscilla and David, they left this morning, saying they would be late and would get a sandwich somewhere, so I was completely on my own for dinner tonight. It was a very unusual experience.*

⁂

Gilda showed up at the manor the next morning at her regular time, and she was as subdued as the others. The men in the afternoon breakfast line were gracious to their servers, as always, but the worried brows of the officers reminded Eleanor and Gilda of just seven months ago, before D-day, when even the air had been electric with anticipation and anxiety.

The three women sat down to their tea, and just as Eleanor was going to say that they needed to get more flour and other staples, the telephone rang. Eleanor got up and moved to the little chair beside the telephone table, just inside the door separating the kitchen from the hall. Knowing it would be Edith, she cheerfully answered, "Hello?"

"Mum?"

"Yes, Edith, what do you know?"

"Not much. Larry rang me, but I don't think he felt at liberty to tell me what was going on. He's not going to be able to take leave right away."

"I'm so sorry, Edith. I'm sure you're disappointed."

"Yes, I truly am, but more than that, he sounded so terribly worried."

"What will you do? Can you come home, dear?" asked Eleanor hopefully.

"I think I will," said Edith. "Mr. Banks is letting all of us go at once. His family is coming in, and they will help him with the milking. Our leaving will free up the attic space for his family."

"When shall we expect you, dear?"

"We're all trying to head home on Thursday."

"I've prepared your old room, so at least you have that to look forward to. And Jane is coming Friday, as far as I know. I'm putting them in the room beside yours. Try not to worry too much."

"See you then, Mum."

Eleanor returned to the table, where they talked of the war until Gilda changed the subject, for the benefit of all of them. When she asked Dotty about Emma, they all instinctively looked at the doorway, to make sure that Priscilla was not standing there, before they delved into the entertaining antics of Emma May Cooper.

Dotty shared that Emma had taken to singing hymns around the house, and before she could begin telling the story, she was laughing to the point of not being able to tell it at all.

Calming herself, she said, "The poor child needs a new dress. Hers is getting too small, but Sunday last, I moved a button over, so she could wear it, you know, comfortably. Well, then I noticed there was some puckering around the waist that I thought would never do, so I took some shiny, blue ribbon I'd been saving for a special occasion, and used it for a sash to cover the puckering. I had a little left over to put in her hair, and she thought she looked beautiful. Stared and stared at herself, she did, in front of her little looking glass."

Dotty laughed as she neared the punch line, so Eleanor and Gilda smiled, waiting patiently. Dotty regained control to say, "Well, at church, we sang this hymn."

Singing now, Dotty went on, "Praise God from whom all blessings flow."

She stopped singing to ask, "You know the one?"

Eleanor nodded encouragingly, and Gilda shrugged,

having not spent any time in church.

Dotty patted her chest, in a futile attempt to stop laughing, and managed to say before bursting, "Well, after church, we heard her singing, 'Praise God to whom all *dresses show*.'"

Dotty shook with laughter and mopped the tears that coursed down her cheeks. The others laughed enthusiastically, too, but, beyond the humor of the sweet story, Eleanor and Gilda had found great pleasure in seeing Dotty's overwhelming joy in motherhood.

Later that day, Eleanor worked in the large children's bedroom next to Edith's in preparation for the arrival of Jane, her mother, and Willy. She gave the furniture a final going over and put fresh sheets on the three single beds. She was ashamed of the patched sheets, recently sewed sides-to-middle, but she was pleased that they were still very white. Smiling in the looking glass over the dressing table, she said to herself, "William is alive, Jane is bringing Willy for Christmas, and even Edith is coming."

As Eleanor walked past the door to Priscilla's sewing workroom on her way back downstairs, she was surprised to hear humming. Wondering if Priscilla was feeling better, she was tempted to knock on the door but

*At Willows Edge*

changed her mind. It occurred to her that sewing machines could hum, as well as rattle and thump, so she decided to leave Priscilla to her work. She had been keeping very much to herself, and Eleanor felt she should not intrude upon her. Carefully descending the steep steps, Eleanor thought, "She will come around in her own time."

ಶಿ⋟ಶಿ⋟

That afternoon after work, Gilda took the time to write in her journal. She was cooking some potatoes and carrots in a covered pot on the cooker, so she seated herself at her table in the sitting room by the south window. From there, although she couldn't quite see the cooker on the north wall of the kitchen, she would be able to hear if her pot began to boil over. She opened her journal and began to write.

*December 18, 1944*
*Dear Diary,*

*Thomas has invited Richard to have dinner with us again this evening, but I am no longer alarmed by such invitations. Once again, he is bringing a little game for our meat, which I can now eat without feeling sick. In fact, I crave it.*

*Richard has insisted that we call him by his first name, and we have spent many wonderful hours talking into the dark winter nights. I'll be grateful when the days lengthen out again. It has been a little too dark, for my liking, going to the manor each morning, but I hadn't mentioned it to anyone. I was quite surprised when, last week, Thomas insisted on walking me halfway. Then David and Spanky met us and walked with me the rest of the way. I was touched that they had made the arrangement without my knowing.*

*Having David meet us, enables Thomas to get to work on time, too. Of course, I always have my torch, but Thomas was adamant that I not make my way in the dark anymore.*

*I have felt very healthy. I can feel the baby moving in little flutters, from time to time, and it thrills me. The slight movements aren't enough for Thomas to feel on the outside, yet, but he likes it when I tell him that the baby is moving. He always puts his hand on my belly in the hope that he'll feel the baby kick for the first time.*

*David talks to me each morning about my condition and has come by the cottage for regular visits. I have been asking him if I can count on his being here for the birth, and he hesitates to promise, because of Priscilla. He told me today, though, that he thinks Priscilla is doing a little better. He says she is more talkative and has been working hours on end in the workroom. I told him I hadn't been up to help in a long time and asked that he tell her I would try to dedicate my Saturdays to the sewing room as soon as Christmas was over. I was certainly glad to hear she was doing something again. That's a good sign.*

Looking up from her journal and out the window into the near-darkness, Gilda jumped when she saw someone in the open field, just standing there, staring at the cottage. Gilda's heart started to pound, and she darted to turn off the light and lock the cottage door. She still had no window coverings in the sitting room, because until now, they simply had not been needed. In jumping to kill the light, she knocked over the chair she'd been sitting on and bumped her hip against the wooden settee in the middle of the room.

For the first time, Gilda was sure that she was being stalked, and she was absolutely certain of two things. The figure was a female, and she was the same person Gilda had seen on the other two occasions. She was determined to make some curtains for the cottage windows immediately.

She was still shaking and rubbing her hip where

she'd bruised it, when someone rattled the door. With a trembling voice, she asked, "Who's there?"

"It's Richard."

Gilda unlocked the door, and Richard came in carrying a small platter of cooked pheasant. Before they had time to speak, Gilda heard the rattle of the pan lid and hurried into the kitchen to check on her vegetables. Richard got rid of his coat and joined Gilda in the dark kitchen, where she was standing motionlessly by the cooker.

Moving toward the south side of the kitchen, keeping out of sight from the window in the sitting room, Gilda turned on the kitchen light and said shakily, "Since the kitchen is warmer than the sitting room, let's eat in here tonight."

"I'll be glad to move the table, but I can get the fire roaring in the sitting room in no time," offered Richard, watching Gilda carefully.

Turning toward the cooker and staying just east of the doorway, Gilda uttered, "I was writing in my diary when I should have been building up the fire."

Richard began, "There's something wrong here…"

He was interrupted by Thomas storming into the cottage, completely out of breath. Coming into the kitchen, he took Gilda in his arms and held her close.

*At Willows Edge*

Once he'd caught his breath, he said, "You should have locked the door, darling."

Turning to Richard, he said, "I was almost home when I saw a woman, standing on the south side of the cottage. You had the light on, Gilda, silhouetting the woman, and I saw you get startled and jump to douse the light. When I saw Richard approaching the house with his platter and torch, I knew you'd be all right, so I went in pursuit of the woman, but she disappeared completely into the darkness, so I gave up and came home."

Gilda admitted, "I should have told you, Thomas, that I'd seen her twice before. The first time was the night before we went to fetch Emma. I wasn't entirely positive of what I'd seen in the willow trees, so once inside the cottage, I ran to the back window to see if I could spot anything. By then she was gone, and I pushed it to the back of my mind."

"When did you see her next?" asked Richard.

"It must have been the very end of October, but not since, until just now. I decided not to worry about it. I have no enemies."

Thomas met eyes with Richard before confessing, "I've seen her before, too, Gilda. It was the first day Richard came, so I thought, at first, that the person must have had something to do with the opening of his house."

"But then, you heard me ask him about it," said Gilda, nodding.

Richard explained, "Thomas talked to me about it when he walked me home that night."

"Why didn't you tell me?" asked Gilda accusingly.

"My God, Gilda, why didn't you tell me?" exclaimed Thomas, reaching for her hand.

"You were each protecting the other. Gilda didn't want to fuel another nightmare, and you, Thomas, could see no point in alarming your pregnant wife," said Richard wisely.

Thomas said, "I even checked the local inns, believing the person to be on foot, although I suppose there could have been a car parked somewhere. There was no one that any of the innkeepers considered suspicious. Most of their guests have been permanent residents since the beginning of the war."

"You went so far as to investigate?" asked Gilda. "I just thought I was being jumpy because of my pregnancy and tried not to think about it."

"I don't really know how to explain the way I felt about it," said Thomas, "but the individual seemed almost menacing."

"I thought the same thing," said Gilda, shaking her head. "But who would want to bother us?"

"I don't know, yet, but I'm going to find out," said Thomas angrily.

Richard suggested that Thomas help him bring the little table back into the kitchen, which they did, also checking quickly that no one lurked outside the cottage. Returning to the kitchen, Thomas saw Gilda tenderly rubbing her hip where she'd hit the settee. As soon as they put the table down, Thomas asked her, "You hurt yourself, didn't you, darling?"

To everyone's surprise, in an uncharacteristically irritable tone, Gilda said, "I just caught my hip on the corner of the settee. It's only a bruise, so don't go calling in the medics!"

Her comment brought an unexpected burst of laughter from the men, so she laughed, too, dispelling some of the tension. She sat down with the men to partake of their meal, and they ate in relative silence, each trying to make sense of the afternoon's events.

## Chapter Fourteen

When Edith arrived at home on Thursday night, she was too preoccupied to do so much as acknowledge Spanky, so he slinked off to his bed, feeling sorry for himself. She and three other Land Girls had driven through intense fog and rain and admitted that, if they'd had more sense, they would have given it up, or better yet, not started out at all. Mr. Banks had given them, for a Christmas present of sorts, the use of his old milk lorry during Christmas. Margaret had been given the keys, because she was not only the best driver, but she also lived the furthest from the farm. Having been spared the dreaded train ride, the girls had squashed together inside the cab of the small lorry and had worked out how to get everyone home and picked up again after the holidays, using the least amount of petrol.

Desperate to leave as planned, they had assured Mr. Banks that they would drive out of the fog in no time. Against his better judgment, he had agreed, and they had been inching their way south for what seemed like hours. Greystone Manor was a far as they could get, so Eleanor found herself with three Land Girls to feed and bed down for the night. She was glad she'd gotten Jane's room ready ahead of time.

Eleanor led the shivering young women upstairs and installed them in the children's bedroom, as it had always been called. They exclaimed their thanks for the use of the warm bedroom and beds of their very own.

With David's permission, two of the girls bathed in their bathroom and Edith and the other girl used the bathroom in the hall downstairs. Advised to go easy on the hot water, or it wouldn't last, the girls did as they always did at Banks Farm, and opted for a deep bath, used twice, rather than a shallow one. Tonight, it was Edith and Anne's turn for the first baths, so the others, Margaret and Jean, hung around the kitchen listening to the wireless with Eleanor. She learned that Anne had been Marva's replacement at the farm, after her marriage to Jack in May. They talked of Marva warmly and had plans to see her and her new baby, Victoria, before returning north, in January.

Eleanor enjoyed talking with Edith's comrades and thought the girls looked pretty, even dressed as they were in their green jerseys, brown breeches and brown felt hats. Their young bodies were lean and muscular from their heavy labor, and thanks to them, thought Eleanor, the country had not starved to death.

## Meredith Kennon

It wasn't until late, after the others had gone to bed, that Edith and her mother had a chance to talk. It was then that Edith finally had a little interest in the dejected Spanky, so with him on her lap, mother and daughter sat beside the wireless with a cup of hot tea and talked.

Edith found some soothing music on the wireless, and turning the volume low, said, "The Germans took the Allies by surprise, and they are cut off from supplies in Bastogne, Belgium. Larry was frantic about his brother, because news had come that a unit was massacred at a place called Malmedy. He didn't have time to say more, and I've not been able to learn anything else from any source."

Her mother replied, "I've listened faithfully to the news since Monday, and I've not heard any mention of Malmedy. They have reported the attack that took the Americans by surprise and the two-day advance of the Germans through the Ardennes Forest to Bastogne."

Edith said, "Larry told me that the Americans are having the British equivalent of Dunkirk."

"How awful! Where is Larry now, do you know?" asked Eleanor.

"His last contact was Tuesday from London. There is just the slightest chance that he'll go over to the continent, and he'd like to, if it meant he could learn more about Craig. The Americans are completely cut off. Larry said that they have to wait for the weather to clear before air support can begin."

"This fog must be everywhere, then," said Eleanor wearily.

"It's been hovering over the Ardennes Mountains since Sunday, making things just right for the bloody Nazis. Now, it covers us all like a giant blanket, giving the Allies no possible way to go in yet."

"I know, Edith. It's troubling."

They sat sipping their tea for a few minutes in silence.

Looking at the clock on the wall and putting Spanky on the floor, Edith said, "You've got to get to bed, Mum."

"I'd better. Tomorrow is fast approaching."

"I'll help Dotty with the early breakfast," offered Edith. "I want you to have a lie in."

When Eleanor began to argue the point, Edith said, "I'm quite used to waking early, and I insist, Mum. Thanks for all the trouble you went to for the other girls tonight."

Rising from her chair, Eleanor smiled and said, "I had the room all ready for Jane, so it worked out perfectly. No last minute rush."

Briefly kissing her mum's cheek, Edith said, "Try to sleep in. The girls will probably leave before you get up, but that is fine. I'll see them off. They want to get at least to Jean's place, just twelve miles east of here."

"But the fog," argued Eleanor.

"I know," said Edith, "but if it isn't too bad, they can surely make it twelve miles. They know you've got Jane coming in."

"You girls really should have taken the train. What made you so determined to drive?"

Gathering their cups, Edith laughed and said, "We thought we'd make better time."

Eleanor retired with a prayer for better weather for the sake of the Americans and anyone else trying to travel. She thought about Jane's coming and was glad the fog wouldn't upset the train schedule too much. Eleanor's final thought, before drifting off to sleep was, "My grandson is coming to Greystone Manor, at last."

❧❦❧❦

The next morning, protected by their anoraks and umbrellas, Thomas and Gilda walked through the dense fog and cold rain with their torches on. Heads down, they nearly bumped into David, who was coming to meet them.

After a quick farewell, Thomas was off to the airfield in long, purposeful strides.

Richard had placed a telephone call to the manor from his cottage the night before and had talked to David. Having gotten Thomas's permission, Richard told him about the stalker.

As soon as Thomas turned in the opposite direction toward the airfield, David said, "Now, Gilda, I want you to tell me everything about this stalker, starting at the beginning."

Keeping details to a minimum, because of the steady rain drumming on their umbrellas, Gilda told David what had transpired. David nodded his understanding and promised Gilda he wouldn't trouble Priscilla with any of the disturbing events.

When Gilda and David arrived at the kitchen door, Spanky looked at them accusingly for excluding him. To the dog, David said, "Go out, then, and see how much you like the cold rain."

Dotty said, "Oh, he's been out, but only long enough to do his business. He's just trying to make you feel guilty. Don't pay any attention to that one."

When David and Gilda laughed, Spanky barked defensively and returned to his bed in a sulk.

Not long after, while Gilda was still scrubbing down the tables in the dining area, Eleanor called her to the telephone.

It was Thomas. Hurriedly, he said, "Darling, I'm on call to join a bomber group, so I have to stay right here at the airfield until the weather clears. Not a damn thing can happen until this bloody weather breaks."

With a sinking heart, Gilda asked, "Do you mean you're going to fly a mission?"

"Just one or two, dear," said Thomas with excitement in his voice. "They are short of men. You know the state of the Americans in Belgium. I'm going to be part of the relief effort."

"Oh, I see," said Gilda quietly.

He said, "I'd rather you didn't go home tonight, darling. I want you to arrange to stay there at the manor. I'll ring Richard and tell him, so he doesn't worry about us. He plans to go to his brother-in-law's place tomorrow, but he'll worry if he sees no one at the cottage tonight."

"I'm sure I can stay here. And, Thomas, Richard and I have told David everything."

"That's good. I think you should tell Mrs. Wood, too."

"I will. Promise you won't worry about me,

Thomas. I'm sure I can stay here."

"I'll try to ring you, if at all possible."

When Gilda put the receiver down, Eleanor said, "Of course, you can stay here. I'll give you something to sleep on. The rain has eased and yet the fog is thicker than before. It's certainly poses a hazard for walking."

"It's not just the fog he's worried about. Since last week, Thomas walks me halfway here in the morning, and David meets us to walk me the rest of the way. It was first planned because of how dark it is when I leave the cottage, but now it's more than that. We've had a bit of a scare. I suppose I'd better tell you about it."

Guiding Gilda to the kitchen table by her arm, Eleanor said firmly, "I suppose you'd better, indeed."

Edith had done the early stint with Dotty and had gone upstairs to her room for a few minutes, and Dotty had been wiping down the table in the serving area. They both returned to the kitchen in time to hear Eleanor say, "I suppose you'd better, indeed."

Knowing that no special invitation was required, Edith sat down at the table, and Dotty joined them, too, as soon as she put the kettle on the hob.

Eleanor said, "Tell us everything."

Gilda began, "It was the night before we went to

fetch Emma, that I first saw the mysterious figure between the hedge and the willows. It frightened me, but I dismissed it, thinking my pregnancy was making me particularly jumpy. Then, about a month later, I saw her again."

"Her?" asked Edith.

"I didn't actually know it was a woman, at first. I'm only sure of that now. The second time, she wore a long hooded coat, her face hidden from view. In spite of telling myself repeatedly that a person walking alone was nothing necessarily to be feared, she frightened me.

"It turned out that Thomas had seen her, too, the first day he met Richard. We both thought that perhaps he'd had someone open the cottage for him, but he had not. He said no one knew he was coming ahead of time."

"When did you last see her?" asked Eleanor.

"Monday, before dinner. It was almost dark, of course. I was sitting by the window, writing in my journal. I looked up and she was just beyond the south gate, staring right at me. I could barely see her, really, but I knew she was a woman, and I knew she was staring at me. I still have no curtains in there, so I bolted to turn off the light. Soon after, both Richard and Thomas came. In fact, Thomas saw the woman, too, as he was walking home. With the light from the window behind her, he got a better view of her than I did. He went in pursuit when he saw that Richard was at the door to look after me. We had asked him to dinner again, so I let him in, and before long, Thomas came. It was too dark to pursue anyone, and before anyone asks, we have yet to have real cause to call in the authorities."

Exclamations came from each of the other women.

Gilda said, "We have moved directly from the kitchen to the bedroom each night since, keeping the cottage dark and avoiding the sitting room as much as possible. I've just got to get the sitting room window covered!"

"Have you checked into anything, as to who she could be?" asked Edith leaning forward.

"Actually, Thomas did so the first time he saw her. He called local inns but learned nothing. The bulk of their residents have stayed with them a long time, waiting out the war. Thomas was going to do more, but this week has been bad, what with the weather and the German attack. David knows everything, too. Richard rang to tell him last night, and I told what I could this morning when he walked me to work."

Looking at Dotty and Edith, Gilda explained, "As I told Mrs. Wood, he's been meeting us in the morning, so

Thomas can get to work on time, and I don't have to walk alone in the dark.

To Edith and Dotty, Eleanor said, "You should also know that Thomas is on call to fly a couple of missions and will be staying at the airfield until he gets his orders. Gilda will stay here until he gets back."

Gilda added, "Thomas will ring Richard, so he won't worry."

Eleanor asked, "Are you sure you can trust this Richard fellow?"

Shocked, Gilda replied, "Of course; he's become a great friend."

Smiling, Eleanor said, "I was just trying to be a detective, you know, everyone's a suspect."

Gilda said, "I've never once thought of that, and you wouldn't either, if you knew him. He did arrive here within days of my first sighting of the woman, but it's not him stalking us. He's over six feet tall and the woman is much smaller."

Dotty said impulsively, "Maybe the woman is stalking him, instead of you."

"That's clever thinking, Dotty, really" said Gilda, "But he has yet to even see her."

Under her breath, Eleanor said, "So he says,

anyway. Interesting that he appeared at your door just after you saw your stalker on Monday night."

Gilda laughed at the remark, so Eleanor changed the subject, saying, "There's a little bed in Priscilla's workroom, Gilda. How would you like to sleep in there, among the apples?"

"That will be perfect. And ladies, I don't want Priscilla to know about the stalker, yet. As it is, I'll have to tell her about Thomas's assignment. That will be news enough. I wonder where David is."

At that, the group arose as one and attended their individual duties.

֎֎֎֎

Late that morning, after taking a telephone call, Eleanor found Gilda and Edith straightening the bedroom that was occupied the night before by the Land Girls. It greatly pleased her that Edith and Gilda were chattering like old friends. Edith was older and, as the girls were so different in personality, they'd never really had anything in common. But, now that they were twenty-one and twenty-five, the four-year gap had become insignificant, thought Eleanor happily.

"Girls," she began, "we've had another change of

plan. Who do you think just rang?"

Looking at each other first and then at Eleanor, they shrugged.

"It was your mum, Gilda. She wanted me to tell you that the trip to Shrewsbury is off. She wants you to ring her to see about getting together for Christmas. I took the liberty of inviting them here, because I know Priscilla and David want to celebrate Christmas with you, too."

"This is too much for you, Mrs. Wood," cried Gilda. "Mum could have us all over there, and you wouldn't have so much on your plate."

"If I get many more guests, no one is going to have much on their plate," said Eleanor, laughing.

"That's what I mean. We can take Priscilla and David to Mum's, and that will solve the sensitive issue of Priscilla and Emma being thrown together. In fact, I'll go chat with Priscilla now. I have to tell her about Thomas's flying assignment, too. I've been procrastinating."

Edith added, "There's that, but what about Jane, Mum? She's expecting a small group, isn't she? You were the one so worried that she'd be completely overwhelmed by a crowd."

"I know you're right, on both counts" agreed Eleanor, feeling slightly relieved. "I have to admit that nothing has gone as planned for the last few days, and I'm so flustered, I can't even recall what time Jane is coming in today."

Gilda left them and walked down the hall. She peeked into the workroom, finding it empty and still smelling of dried apples. She went on to the sitting room door, and knocking lightly, heard a voice say, "Come on in."

Gilda entered and saw Priscilla sitting in her chair, under the light of the standing lamp, hand-stitching a garment made of beautiful, royal-blue velvet. Priscilla looked up and said, "Gilda, what a pleasant surprise. Come in, my dear."

"What a beautiful piece of fabric!" exclaimed Gilda.

"I know, isn't it?" asked Priscilla eagerly.

Completely taken off guard by Priscilla's happy mood, Gilda said, "It's very lovely. One of your recent finds?" She noticed that Priscilla did not show her what she was working on, but rather tucked it away in the basket on the floor by her feet.

"No, I've had no recent finds, but as Eleanor has said, Mrs. Adair can get her hands on anything. She found the blue for me. Pretty wools and cottons are difficult to come by, of course, but if you know where to look, as does

Mrs. Adair, you can still find some real treasures."

"So, she's on the hunt for you, now," said Gilda with a smile. Priscilla's talkativeness had surprised and pleased her.

"No, not really, just one transaction, but if our relationship continues, we may have to make her a partner," said Priscilla cheerfully. "You know," she continued, "I paid top dollar for the last group of old gowns I bought, or I could never have gotten them at all. Exquisite material! The only reason I was able to buy them, I think, is that so few know how to remake them into something special. I meant to bring them here, but the car was too full to bring everything. Of course, those kinds of fabrics are impractical for wartime, anyway."

Gilda thought, "What a surprise to find this new Priscilla, or rather, the old Priscilla."

Seeing Gilda's confusion, Priscilla bid her to sit down. She told her she didn't really want the others to know how much better she had become, of late, because it was buying her time to make something for everyone for Christmas. Gilda was floored.

Priscilla's eyes sparkled with excitement. She said, "I'm working on the last two gifts now. I even have something for your family at Cottage on the Lane."

Just as Gilda was opening her mouth to tell Priscilla of the change of plans for Christmas, she stopped herself. Even if she couldn't tell anyone about her mother-in-law's new mood, this development required some time to pause and reflect. Maybe she should leave well enough alone until she talked to David. Instead, she braced herself to tell her mother-in-law about Thomas's flying assignment.

Fearing she might set Priscilla back, Gilda said gently, "Thomas is on call to fly a couple of missions this weekend." She watched as Priscilla absorbed the information.

"I bet the scoundrel volunteered, don't you?" asked Priscilla, shaking her head.

"The thought did enter my mind," admitted Gilda, nodding.

"Men will do what men will do, Gilda. There's no sense trying to stop them, either," said Priscilla wisely.

"I'm going to sleep in the workroom until he's back, if that's all right."

"Excellent. I'm glad you won't be all alone over there, worrying yourself sick about Thomas."

Relieved that Priscilla didn't seem to know anything about the mystery lady, Gilda asked, "Shall we agree not to worry unnecessarily, then?"

"Yes, let's," said Priscilla. "What did you have planned for his birthday?"

"He just wanted it blended into Christmas without a fuss. What's that supposed to mean, anyway?"

"He wants it to be downplayed, for the sake of simplicity," said Priscilla knowingly. "He's done this before. He's always thought that Christmas can get a little overwhelming."

Gilda smiled and nodded, while aching with worry for her beloved husband.

They chatted for a few moments in the quiet room, hearing Dotty's voice call Eleanor to the telephone. This reminded Priscilla to tell Gilda that, as of tomorrow, she would be free to help some in the kitchen, and that David was making arrangements for some bread at the bakery and some chickens from the Morrises. She asked, "Will you pass that along to Eleanor?"

Gilda nodded and said, "Would you tell David about Thomas's assignment?"

"Certainly."

Seeing Priscilla's interest and involvement in the Christmas plans and firmly deciding not to mention anything now about any changes, Gilda said she must get back to work. She left Priscilla with her needlework and walked carefully down the stairs, not knowing what to do next. She supposed she may have to tell Eleanor about Priscilla's great enthusiasm about Christmas, so that together they could decide how best to proceed, but that would mean she would betray Priscilla's confidence. Gilda found Eleanor, sitting on the little chair by the telephone, seemingly void of emotion.

"Mrs. Wood?" asked Gilda carefully.

"Another change of plans, Gilda," said Eleanor, shaking her head. "Do you know where David is? Is he out right now?"

"I don't know. Why?"

"That was Jane. Her mother became very ill last night. Jane can't come for Christmas after all, but she was wondering if Willy might still come. She has to take care of her mum. She said she was not doing well at all and fears they'll lose her."

"Oh, how awful! Do you want me to fetch Willy?" asked Gilda.

"No, no, I'll ask David first, if I can find him. It's best for Jane if we get the child as soon as possible."

Edith had entered the kitchen and overheard the last of the conversation. "I'll go for him, Mum. He's used to living with women and might not even be willing to go with David, once he got there. Besides, David can't drive that far in this fog. I can take the train as easily as he can. I'll bet he's here somewhere right now. I'll see if he can take me to the station. It will be good for me, Mum. It will keep my mind off my worries. Will you check the timetable for me?"

Knowing that Edith was right and not wanting to take advantage of David, anyway, Eleanor nodded her head and got up to go to her room for the train schedule. When she came back into the kitchen, Edith had gone in search of David, and Gilda was looking very perplexed.

"What is it, Gilda?" asked Eleanor.

"Things are changing by the minute around here, and for some reason, I cannot even think straight. I feel like I'm losing my mind."

"That happens when you're pregnant. You aren't ill, are you?"

"Oh no, but I was just now upstairs with Priscilla, and I can't say why, but I couldn't bring myself to tell her about the change in our Christmas plans."

"Like an intuition?"

"You might say that. For some reason, I just couldn't go through with it. Partly, it was because she said that David was making an order at the bakery and arrangements for some chickens from my dad. I had to tell her about Thomas's assignment, which she took surprisingly well, but I hesitated to say more."

"Well, if you think she can handle Emma better than she can cope with a change in plans, let's trust it. Jane won't be here to be overwhelmed, anyway. She was my main concern."

"Well, I don't know what to think. That seems to be the problem."

Dotty came into the kitchen to start the second breakfast, so Gilda put on her apron and went into work mode. Soon everyone in the house knew the latest developments, and all minds were working on different aspects of preparation.

Although, everyone seemed to be bustling, the house was unusually devoid of conversation. Besides concentrating on the work at hand, in the back of everyone's mind was the worry of Thomas's imminent call-up, the arrival of little Willy, and anxiety over Larry Bradford's brother and the Allies on the continent, fighting for their lives.

Eleanor was anxious on all those counts, in addition to the ever-present ache in her heart for her poor son and his family who needed him so. Standing in the middle of the kitchen, she found herself quite unable to decide what to do next.

Gilda approached her and said, "Mrs. Wood, Edith says that Willy can sleep in her room, so she's having Sam move the cot in there. I'll put the bedding on it."

"Do we have a cot?" asked Eleanor.

Gilda laughed and said, "Remember Sam finding it in the shed? He was going to get it down and clean it up for me."

Eleanor shook her head, saying, "I, too, am losing my mind."

Gilda said, "I doubt that, Mrs. Wood. Now, here is the plan. David takes Edith to the station in a few minutes, and if things go smoothly, she might even get back tonight. I'll stay in the workroom as planned, so that gives you yet one more room for the next unexpected guests."

Eleanor chuckled and went to tell Dotty the recent news and talk to her about food, since everything else seemed to be in hand. She knew that Dotty would be delighted to hear of David's promised contributions.

After dinner that night, Gilda was feeling lost without Thomas and trying not to show it. Edith was gone, and the Armstrongs had gone to their room early, as usual, so it was just Eleanor and Gilda, sitting by the wireless.

Gilda asked, "Are we going to have plenty of wood for our traditional crackling Christmas fires?"

"I think so. Sam is working on that. He's also checking the flues and getting any birds out of the chimneys." Noticing a faraway expression on Gilda's face, Eleanor asked, "Are you all right tonight, Gilda?"

Just as Gilda was going to lie and say she was doing fine, the telephone began to ring. Eleanor answered, thinking it might be Edith, but it was Thomas for Gilda, instead.

Her eyes glistened with gratitude as she took the receiver and uttered, "Hello?"

"Darling, I have to be quick, but I wanted to tell you that I love you. We are standing by for our orders and may even be sent down to Bramcote Station to depart from there. I may not have another chance to talk to you."

"I see. I love you, too," said Gilda, clutching the telephone receiver with both hands.

"Please don't worry, Gilda. The Jerries have made no progress since the second day of the attack, and their air defense is nothing to brag about."

"I'll be fine; I'll try not to worry. And you," said Gilda firmly, "Don't you be worrying about me, either. Keep your mind on the job."

Before hanging up, Thomas said, "When I talked to Richard, he said he would keep an eye on the cottage for us while we were gone. His own plans for Christmas have fallen through. Do you think you might invite him to join the festivities at the manor? Run it by Mrs. Wood, and if she agrees, you make the invitation, all right, darling?"

"Sure," said Gilda, rolling her eyes at Eleanor, "I'll ask her right now."

"And there's one more thing, Gilda," added Thomas hurriedly. "Tell mum I'll be careful and that I love her."

"I'll take care of it. Be safe, Thomas, and happy birthday, tomorrow."

When Gilda got off the telephone, she told Eleanor about Thomas's request to invite Richard for Christmas. When Eleanor agreed enthusiastically, they collapsed back in their chairs and laughed, not knowing whether the hysteria was driven by the actual situation or the underlying angst.

Wiping the tears on her cheeks, Gilda said, "So much for your small, intimate gathering."

The telephone began ringing again, and this time it was Edith. She was staying the night with Jane, who was still with her mother in the hospital. She was using the neighbor's telephone and wanted her mum to have that extension. Eleanor wrote down the information and repeated it back to Edith before asking, "How is Willy doing?"

Edith answered, "Willy and I are already getting along wonderfully. He's a trusting little fellow. Soon, we'll go to his house to wait for his mum to come home from the hospital."

Eleanor said, "I'm so glad you called. Was your journey awful?"

"Of course," answered Edith candidly. "I've booked our trip home. We should be there about four o'clock tomorrow afternoon."

"I'll send David to fetch you."

Eleanor hung up the telephone, but before she could even sit down, it rang again, and this time it was Larry. Eleanor explained, "Edith went to collect my grandson today. She rang here moments ago. She was phoning from the neighbor's house, because theirs is out of order."

She listened for few seconds and said, "Let me give that to you. I hope you can catch her before she leaves."

Eleanor carefully gave him the information, and when she sat down, she said, "I hope his brother is safe. I hated to ask. He hardly knows me."

"Perhaps," said Gilda.

"Say, Gilda?" asked Eleanor.

"Yes, Mrs. Wood?" replied Gilda.

"He said he might surprise us and join us in a couple of days."

"That's nice," said Gilda, yawning. She then added, "Apparently, he knows you well enough to invite himself for Christmas."

"That's a good point. We can put him in the RAF wing. Since Jane's not coming yet, I suppose we could put him in the children's room."

"She may yet come, and bring the village of Trubury," said Gilda, smiling at her mentor's great calm.

"Now, that would surprise me!" exclaimed Eleanor. Eyeing Gilda, she asked, "So, you're really all right?"

"I really think I am."

"Let's go to bed, then. This has been the longest day of my life."

## Chapter Fifteen

Arriving at St. Martin Station, Edith had hired a ride into Trubury. Jane's house was dark, but Mr. Jameson had watched for her arrival and invited her into his own house next door, where Willy was playing quietly on the floor. Mr. Jameson had suggested she ring Jane at the hospital from his house, before taking Willy home, reminding her that the telephone was out next door.

Talking to Jane for the first time, under such circumstances, had been a bit surreal, Edith thought, but she'd assured Jane that Willy had taken to her and would be fine until her return. Then, getting permission, she had called Greystone Manor to make her mum aware of her return plans.

As she gathered up Willy's things and prepared to leave, Larry rang, and although they spoke very briefly, Edith's optimism was restored. Happily, she managed to put Willy to bed and meet all his needs in a house she had never seen before. Waiting there in Jane's quiet sitting room, Edith relived her conversation with Larry, in which she'd learned very little, but had been comforted, all the same.

Jane didn't feel she could leave her mum alone at

the hospital until well after midnight, when she caught a taxi home. When she finally arrived, disheveled and emotionally exhausted, she used her key to get in and found Edith reading a book in her sitting room. Under the circumstances, all that Edith could think of to say was, "Do come in and make yourself at home."

Jane burst into laughter, followed quickly by tears. Digging for her handkerchief and dabbing her face with it, she exclaimed, "I'm so sorry. I've had a horrible day!"

Edith helped Jane remove her coat and said, "I know. Why don't you sit down, and I'll get you some tea."

Jane complied, because she needed some time in private to pull herself together.

A few minutes later, Edith brought in a tray of tea and toast. Jane ate the toast eagerly, not saying anything. The hot tea had a soothing effect, and Jane wound down from her emotional crisis. She finally said, "How can I thank you enough, Edith? Poor Mr. Jameson! I just couldn't ask him to keep Willy all night. And yet, when it came down to it, he was my only option."

"Everyone else was gone for the holidays, already?"

"Oh no, there really is no one else. There never has been. Mum and I were judged pretty harshly when we got back here from Singapore. Mum's old friends shunned her, and after all we had been through, it made her furious. She vowed never to speak to them again, and she hasn't. Our dear neighbor, Mr. Jameson, has been our only real friend."

"I'm so sorry, Jane," said Edith sincerely. "I'm sure my mother doesn't realize that."

"No, I never told her. We couldn't change the way people felt about us, and we wouldn't have changed the circumstances, either. Our mutual love for Willy has kept us sane, as we've waited for information about my dad and William. I think we'd have gone somewhere else if we'd thought it might be different, but Mum owns this house, so we needed to stay and endure."

"It's been so long, too. I don't know how you've stood it."

"Oh, it's been terrible, all right. It's been hard on me, but maybe even worse on Mum. The coldness of the community here, on top of our harrowing experience getting out of Singapore, has added vastly to our ordeal, and the sum total has taken a huge toll on my mum."

"You've not heard any news at all about your father?"

"Nothing, but whether he was captured or even injured at the beginning, the outcome was the same. He's gone; I'm sure of it. He was not a healthy man when we last saw him. I think William and I would have gotten married before it all fell apart in Singapore, if I hadn't been so afraid to tell my father that I was pregnant. I didn't fear him at all, of course. He wouldn't have been angry, but his health was fragile. I honestly was afraid that telling him would kill him. In fact, I never did have to tell him. I have the Japanese to thank for that."

"He should have gotten on the boat with you."

"I know. He just couldn't, he said."

"Your father could be alive somewhere, Jane."

"He isn't; I promise you. And I think Mum has finally come to that conclusion herself. She told me that yesterday's post had something in it that made her think it was from the Royal Navy about my dad. It turned out to be nothing important, but she didn't know that right away. She was here with Willy alone, because I had to get some food in. She suddenly felt ill, she told me later, and went to use the telephone to call for help, but the line was dead. When she collapsed, Willy went to get Mr. Jameson on his own."

"He is precious, Jane. He's a beautiful little boy, and a smart one, too. Since when do two-year-olds have the presence of mind to do what he did?"

Smiling proudly, Jane said, "I'm pretty amazed

myself."

Edith asked, "Do you have any other family nearby?"

"None, my mum was an only child. My dad had a brother here, but I never knew them. He and his wife were killed in a car crash just before my parents married, and my grandparents are long gone. But, from the time she married my dad, Mum's life has been a happy one until I got pregnant and we had to leave Singapore. It all fell apart on us then. Mum hopes to be able to come home tomorrow, because she hopes to meet you and see Willy before you both go."

"You must have a very strong bond between you after all you've been through with no one but yourselves to rely on."

"We do. She's resigned to the idea that Willy will go with you. She knows she's dying and doesn't want him to be here when she does. We've been given little hope that her heart will hold out for very long."

"I'm so terribly sorry, Jane."

Nodding, Jane said, "Before I forget entirely, please tell your mum that I will bring William's letters with me when I come for Willy. If my mum gets through this crisis and survives the next few days, I'll have Mr. Jameson sit with her for a day, so I can come get Willy myself. Your mum wants particularly to see the last of William's letters with her own eyes, and I don't blame her. I don't want to part with them right now, so tell her I promise to bring them. Sometimes I go to sleep at night with his letters in my hand."

"I'll tell her. She'll be so pleased to see you. You and Willy have been very good for her."

"We are so grateful that she found us, and I'm truly thankful that you came today, Edith. It was very kind of you to save the day," said Jane, smiling weakly.

Nodding, Edith said, "I'm happy to have been here when you needed me. I think we should get you to bed, now, so why don't you show me where to put you."

Chuckling at the strangeness of the situation, they made their way to bed.

The following morning, Edith awoke in the tiny, ground-floor guestroom and took a moment to remember where she was. She again heard the knocking that had awakened her in the first place, so she grabbed her dressing gown and hurried to answer the door.

She opened the door to Mr. Jameson. He, too, was in his housecoat and slippers, with the addition of a ratty, old shawl wrapped around his shoulders. Edith noted that

## At Willows Edge

his appearance was startlingly different than the night before and exclaimed, "Mr. Jameson, come in out of the freezing air."

Once he was inside and Edith had tightly closed the door against the icy breeze, she was alarmed that his face had no color. "Are you ill, Mr. Jameson?"

"No, I have a telephone message for Miss Jane," he explained breathlessly.

Jane had suddenly appeared and asked, "From the hospital?"

The old man nodded sadly and said, "I'm so sorry, Miss Jane. Your mama passed away a few minutes ago. I told the hospital I'd tell you right away."

"Come sit down, Mr. Jameson," said Edith, leading him into the sitting room. "Just rest here a little while. I'll bring you some tea. Come, Jane, and sit."

Jane slowly followed them into the sitting room and sat down with her neighbor, not yet realizing that she was in her nightgown only. Edith asked her if she was all right, but Jane didn't even hear her. She just stared straight ahead, tears streaming down her face. Edith left them.

"Now, Miss Jane," said her neighbor, "your mama was a wonderful lady, and until the war, she had a lovely life. I liked your parents from the time they bought this house, years ago." He paused and added, "I was always a little in love with your mama, you know, but she was way too young for me, of course."

Surprised by his admission, Jane better understood his great distress at her mother's death.

"You need to sell this house and move to a friendly village, where people won't treat you like they've done here."

"I don't want to move away from you, Mr. Jameson. This is the only home I know. Who will be here for you if we move?"

"You needn't move far, but go somewhere else. When Willy goes to school, you don't want to be here. He'll be picked on awful. I won't have it. I'll even buy your house here, so you can leave at once."

"Why would you do that?"

"I can't have it, Miss Jane. You need to get out of here, now. You should call yourself Mrs. William Wood and move away from this hateful place."

Having heard none of the conversation, Edith returned with the tea and quietly and unobtrusively laid it out on the oval tea table. She didn't know what to do then, so she turned to go back to her room.

"Wait, Edith," said Jane. "I want you to take Willy

today as planned. He is too little to understand any of this, anyway. I'll come join you at the manor as soon as the burial is over."

"Don't you want me to stay here and help you?"

"Mr. Jameson will take care of me, and I would like for you and your mum to take care of Willy."

Edith looked at the poor disheveled man and wondered if he could even take care of himself, but she nodded her agreement and left the room when she heard Willy awake upstairs. She said, "I'll get us packed up for the journey. I hope to see you again, Mr. Jameson. Thank you for your kindness."

❦❦

Willy seemed confused when he said goodbye to his mama later that morning, but he seemed reassured when Jane promised to join him and his grandmother in a few days. Trying to appear excited for Willy's first train ride, she waved them off at the station. Mr. Jameson had driven them all to the station in St. Martin, although Edith had insisted she could hire a ride just as easily as she had done the night before.

Waving from the train window, Edith thought that Jane and her neighbor did not appear to be up to the task before them, but she had no choice but to leave them to it. Returning to her own responsibilities, Edith reminded herself that Willy, although smart enough get help for his grandmother in an emergency, probably wouldn't tell her if he needed to use the loo, so she would have to be alert to his needs, as well as her own.

Thinking to herself that one little child was probably more work than a barn full of cows, she asked, "Willy, have you ever seen a cow?"

Loudly, he said, "Moooooo," and then he giggled uproariously at himself.

"Oh, to be a little child again," thought Edith as she laughed, too.

༺༻༺༻

Richard had contacted his brother-in-law and had cancelled going to Birmingham for Christmas. He hadn't exactly explained it that way to Thomas, but with the Gardners out of Willows Edge, Richard wanted to watch the place and take an active part in solving the mystery of the stalking woman. The empty cottage seemed to him like an opportunity to lure the stalker into some kind of action.

He had already asked residents of the village about any transient population and had gotten nowhere. One woman had gone on about a gypsy camp, piquing his interest, but her daughter shushed her, saying the event had happened more than twenty years ago.

Richard's first idea was to do as Thomas had already done and talk to the innkeepers in and around Englewood. He rang the estate agent in Nuneaton, who he and his wife had used to purchase their cottage. He had been an elderly fellow, five years ago, so, assuming he had not been called up to serve in the war, and hoping he had not died in the meantime, Richard placed the call with optimism.

After being told all that had happened to the old man in the past five years, Richard was rewarded for his patience and given a list of four inns that were within walking distance of Englewood. Three of them were the same ones that Thomas had already contacted, and having no car, Richard rang the desks at the inns on his list. By three of the desk managers, he was told the exact thing that Thomas had been told. The residents were mostly permanent, with the occasional couple passing through, but more often, men traveling alone.

Codgett's Country Inn was not only the closest hotel in the area, but the manager there said that they did have a single female guest, who traveled up from London from time to time. At first, the manager mistook Richard's line of questioning for inquiring about appropriate accommodations for a female family member of his, but when asked if the woman was there now, the manager clammed up. He suddenly feared that he had already revealed too much about his reclusive guest, who always paid up front, in cash, and left generous tips.

Richard knew that he'd get no more help from him, so he thanked him and hung up. He determined to walk to the inn and stake it out, so to speak, but then realized that he'd be staking out the inn for a woman he had not yet seen with his own eyes. Concluding that such a tack was a bit absurd, Richard decided to stake out Willows Edge, instead. Having an educated guess about what direction his mystery woman might come from, he found the perfect hiding place in the thick hedge, made himself a comfortable nest, and waited.

ೀೀೀೀ

In the sewing room that night, Gilda went to bed exhausted and missing Thomas terribly. She had retrieved her own clothes and diary that day from the cottage when David had agreed to go there with her. He'd had the desire to meet Richard Fitzgerald to whom he'd spoken, but once, on the telephone, and hoped to introduce himself.

Trying to ignore the masses of now-dried apples hanging from the ceiling, Gilda recorded the strange events of her week.

*December 23, 1944*
*Dear Diary,*

*This week has been full of events, none good, from my point of view. As I was finishing up writing in my diary on Monday evening, I looked up to see a strange woman some distance away from our southern window. It was quite dark, but the little light from the airfield reflecting off the low clouds put her in a vague silhouette that I would have never seen, anyway, if I hadn't felt her gaze upon me. She was facing the cottage, staring right at me; I'm sure of it. Although, I'd seen her twice before, this time I knew she was a woman. If you asked me to explain how I know that absolutely, I'm not sure I could put it into words, but Thomas saw her, too, as he was coming home from the airfield, and he agrees. She could see me much better than I could see her, because I still have no curtains in the sitting room, and I had a light on. Thomas could actually see her more clearly than I could, because of the light from my window behind her. Of course, when I turned off the light, he lost sight of her. He tried to pursue her, but she disappeared into the night.*

*Mrs. Wood has been planning Christmas for weeks, but her planning has been in vain. Everything has changed, and everyone seems to be descending upon her, except Jane, whose mother died this morning. Edith brought Willy to Greystone today, but I have seen little of him. He was exhausted from the train ride, which ran late, so he was bathed and put to bed hours ago.*

*I'm sleeping in the sewing workroom this week, because Thomas is flying missions. The Americans have been in trouble in Belgium since Sunday, and the Allies have been unable to provide air support until today, when, at last, the weather cleared and that impenetrable fog finally lifted. I'm trying to stay calm and very British over this development, for which I commend myself.*

*David walked me to the cottage to get some clean clothes and my journal this afternoon. We dropped in on Richard, but he was out. I had already invited him to the manor for Christmas by telephone, but David wanted to meet him. Thomas and I know Richard well, by now, but he has not yet been introduced to any of the others at the manor. Priscilla hasn't been up to anything social, yet, so we have respected that.*

*As for Christmas, I want to give a gift of some kind to everyone, and I haven't so much as given it a thought until tonight. I'll work at that tomorrow. The RAF is feeding all the airmen for the next two days in honour of Christmas (and to give Mrs. Wood a reprieve) so I will have all day to get into the Christmas spirit. It will keep my mind off Thomas. Today is his birthday. Please God, watch over him.*

*My Christmas list includes the Coopers, including Emma, of course, my parents and their foster children, Priscilla and David, Richard, Eleanor, and Thomas, for whom I don't even have a birthday gift. Alas. I should try to come up with something for little Willy, too.*

*I suddenly remember that Richard has boxes of books that he has been going through, some of which he no longer wants. Perhaps, he would sell some of them to me. Having some kind of plan, now, maybe I can get to sleep, that is if I can ignore the aroma of the apples above me and the ache in my heart for Thomas.*

∽∾∽∾

Picking up her diary that same evening, Eleanor wrote, *I will have no airmen at the manor for Christmas, and yet, because of prolonged bad weather, I expect a crowd. The fog actually lifted today, so I was half-expecting everyone's plans to change again, but they have not. Edith and Willy are sharing her room, and Gilda is in the sewing room until Thomas's return. David and Priscilla are here, and Gilda's family will join us for Christmas Eve and again for Christmas dinner. Of course, Dotty and Sam will join us. Emma and Willy can be playmates, which will make it all that much more fun for them. We've had no word from Larry or Thomas, so I have no idea, whether or not to expect either of them, but I do expect Gilda and Thomas's new neighbour, Richard, to join us. I'm a little wary of him, in spite of Gilda's assurances. His arrival coincides exactly with the appearance of the woman, who has so unnerved Gilda.*

*When Willy arrived this afternoon, I feared he would think me a stranger, but he remembered me. My heart nearly burst with joy. I wish I could make his Christmas magical, but all over England, it will be predictably lack-luster after five years of war. Dotty has shamed us all by suggesting we concentrate on the true meaning of Christmas, for which I applaud her. She wants to perform a nativity play, and I have given her leave to do so. Apparently, according to her, we'll be having a pantomime on New Years, too. Sam has found a Christmas tree, which he has already put in the big hall. Lucas and Matty have agreed to help me decorate it tomorrow. I welcome their help. Dotty, Agnes, Edith, and even Pris have taken over the food preparations. Gilda hasn't had a day off all week, so she has tomorrow to prepare herself for Christmas, and hopefully, Thomas's safe return.*

*I'm concerned about Edith. She shares Larry's concerns for his brother on the continent and seems worn down. Willy's presence will help keep her mind off of her worries.*

*I will miss Wilbur, Andrew, and William again this Christmas. Poor Jane is separated from her son, too, on his third Christmas. She rang today to say her mother will be buried on Tuesday. From what Edith has shared with me, Jane and her neighbour will be on their own for Christmas and the intimate burial service, because Ruth became estranged from the village people when Willy was born. I remember her as such a docile creature, but apparently she had more than enough of a mother's protective instinct.*

*Jane was so kind as to tell Edith that she will bring William's letters when she comes next week. I'm sure she didn't want to be separated from them, as well from William, himself. She has just lost her mother, and her little lad will not be with her on Christmas morning. Poor Jane.*

## Chapter Sixteen

The following morning, Lucas was pounding on the door by eight o'clock. He and Matty, bundled warm against the cold, had come to decorate. Eleanor wasn't up yet, thanks to the Royal Air Force for a luxurious lie-in. Dotty was in the kitchen, though, so she sent the children in search of branches of holly and bows of fir. They took a basket and were off to the trees that surrounded the estate. They returned for breakfast, lugging a full basket of branches, berries, and pine cones.

David saw Gilda start out for home again, so he offered to walk her. With Spanky at their heels, they went first to the cottage, where Gilda gathered a few things and put them together on the kitchen table to be fetched later. Then, they walked to her neighbor's cottage, where she intended to spend the morning looking through his stash of castoffs. She introduced the men and left them to talk, while she got to the task at hand.

Richard offered David a cup of tea and invited him into his tiny sitting room. His cottage was much like Gilda's, next door, but not as tidy, having no woman to care about such things.

When they were settled in their chairs, Richard said,

"I'm glad you walked with Gilda."

"Well," said David, "in her condition, we haven't been letting her walk in the dark. As you know, before Thomas left, I'd been meeting them halfway in the mornings. Now, of course, there is the added anxiety over the mystery woman that I find downright alarming."

"I changed my Christmas plans, so I could do a little detective work on that issue."

"Glad to hear it. Gilda and I came by yesterday, but you were out."

"I hadn't gone far. I determined the hedge to be the best place to watch for the approach of the mystery woman, who I do not deem harmless, by the way."

"You think she means to harm Gilda and Thomas?" asked David incredulously.

"I believe she means to harm them emotionally, if nothing else," said Richard.

"Have you thought about the possibility of this woman being unstable?"

"Of course," exclaimed Richard. "Of course, she's unstable. Look, I have talked to the local police. No one else has reported anything like this."

"Who could have ill will toward Gilda or Thomas? They are the nicest of people. Pris says that Thomas was always such a mild-mannered little boy." Quietly, so Gilda wouldn't overhear, he went on, "When he got engaged to a selfish woman by the name Gates, it was almost too much for Priscilla. Thomas broke it off last summer and married Gilda, instead, but I would have thought you'd have heard all this by now."

"Remember, I just got here. I know some, but not all of their history. I don't imagine Thomas and Gilda speak of her often."

"No, I don't think they do. So, did you see anything yesterday?"

"No, I didn't. I made myself a comfortable nest in the hedge and fell asleep, damn it."

David laughed heartily and said, "It must have been chilly and miserable on the ground. You must have needed the rest."

"I'll admit I don't sleep very well, lately. I don't know what you know about me, but I have a son missing in the Pacific. The last communication we had of him was before we left here in '39, and the navy knows nothing. He had signed up with the Royal Navy before the war had begun, in earnest. The trail ends in Singapore. I've tried to find out what happened to any of the personnel on his ship, but information is hard to get. All they can tell me is that my son is missing in the east. I went to London directly from Liverpool, when my ship came in a few weeks ago. You see, my son might never have gotten our letter saying his mother and I were going to America to visit our daughter, and once there, we couldn't get out again."

"Does he know that you intended to settle here?"

"We never received a letter from him that indicated that, so how would we know?"

"How did you get home?"

"The Royal Navy worked out something with the Americans, and they let me come in on a military ship, the USS Wakefield."

"So that's why you don't sleep."

"That, among other things, I suppose."

"I can give you something for sleep. I'm an orthopedist, but I was a family doctor, first. I'm working with the wounded and provide some rehabilitation therapy. I boarded with a colleague before I married Pris. I base myself out of here, now, although Pris has a home in Surrey. Hitler's newest vengeance machine was our excuse for leaving there and coming here, and it's been good for Priscilla to be near Thomas. We haven't met you, because Pris has had to overcome some recent heartache. I didn't think she'd come back to us, but just recently, she's been acting more like her old self again."

"I hope she recovers quickly. You'd better save your sleeping draughts for the wounded. I'll be all right in time. You should probably know that Thomas has confided in me. I know about your wife's ordeal, as well as the situation surrounding Mrs. Wood's grandson and his missing father. Not knowing is a condition that allows no rest. It's something that never leaves you. You are haunted by it. My wife was glad to be in America, at first, but once the war actually started, she was afraid of going home. And yet, she was so worried about what might have happened to Alec, she lost her vitality. She died two years ago."

"I'm sorry to hear that. I lost my first wife to cancer before the war. Pris and I married last summer soon after Thomas and Gilda's wedding."

"I knew that, as well," said Richard nodding. "Thomas and I have become great friends, and I've become something of a father figure to him, I think."

"He's needed one," said David honestly.

There's more to war than war," said Richard wisely.

"You know," said David, "for some time now, I've been thinking about taking Pris to my sister's house for Christmas, or even back to Surrey, to her home. I've been worried how she will handle being in the same room as the child. I think I've given myself stomach ulcers over it."

David looked up mischievously and added, "And don't say, 'Physician, heal thyself.'"

"I wouldn't dream of it."

Looking around the snug, little room, David asked, "What do you make of the Germans coming against the Americans so suddenly?"

"The Allies should have seen it coming, by God," said Richard angrily. "It was a fool-hardy thing for Hitler to do, but he's insane. The Allies keep forgetting to factor the insanity into it. Hitler's got no chance, because, although he may have cut the Americans off, for now, the Jerries won't be able to get supplies in, either. A lot of hope their armored attack will have without a fuel supply. There's no hope of sustaining it. They are buying time, no more."

"Well, it seems they had the weather on their side," said David shaking his head.

"Until yesterday," said Richard. "We're going after them now."

"Thomas is part of that, you know," said David nervously. "Pris is handling his going far better than I'd hoped."

"Gilda seems to be doing all right, too," said Richard.

"Yes, she seems to be doing quite well," said David, emphasizing the word "seems."

Richard nodded agreement, and David said, "I need to go on home and help with Christmas. Come along any time you want. Considering the size of the crowd already there, it appears the party has begun."

"It's very gracious of Mrs. Wood to invite me, considering we have yet to meet."

"You'll meet the great lady today. Tell Gilda I'll take her things that she sat aside at the cottage. Should I come back for her, then?"

"I'll just accompany Gilda when she's done in there," said Richard pointing in the direction of the storeroom. "She can't go alone, and this way, you won't have to come back for her."

After showing David out, Richard found Gilda in the unheated storeroom. Seeing her sitting there on the floor, amid the stacks of books in the near-dark, he opened the curtains of the single, small window, and a bit of indirect light found its way in, revealing the tears that streamed down her cheeks.

"He's flying now, Richard. I can feel it," whispered Gilda.

"Have you been in here crying all this time?"

*At Willows Edge*

"Not the whole time," answered Gilda sheepishly. Thinking of Richard's missing son, she added, "I'm not the only one with reason to cry."

"That's not to say you shouldn't indulge yourself from time to time. I'm going to help you with your project, and you are going to help me think of something I can do for Mrs. Wood, since she is so kind to extend a Christmas invitation to a total stranger."

"Thomas and I have been keeping you to ourselves," admitted Gilda. "You've been good for Thomas."

"Well, it looks like I'm going to meet everyone today."

"Recovering herself and taking in the bounty of Richard's castoffs, Gilda said, "This room is a veritable treasure chest."

"I've left the door open quite a lot since I've been here, so it doesn't smell too musty anymore, does it?"

"Oh, I don't think so," said Gilda. "I'll have to figure out what I can wrap these gifts in, once I've persuaded you to part with them."

"I'm willing to part with anything in this room. Furthermore, since I've not been here for years, I have an ample supply of wrapping paper, Christmas wrapping paper, in fact. I'll get it, and I'll bring some ribbon, too."

"Everyone will be so jealous," exclaimed Gilda. She smiled genuinely, and Richard squeezed her shoulder affectionately, as he turned to go in search of the paper. When he returned moments later, he helped Gilda get up from the floor, and together they gathered up her treasures and took them to the kitchen table for wrapping.

৵৽৵৽

At eleven o'clock, when Eleanor finally entered the kitchen, it was full of breakfasters. To her pleasure and surprise, she discovered that even the Armstrongs, who usually took breakfast alone upstairs, were there among the crowd.

Donned with an apron, Sam was tossing pancakes to the squeals of delight from the children. Emma and Willy stood on sturdy chairs behind the chef, wearing large aprons that reached the tops of their feet. Sam was in his glory, making a regular production out of the process, and Lucas and Matty were positioned behind the little ones, making sure they didn't fall off or tip their chairs in the excitement. Dotty was seeing to other things and leading the cheers as Sam perfectly flipped the thin pancakes every time.

Edith was busy at the cooker, frying up a few rashers of bacon that smelled heavenly to Eleanor, and she smiled when she thought, "I should really enjoy the smell of the bacon and savor it, because there will be no more than a bite or two for each of us."

The Armstrongs were setting out the syrup that had been made from wild damson berries by Gilda's dad and Lucas, when the berries peaked in September. Seeing all this productivity reminded Eleanor that she must get the dried apples down. She intended to bag them up and give them to any of the airmen, who might seek her out and wish her a Happy Christmas in the next few days.

Dotty had prepared for Eleanor's comfort by setting up a little table in the corner by the wireless. The food was being laid out on the kitchen table, and rather than take their plates to one of the long military tables in the dining hall, everyone seemed to prefer carrying their plates around the kitchen and trying to keep track of which cup of tea was theirs. Eleanor thought it looked like a joyous kind of chaos that she would enjoy sharing with her diary. It was apparent that the four children present were having tremendous fun, and it occurred to Eleanor that Christmas itself might prove to be a bit of a letdown.

Scanning the noisy group, Eleanor noted that Gilda

was not there. She remembered Gilda saying she had much to do, so she assumed she had breakfasted early. Eleanor worried briefly if she had gone home alone, but amid the clamor, she didn't attempt to ask anyone.

༄༅༄༅

That afternoon, before making a short trip into Nuneaton to check on two patients, David popped into the kitchen looking for his wife. To his surprise, he found her making Christmas treats with Dotty.

"Hello, ladies, what's happening in here? And where did everyone go?"

"We kicked the lot of them out," said Dotty chuckling. "Didn't we, Mrs. Armstrong?"

"We most certainly did," said Priscilla. "We had to. The children were underfoot, something awful. The older children helped Eleanor with the tree, took down all the dried apples, and went on home awhile ago. Edith took the little ones and Spanky out for a walk in this glorious sunshine."

"Where is Eleanor now?" asked David.

"She's been holed up in her room and won't open up for anyone," said Dotty.

"She's not ill, is she?" asked David.

"Not at all," said Dotty. "She's wrapping presents. She's having a double dose of Christmas spirit this year, and I, for one, couldn't be happier about it."

"Well, I'm off to Nuneaton," said the doctor. "If you need anything, I'd be happy to try to get it for you."

"We won't impose on you, Doctor," said Dotty. "We'll manage with what we've got."

"I'll run along then," said David, kissing his wife on the cheek.

As he was heading down the hall, he heard his wife's voice call out, "Don't forget to bring a newspaper, David."

Turning, he answered, "I won't."

He saw Eleanor emerge from her room, and coming toward him, she said, "I heard your voice, David. Do you have any idea what's become of Gilda? I'm worried about her."

"I walked her to the cottage and then to her neighbor's house to do her Christmas presents this morning. He's walking her home this afternoon. She'll need his help carrying her gifts."

"You left her all alone with Mr. Fitzgerald?"

"Of course, shouldn't I have?" asked the doctor perplexed.

"We don't know anything about him, David. He showed up here at precisely the same time as that woman began stalking Gilda."

"He's been trying to help solve the mystery. He cancelled his Christmas plans for the sole purpose of watching the cottage for them. He's even spoken to the constable."

"So he says," said Eleanor skeptically.

"Well, I never," said the doctor, now flummoxed.

"We should have looked into the background of this man and found out who he really is," insisted Eleanor.

"Mrs. Wood, I mean, Eleanor, please calm down. There is nothing to worry about. You'll meet him soon and know for yourself."

"I'm not so trusting. For all we know, he's a spy."

At that, David burst into laughter, put on his hat, and said he must be going. He chuckled all the way out to his car, stopping only briefly to admire the tall tree in the great hall.

༄༅༄༅

In Shrewsbury, Dr. Hughes, the Davies's family doctor, stopped by Jane's home to see how she was faring. Most of the burial arrangements had been made the day before, so Jane had been at loose ends, finding it hard to know what to do next. She was resting in the sitting room when the doctor called on her.

She invited him into the genteel room, saying, "Can I get you something to drink, Doctor?"

"No, I don't need anything. I just wanted to see how you're doing, considering you are here alone on Christmas Eve."

"Mr. Jameson and I are going to spend Christmas together," said Jane. "I didn't even have the presence of mind to send Willy's Christmas present with his Aunt Edith when they left."

"You can give it to him when you see him. You want to see him open it, don't you?"

"I was very excited about that prospect just a few days ago," said Jane quietly.

"How about I come round and remind you to take it with you after the burial service?"

"That's good of you, Doctor, but unnecessary, really."

"I'm worried about you, Jane. You seem very much alone, except for your dear Mr. Jameson, of course."

"He's so kind," said Jane.

"Is there anything at all I can do for you? Have you

heard from William, lately?"

We have had two letters now. You know, when the first one came in May, his mother and I had this notion that we'd get one every month. I think he may be writing often enough, but I have recently learned that we are very fortunate indeed to have gotten two of them."

"That is true, from what I hear, too."

"Weeks after I got the last letter, it dawned on me that it wasn't written by William at all. It was written and signed for him, but I didn't notice the difference in the handwriting for weeks, probably because the writing is so small, as there is very little space in which to write. Looking at it now, I don't know how I could have missed how different the handwriting was, and even how different the poetic writing style was from William's own practical style. I'm better now, but I was initially very upset, thinking he had been terribly sick or something worse."

"You will feel much better once you've heard from him again."

"Yes. You know, Doctor, there is something at the bottom of that same letter that I can't make out. In fact, I didn't even see it there until it hit me that the writing was not William's."

"I have a friend who could put the letter under

intense magnification. Let me show it to him tomorrow when my wife and I go there for Christmas dinner. I'll be at the burial service and give it back to you."

"You won't forget?" asked Jane worriedly.

"I promise," said the doctor kindly.

"You have been a good friend, Dr. Hughes. You delivered Willy and have taken care of him. And, you have taken care of me and Mum."

"You've had few enough friends, my dear. I think you should consider getting away from Trubury for awhile."

"Mr. Jameson wants me to sell the house to him. He wants me to go somewhere more friendly and call myself Mrs. William Wood."

"That would be a splendid idea as long as you engaged and made friends, but as reclusive as you and your mum have been for so long, you might not get to know anyone. That wouldn't be good for you, either."

"I now know William's family in Warwickshire. That's where Mr. Jameson thinks I should go."

"He loves you like a daughter, doesn't he?"

"Yes, and he loved my mother in another way," said Jane making eye contact. "I just learned that."

"I never knew. He was content to look over you all.

He'll be a lonely fellow when you leave."

"He's thinking about going to his brother's home in Dorset. He says he'll lease these two houses and leave here himself. He says as long as he's here, he'll never get over his grudge about the way people treated my mum and me." Remembering the task at hand, she said, "I'll get William's letter. You promise to bring it back to me?"

"I'll even give you a receipt," offered the doctor.

Jane smiled for the first time that day and told the doctor that a receipt would not be necessary.

※※※※

When Richard and Gilda arrived at the manor that afternoon, they caused quite a stir. Richard had put all of Gilda's packages into an old pillowcase and had easily carried it the quarter mile by heaving it over one shoulder. The eyes of the four children lit up when the stranger with the kind face and bagful of presents arrived. Emma approached him saying, "Aren't you worried that we'll see you and ruin everything?"

It took Richard only a second to know that he had been mistaken for Father Christmas. He said, "Oh, I'm not the official Father Christmas. I'm just a close relation of his. In fact, I've been invited to spend Christmas with you, here, if that's all right with you."

Stepping forward, Matty asked, "You're kin to Father Christmas?"

"It's a distant relationship," explained Richard vaguely.

Emma looked directly at Priscilla to see if she concurred. Emma wasn't going to believe this man, unless Mother Christmas vouched for him. No one, but Emma, saw Priscilla nod her head in confirmation of Richard's status, which satisfied Emma completely. Mother Christmas had never given her secret away, and Emma felt she was as trustworthy of an adult as she had ever known.

Everyone laughed when Emma exclaimed, "Of course, it's all right with us. Come on in."

Richard carried the bag of the gifts to the tree and took from Gilda the parcel she had carried for him. He stepped back toward the doorway, so he could more easily enjoy the ancient grandeur of the great hall and the hubbub of familial activity.

Eleanor approached him and said formally, "Welcome to Greystone Manor, Mr. Fitzgerald. I am Eleanor Wood. We are glad you could join us."

"I thank you for the invitation. I think you may have been coerced, but I thank you, all the same."

"Well, many of us here tonight intended to be elsewhere, but the weather has brought us all together," said Eleanor feigning enthusiasm at the end of a long day.

When she inadvertently sighed with resignation, Richard laughed and said, "Your generosity and your safe haven are humanity's last hope on a cold December night."

Deflecting the compliment, Eleanor said, "Perhaps, something like that."

Richard turned their conversation to the old home. Pointing to the high, paneled ceiling, he said, "The first floor must be a horseshoe shape."

"Yes," replied Eleanor, "There are numerous bedrooms above. Until a few weeks ago, the Royal Air Force had the entire use of the two upper floors. A temporary wall now partitions the western side for my use."

"I wonder if this was once a balcony all the way around," said Richard, pointing upward. "I was interested in architecture at one point. This is a fascinating house with an interesting history, I daresay."

"I know little of the history of it, having been here only seventeen years now, but another thing I find interesting is that both the staircases to the upper level are behind closed doors. No grand staircase, anywhere."

"That is interesting, indeed," said Richard gazing

upward again. "How is it heated?"

"When we bought the place, we had electric heating installed everywhere, except for this cavernous room."

"It's a remarkable house, Mrs. Wood. I won't even have to watch my head while I'm here," said Richard. Then, handing Eleanor the parcel containing a particularly fine bottle of wine, he said, "For the hostess."

Eleanor accepted it graciously and returned to the others. The sun had gone down, and she decided it was time to light up the tree. She had strung a few lights on it, and the children could wait no longer. When the colorful lights came on, a great cheer went up, causing the children to act enormously silly.

Gilda took this opportunity to invite her mother into the library. She had realized that her mum needed to know all the complexities concerning the people in attendance, especially the children.

Before she could open her mouth, her mother said, "Dotty told me everything this afternoon when I arrived. I know all about Willy and Emma. I know very little of Richard, but I'm not alone in that."

Gilda smiled and said, "Oh, he's a darling. Don't worry about him. I'm glad you know about the others, though. It wasn't my business to tell you, but when Richard and I walked in, I realized that you needed to know what was going on around here. Now you know why Priscilla and David have been keeping to themselves. It has been a very tough go for her. She's doing very well today, I think, considering it's the first time she's been in the same room as Emma."

"I wouldn't have thought it," said Agnes surprised. "But," she added, "I've just been here an hour or so."

"If you were with Dotty for an hour, it was long enough for you to learn everything you need to know," said Gilda, chuckling. "Let's go find the others."

Agnes grabbed her daughter's arm gently and said, "I know you are worried about Thomas. I'm worrying with you, child. You aren't alone."

"Oh Mum," cried Gilda, "I almost can't bear it!"

"I know. I do know," said Agnes genuinely. "It will be all right."

Gilda's mum put her arm around her daughter and led her to the door saying, "You are going to need some new clothes soon. Look at you, a little mother."

## Chapter Seventeen

After Richard thanked his hostess and said goodbye to the others that evening, Gilda walked him to the front door of the manor. They stood for a moment gazing at the moon in the clear sky. Richard explained the phases of the moon, pointing out that the one before them was called a Waxing Gibbous Moon. Gilda tried to be cheerful, but she was suffering, and Richard knew it.

He said kindly, "Gilda, I know how you are worrying about Thomas tonight. I'm sorry he wasn't here with you on your first Christmas Eve together. And now, my dear, you must go in, before you catch your death."

He kissed her on the cheek and walked home in the light of the oval-shaped moon, not needing his torch. He let himself into the little cottage, remembering how his wife had found it irresistibly charming, in spite of his tendency to hit his head on the low ceiling beams and door headers.

Sleep was far from his mind, so he started a fire in his rustic fireplace and got comfortable in his over-stuffed, leather chair. Reaching for pen and paper, he determined to emulate the detective, Hercule Poirot, and use his little gray cells in a methodical manner.

He wrote: *Who is stalking Gilda and Thomas?*

*Meredith Kennon*
*First seen by Gilda on September 29$^{th}$*
*First seen by Thomas on October 1$^{st}$*
*Second sighting by Gilda about Oct 30$^{th}$*
*Seen by both on December 18$^{th}$*

*If the person meant to harm Gilda, there had been two opportunities, but no contact, why?*

*Who would be interested in the Gardner fortune? Someone involved with the child, Emma? Isn't her mother dead, after all? Perhaps the old aunt? Thomas's father, John, couldn't be alive, could he? Other relatives?*

*Who from their past would have hatred towards them? Someone from Thomas's RAF past? Something war-related? Is there someone who would resent the life that Thomas and Gilda have built together? Someone from their personal histories?*

Suddenly, the beginnings of an idea began to form in Richard's mind. He wanted to read something that Thomas had shown him once before. He had a key to Willows Edge, and he determined he would use it in the morning. Banking the fire and turning off the light, he thought, "Need I get Gilda's permission to go in?"

※※※※

Gilda had been invited to go to the Christmas Eve midnight service with Dotty and Mrs. Wood, but she opted to go to bed and write in her journal.

*December 24, 1944*
*Dear Diary,*

*Except for the absence of Thomas and the ever-present war, I had a lovely Christmas Eve. The nativity play, which was put on by the children, was a real treat. Bursts of laughter interrupted its sacred solemnity from time to time, as the donkey (Emma) and sheep (Willy) were particularly vocal. When the two little ones became too tired to bray and baa, we sang carols and David read from the Bible.*

*My heart ached for Thomas, and I could see that Edith felt as I did. She does not fear for Larry's life as I do for Thomas's, but she is sharing Larry's anxiety over his brother on the continent.*

*On another plane, I have made a complete breakthrough. I can no longer be jealous of my mum's love for Matty. That little girl has made my mum into the person she has always longed to be. When I took her aside to explain the histories of Emma and Willy, she had already been put in the know by Dotty. She took that opportunity, though, to tell me that she understood how I was feeling about Thomas flying, and that she was concerned about me. She referred to my growing belly, but in a nice way. I believe I have developed a real love for my mum that I thought never to achieve in this lifetime. In spite of my dad's seasonal cough, he was especially cheerful tonight, too, taking part in the nativity.*

*I have a few gifts (books, mostly) wrapped to give to my family and friends here at the manor tomorrow afternoon, but I'm most excited to give Thomas his present upon his return. He's going to love it.*

*I so wish Thomas had been here tonight, but I also respect his desire to help the cause. Please God, bring him safely home to me.*


Eleanor, too, went to bed with her diary on Christmas Eve, writing, *I thought I'd be exhausted tonight, but I am not. In fact, I'm still quite stimulated from all the goings-on of this evening. Maybe that is because it was determined by the others that I should not do any of the actual work. They wanted me to have a relaxing first Christmas Eve with Willy, and it was truly wonderful. Jane rang here before dinner, so she could wish Willy a Happy Christmas. He was pleased to talk to his mama, but, thankfully, did not make a fuss when she hung up. Edith and I were most grateful for that. I talked to Jane just briefly and learnt that she and Mr. Jameson were managing all right.*

*I was ordered not go into the kitchen tonight. For one reason or another, all the guests were here by five o'clock. With so much help, we soon had big fires roaring in the hall and the drawing room. Lucas and Matty had beautifully decorated the tree in the great hall, and evergreen and holly branches on the drawing room mantel were lovely to see as we entered the room. It felt strange and wonderful having that room for our own use again. We did have one airman wander through, and we invited him to join us, but he was just popping in to change his clothes for a party.*

*We put white tablecloths on the remaining tables in the great hall and holly berries and greenery were placed down the centres of the tables. Everyone cheered when I lit the Christmas tree. The children loved it!*

*At seven o'clock we ate chicken, potatoes, and vegetables from the garden. Several kinds of breads were on offer, courtesy of David and Priscilla, and although they looked unique, they all tasted about the same, thanks, of course, to the hardships of war. We all had a good laugh over that when Gilda's mother, who still works at the bakery where the breads were purchased, assured us that there was indeed nothing particularly unique about any of them, except, perhaps, for their shape and a few dried herbs sprinkled on top. For pudding, my apples found their way into everything, and we appreciated the bounty, if not the abundance of choices. Everyone contributed something to the festivities, and it was enjoyed by all.*

*To my delight, Dotty, Priscilla (yes, Priscilla) and Agnes had coordinated the nativity play. It was the highlight of the evening. Willy played a sheep and was very serious about it. After all his baaing, he was exhausted and willing to go to bed (for the second night in a row) without a fuss. The Smith children, Matty and Lucas played Joseph and Mary, and Emma played a donkey, whose braying competed heartily with the vocal sheep. I later learnt that Emma had volunteered her cherished doll baby to be the baby Jesus. Sam and Simon first played the part of shepherds, but soon disappeared behind the backdrop, depicting the crèche under a night sky full of stars, which had been painted by Simon. Moments later, headdresses and all, they appeared as the magi, bearing gifts, having travelled from afar.*

*We sang Silent Night and It Came Upon a Midnight*

*Clear together, followed by David reading Luke's account in the Bible of the Savior's birth. Everyone went their separate ways, agreeing to come for a seven o'clock dinner tomorrow evening.*

*Since Willy was down for the night and Edith was with him, I accepted Dotty's invitation to attend midnight church with her. Sam was staying home with Emma, so I went along, mostly, so Dotty wouldn't have to go alone. I hadn't gone to midnight church on Christmas Eve for a long time, and I was uplifted by the beautiful music. As we walked toward the church, it was so wonderful seeing the gothic windows outlined by the lights within. The street lights were lit, as well, and the presence of the glorious lights, after five years of darkness, was what the attendees talked about more than anything else.*

*I finally met Mr. Richard Fitzgerald, who, I will reluctantly admit, seems incapable of anything menacing. He is still a suspect, though, considering the timing of his appearance. Miss Marple wouldn't allow a man's charm to take him off her list of suspicious characters, and neither will I. I watched him throughout the evening, and I think he sensed my distrust. Well, trust is earned, so he will have to live with things as they are, not as he'd like them to be.*

*I feel a bit guilty about Spanky, because he was*

*banished to the carriage house. He is not accustomed so much noise, and his excited barking became too much for everyone. It was Dotty, though, who finally said, "Either that dog goes, or I do!"*

*Willy's present is under the tree, and Edith filled his stocking at the foot of his bed. She promised to fetch me, as soon as he wakes up in a few hours. I'd better get some sleep, so I'm not too tired to enjoy the big day. Happy Christmas, William, wherever you are.*

⁂

Christmas Day brought sparkling sunshine through the decorative frost on all the windows. David and Priscilla came downstairs with Edith, Gilda, and Willy because everyone wanted to see the look on Willy's face when he saw the painted wagon that Sam had revived for him. Sam had painted it blue and had asked Simon Morris to paint Willy's name on the side in white letters. Found in the back of the carriage house, it had, no doubt, been the favorite possession of a child, who had lived at the manor years before.

When Willy saw the wagon, he squealed with delight. He showed everyone the contents of his stocking, which Eleanor thought was rather meager, compared to her own Christmases past. Even as a grocer's daughter, the Father Christmas of her childhood had been able to provide much more. However, Willy knew nothing different, and Christmas appeared to have exceeded his expectations.

As the day before, Eleanor was banned from the kitchen, so that afternoon, with Spanky once again underfoot, she set the tables and greeted any airmen who happened to wander in and out the manor. For any of her lodgers passing through, Eleanor gave little parcels of dried apples gathered at the top with bits of colorful ribbon.

On previous Christmases, she had received little gifts from some of the airmen, and this year was no different. An officer presented her with a bottle of wine, and a trainee gave her some hothouse roses. She was delighted.

Hearing footsteps behind her, Eleanor reached for another bag of apples and turned to present it. She squealed with delight when she saw that this uniformed officer was none other than Thomas Gardner, himself. Hearing the excitement, everyone from the kitchen dashed through the serving area and into the hall to see what the commotion was all about.

Gilda ran into his arms and surprised herself by crying like a baby. Thomas was wished a belated happy birthday by all, and Spanky barked excitedly. Thomas kissed his mother affectionately and gave hugs and handshakes all around, but he refused their offers of tea. He said that he was taking his teary-eyed wife home for awhile. Dinner was moved back to eight o'clock, and Thomas and Gilda walked home to Willows Edge.

After unlocking the cottage door, Thomas swooped Gilda up into his arms and carried her across the threshold.

"What's this all about?" she asked tearfully.

"It's symbolic, I think," said Thomas sheepishly. "I'll tell you later."

They laughed together and looking towards the bedroom door, Gilda said, "There is another threshold I'd like to be carried through, if you think you could be troubled."

Laughing heartily, Thomas carried his bride to their bed. They had missed each other in every possible way.

ॐॐॐॐ

Waking two hours later, Thomas and Gilda feared that they would be late for dinner if they didn't get cracking. As she was climbing out of bed, Gilda suddenly knew it was time to give Thomas his Christmas present. She said, "Before we go, I want to give you your present."

*At Willows Edge*

"Now?" asked Thomas, pulling on his trousers.

"Now," she answered. She took his hand and placed it on her belly, where the baby had just kicked. As if on cue, the baby kicked again, and Thomas wept for joy.

Holding Gilda in his arms, he said, "Our two missions were without incident, but the whole time I was up there, I promised God I'd be the best father and husband ever, if he would just get me home one more time."

"Oh Thomas, surely you must know that you could never, ever be anything else."

"I didn't always know it. I feared that I might have some of my father in me. In fact, my mother accused me of getting engaged to someone like Candace Gates, so I wouldn't have any happiness to destroy. There was some truth in that. Anyway, I know now, Gilda. I'll not fail you."

"I never thought you would," she said smugly. Then, looking at the clock, she exclaimed, "We're going to be late!"

A few minutes later, they locked their cottage door. Seeing the flicker of their torches, Richard hailed them from a few yards away. After shaking Thomas's hand vigorously, Richard asked if things were going well on the continent.

Thomas said, "Nothing is going well, but things are much better for the Allies than they were a few days ago. The Germans had no real chance at succeeding and ultimately, they won't, but they've caused plenty of death and destruction, especially among the Americans. Supplies are getting into Bastogne now, so that crisis is nearly over. My group was on a bombing mission, my specialty, I suppose."

"Important job, Thomas," said Richard encouragingly.

"Oh, I know. The railway yards were our targets, and fortunately, the attack was amazingly accurate. It helps to be able to see what you're doing. The bombs fell into the railway yards and into the nearby Rhine River, where we sank two barges. The Germans' ultimate goal was to take Antwerp and cut off supplies for the Allies, but, from what I've heard, they've made no forward motion since the second day of their attack. They punched a sizeable bulge into the Allied lines, but they've gotten no further, and now they're being cut off. The fighting is fierce, I'm afraid."

They walked on in the darkness in silence, thinking of the casualties caused by yet another of Hitler's mad ideas.

Richard finally said, "I heard on the wireless this

morning that the musician, Glenn Miller, is missing. He was flying over to Paris to prepare for a Christmas show. He never got there."

Thomas said, "I heard about it. The tragic thing is that if the bad weather didn't take them down, there is every reason to believe that friendly fire did."

It was Gilda, who replied, saying, "It just goes on and on and on."

## Chapter Eighteen

Soon after their lovely, late dinner, any gifts that hadn't been yet exchanged were presented. Once that excitement was over, the tired children were taken home and put to bed. Priscilla, also, retired, and even Edith took Willy up to her bedroom and did not return again that evening.

After Eleanor saw the Coopers and Morrises out, she retired to her room early, too. She was exhausted, in spite of being banned from the kitchen all day. She laughed at herself when she realized that not all of her guests had yet left. Mr. Fitzgerald was still sitting by the fire in the drawing room with David, but she knew that David would eventually see him out.

Upon crawling into bed, she picked up her reading glasses, journal, and pen, and wrote, *The children made Christmas so enjoyable. Their excited, cherubic faces just beamed with happiness. My little offerings from the storeroom were appreciated by all, it seemed. They say if you have to give a secondhand gift, give an old one. "Old has value," Mrs. Adair always says, and I think my gifts were well received.*

*I gave old books, old jewelry, old toys, and even*

*two old clocks, one of which I gave to Edith. I gave the other clock to Gilda and Thomas, who were delighted. I gave the Armstrongs a wireless. That was the one thing that I'd purchased, (which I did with Sam's help), but I'd wanted them to have one since their arrival. They graciously said that they were overwhelmed by the gesture.*

*To young William, I gave an old set of blocks that I'd found. I had Lucas clean them up for me, and Willy and I spent the afternoon building and destroying cottages, houses, and castles. That activity was only interrupted by his demands to be pulled around the great hall in his wagon. Lucas and Matty eagerly helped with that. I was proud of Willy when he shared his wagon with Emma, letting her get in behind him.*

*At dinner, David presented a toast to me. I was flattered to tears. It was excellent wine, given to me yesterday by Mr. Fitzgerald, with whom I've had little conversation. We did talk of his wine, of which he promised there was more where that had come from. He said that he and his wife had left a fine stash of the stuff with her brother when they had left the country. When I asked him if he was sure it was all still there, he said his brother-in-law had proudly shown him that not a drop had been pinched in his absence. When he remarked that his late wife's brother* was a vicar, I told him that his story had become more credible with that additional information, which made him laugh. That is the extent of our conversation. I'm not so very certain that he's as trustworthy as everyone else seems to think he is.

After dinner, Pricilla surprised us all by presenting gifts to everyone. We were shocked by her industry. She had made beautiful, blue velvet dresses for Emma and Matty, a handsome woolen waistcoat for Lucas, and a fine suit for Willy. She presented Gilda with two lovely maternity shirts, and she gave all the adults knitted winter scarves, including one for Mr. Fitzgerald. When I asked her where on earth she had gotten the colourful yarn to embellish the otherwise grey wool scarves, she said she'd unravelled some worn-out sweaters that Mrs. Adair had acquired for her. I should have known, shouldn't I?

We were thoroughly entertained when Gilda opened Priscilla's gift for the unborn baby. I didn't give them anything for the baby, because my mother always preached it was bad luck to do so. However, Priscilla had made a valiant effort. When Gilda pulled the lovely, white, knitted baby shawl from the box, we could see knitting needles poking out from one end, and then a ball of yarn rolled across the floor. Surprised, we all looked at Priscilla, and *she said simply, "I ran out of time." We all laughed and laughed.*

*I just flipped back a few pages to where I wrote about how blissful Christmas would be with an intimate few. Things change quickly around here, and I must commend myself on my flexibility and resilience. It was a wonderful Christmas, though not perfect. Edith is still worrying about Larry's brother, and my heart aches for Jane and William. I long for the day when they will be reunited.*

*On Christmas Eve, Sam and Dotty made a last minute decision to have a small Christmas tree of their own, so we shared some of our lights and ornaments with them, much to Matty's dismay, I might add. Dotty told me that when Emma found her Christmas stocking at the end of her bed this morning, she laughed heartily at the silliness of getting treats in her socks. Then, when she found her new doll and pram under the tree, Emma squealed with delight. She hugged Sam and Dotty, saying that Father Christmas was quite the fellow.*

*When Emma opened her lovely dress from Priscilla, she ran to her and whispered something in her ear. I must ask Priscilla what the child said that made her laugh so. My goodness, I believe that Priscilla and Emma's exchange*

*Meredith Kennon*
*was most definitely a Christmas miracle. Tired; must sleep.*

Gilda and Thomas walked home alone, leaving Richard with David by the fire in the drawing room. The men had found, after their first conversation at Richard's cottage, that they had common interests and enjoyed each other's company. But tonight, David wanted specifically to know what Richard had been doing at Willows Edge that morning. He had seen him while out walking Spanky.

Not knowing how to introduce the subject, he asked, "What do you make of the Glenn Miller disappearance?"

Staring at the leaping flames in the fireplace, Richard said, "Thomas said that he may likely have been shot down by friendly fire."

"There is far more of that in a war than anyone would like to admit."

"David, I've been trying to figure out who has been stalking Thomas and Gilda." Richard reached into his pocket and brought out the piece of paper on which he had outlined the facts, as he knew them, the night before.

He showed David what he'd written on the paper and said, "I've been trying to piece things together. Thomas has confided many things to me, since my arrival, but there has to be a piece to this puzzle that I don't have. I thought of something you had said before and had an idea last night, so this morning I went to Willows Edge to get the newspaper cutting that Thomas had shown me one day."

Richard carefully removed the newspaper cutting from his lapel pocket and handed it to David.

David sighed with relief that his temporary distrust of Richard had been unfounded.

Richard said, "We had been talking about the unexplained blasts in and around London, and Thomas pulled this from a drawer."

David said, "I gave that cutting to him on the day I saw it in the paper. That was the engagement party of the woman who Thomas had been previously engaged to."

"The very one? And she was already engaged to someone else?"

"Yes, she didn't waste any time. She was really quite a horrible creature, and my wife had been most distraught that Thomas was going to go through with his marriage to her. You can imagine Priscilla's delight when Thomas broke it off."

"Was it a friendly breakup?" asked Richard.

"Friendly wasn't part of Candace's vocabulary, but as you can see she was engaged again very quickly. She couldn't have been too upset," said David. "She died, of course, in the blast, as the article says." He handed the article back to Richard, who put both papers away in his lapel pocket.

Richard had some thinking to do, so he said simply, "Well, I must leave you now. Thank you for a lovely time."

David showed Richard out, banked the fires, and went upstairs to join his wife, who had already retired. When David crawled into bed beside Priscilla, she asked, "Is everyone gone now?"

Glad she was still awake, David answered, "Yes, my dear." Then he turned to her and asked, "So how did you keep all those projects a secret?"

Priscilla laughed and said, "As you must remember, I started knitting the dreary, gray scarves in the car, in October, when it was still nice enough for me to ride with you. The apples drying in the workroom were pungent, which made it difficult to work in there for very long. So, I found some gray yarn in the sewing supplies I'd brought from home, and I started to knit. The mindless, repetitiveness of it kept me from going completely crazy. I felt so jittery, you know. It helped if my hands were busy, and yet, I had no energy to take long walks or do anything really constructive."

*At Willows Edge*

"I know, Pris. You've had a terrible time."

"I made myself more miserable than I would have had to have been, I think. I practically wallowed in my misery. I embraced it, for heaven's sake."

"It all caught up with you, darling, and finally you had to deal with all that happened. So, tell me how you accomplished all of this with no one knowing."

"Well, one day, when you and I were in Nuneaton, while you were in the chemist's, I went into a nearby shop to try to find some pretty yarn. They had plenty of the gray, but nothing colorful. As I was about to climb into the car, Mrs. Adair, who I'd never met, walked up to me and introduced herself. I don't know how she knew me. Perhaps it was because I'm the doctor's wife, and she knew the car."

"I'm not so sure I'm particularly known there, but we both have connections with Greystone Manor," said David helpfully.

Nodding, Priscilla continued, "She started talking to me, and I thought she'd never quit. Proceeding to get into the car, I picked up my knitting off the car seat, hoping she'd take a hint and leave me alone. She admired my work and said that if I'd like some yarn, she had some colorful sweaters. She said the garments were completely worn out in places, but that the rest could be resurrected and remade. She also said she had some velvet, if I'd like it. Well, I agreed, thinking that might be the best way to get rid of her. I made her promise to put a note in the parcel when she sent it, so I would know her address and asking price. I thought she'd forget all about it, but one day she brought the parcel out here herself. She gave it to Sam, who was in the yard and left without bothering me. He brought the parcel up to me, and I've been unraveling ever since."

"So, now you are friends with Mrs. Adair," said David laughing.

"In my heart, I am, because I think she knew I was having a hard time and was sensitive to it. I appreciate her for that. I'm not sure I'd recognize her, if I did see her again," said Priscilla shamefully. "I wasn't particularly friendly and made little eye contact with her. Oh David, I've been so rude."

"Now, now, no one thinks that, but please tell me what happened to change your perspective, darling."

"Emma made her way up here one day. She had seen me looking out of the window. Since I had made no effort to meet her, so unlike the others, she determined that the person in the window might be the reclusive Father Christmas she'd been hearing so much about. She sneaked up here and looked around while I was in the workroom. When I came in here for something, we scared each other something awful."

"You never told me."

"I know; I'm sorry, David. I asked her what she was doing up here, and she said she'd been looking for Father Christmas, because she understood that he was watching to see if she was being good. Aware that I'd been avoiding her and using her childish logic, she made the assumption that I must be Mother Christmas, and by the time she left, I was in stitches. She had completely won me over."

"That's amazing," said David shaking his head.

"Well, Eleanor had told me to deal with my feelings, because they existed and were real, and I couldn't just dismiss them, as some might think possible. And, she told me that when the time came to get better, I would know it. She challenged me to take the time I needed to get well, but that when an opportunity showed me a way out, I should take it. She said I should leap."

"What an amazing woman," said David. "Did she know when you made your leap?"

"No, I decided to complete my journey on my own, and I realized that the solitude I was afforded would give me time to make all those gifts. I dug in and worked like there was no tomorrow. When Gilda told me about Thomas's assignment a few days ago, she discovered the change in me but promised to keep mum about it in order for me to finish my gifts in peace."

Priscilla laughed again, the sound of which brought tears to David's eyes. He asked, "How did you know the sizes of the children?"

"I'd seen them all, but Willy, and I knew his age. I can tell a person's clothing size from across the street, dear. Surely, you knew that was one of my talents."

"I don't think I'm aware of half of them."

David gathered Priscilla in his arms and kissed her, thinking, "She's back. My adorable Priscilla is back."

Kissing him back and looking deep into his eyes, Priscilla said seductively, "Happy Christmas, David."

David chuckled and said, "Happy Christmas, indeed."

## Chapter Nineteen

Gilda and Thomas woke up early on Boxing Day, because, as there was no holiday for them, they had to get to work. Back into their normal routine, David and Spanky walked to meet them, wished Thomas a good day, and parted company with Gilda at the kitchen door. She laughed when David said, "I promised Spanky a longer walk this morning, and he's holding me to it."

Coming through the heavy door, Gilda was surprised to see no one in the kitchen, except two small children, having breakfast together at the table. Glad that she was wearing her mittens to conceal her hand, she said, "Good morning, children, where is Dotty?"

Looking up from her toast, Emma said, "She took Papa some breakfast."

Since Willy's arrival, Gilda had not wanted to overwhelm him, so she had given him the same comfortable distance from her as she had always given Emma. By doing so, she believed that, thus far, she had been able to conceal her deformed hand from them. Even throughout the Christmas festivities, she had made every effort to conceal her left hand and was glad for it.

Standing now in the kitchen, she hesitated to take

off her winter apparel, fearing the children might notice, at last, and be frightened by it. Standing there, paralyzed in her indecision, she saw Eleanor appear in the doorway.

Alarmed by Gilda's worried countenance, Eleanor asked, "What's happened to you, Gilda?"

Not looking up from her breakfast, Emma said knowingly, "She's always been that way, Mrs. Wood. That's how she got *borned.* You're not *s'posed* to look at her hand, Willy. Mama says it's not *plite* to stare."

Surprised by Emma's outspokenness, Eleanor and Gilda were speechless, but Willy was not. Offended by Emma's comment, he said, "*Ya dint* have to tell me, Emma. Auntie *Edie* and G*wandmothow* already *asplained* it to me."

Enlightened by the children's frankness and the look of surprise on Eleanor's face, Gilda laughed heartily. She removed her mittens and, with Eleanor's help, proceeded with the morning work, which was light, because they had not had to do the early breakfast.

Edith came into to the kitchen to check on the children, who were once again engrossed in their breakfast. She had become Emma's caregiver for the day, so that Sam could attend to other things. In the short time she'd spent with Willy, she'd learned that providing a playmate for a child presented advantages to all concerned. She was looking forward to a day in which she could think and worry uninterrupted.

Gilda helped Eleanor put away some of the Christmas clutter, but it was decided to postpone taking down the tree, since Larry had yet to see it and the children still seemed so enthralled with it.

The afternoon breakfast for the airmen was served like clockwork, requiring nothing more than going through the motions. As they worked, the women of the house relived the wonderful memories that had been made on Christmas Eve and Christmas Day. Most of their reminiscing was done in silence, but leaning on her broom that afternoon, Dotty asked, "Don't children make Christmas worth all the fuss?"

❦❦❦❦

That afternoon, as Gilda left for home, she looked around for David to walk her, but when she couldn't find him, she headed out on her own. She assumed he had taken Sam into town to conduct his business, and since it wasn't yet dark, she decided to make her way on her own.

Admittedly nervous, Gilda walked toward Gypsy Row, thinking about nothing, except the woman she now feared. The woman's presence had made her feel as if she were trespassing, somehow. Picking up her pace, she wondered who had owned the cottage before their landlords. "Maybe there's a connection there," she thought.

Deciding that she'd present her new theory to Thomas and Richard at dinner, Gilda approached the cottage. The sun was almost gone now, and the dusk surrounded Gilda ominously. Coming closer, she froze. She could see someone walking in the willow trees, and it wasn't Richard. It was the woman again.

Gilda felt the terror she'd felt the last time she'd seen her and broke into a run toward the door, trying, simultaneously, to get her key from her pocket. When she was within two strides of the door, she tripped on a crack in the pavement and fell hard, crying out.

Gilda had protected the baby by falling on her extended right arm, and the pain was intense. She looked in the direction of Richard's cottage, hoping and praying he had seen her fall. She cried, "My baby, my baby."

Someone approached, but it was not Richard. Gilda screamed and fainted.

Richard had indeed seen Gilda's approach from the field, and simultaneously saw the head of the furtive woman in the willows beyond the hedge. He scrambled for his jacket and hurriedly ran out the door, leaving it open in his haste. Running, he heard the scream, and as he approached Willows Edge, he saw the woman kneeling by Gilda's prone body. Coming yet closer, he could hear the woman crying, "I didn't mean to hurt you. I didn't know you were pregnant. Oh God, what have I done?"

The woman turned her head toward Richard, when she heard his approach and cried, "Help me, please, help me. I didn't know she was expecting a baby. I didn't want to hurt anybody."

"Come, Mrs. Gates," said Richard, pulling her to her feet. "Do you think you can help me get her inside?"

She nodded and accepted the key that Richard had taken from the hand of Gilda's broken arm. The woman quickly opened the cottage door.

Carefully noting the unusual position of her arm and protecting it the best he could, Richard carried Gilda into the cottage and back to the bedroom. As he laid her on her bed, she again whimpered, "My baby, my baby."

Richard said, "All is well, now, Gilda. No one wants to hurt you. I'll explain later. I'll go call David, immediately. I think your arm is broken, but you are safe. It's all over. Do you understand?"

Gilda nodded weakly. Looking for signs of shock,

Richard covered Gilda by pulling the counterpane around her and went out to the sitting room. He found Mrs. Gates sitting on the settee, sobbing quietly into her hands.

He said, "Mrs. Gates, I have to run to my cottage and call the doctor. You must sit right there and not move."

The woman nodded, and Richard bolted from the cottage at a full run. Within minutes, he was back, where he found the women, just as he had left them.

Coming in his car, David arrived moments later and burst through the cottage door, just as Thomas approached the cottage, coming home from the airfield.

David went into the bedroom and sent Richard to the sitting room to deal with the woman and Thomas's arrival. He said, "Tell Thomas to wait there until I come for him."

The doctor found Gilda conscious and less traumatized that he'd thought he might. He asked her if she'd fallen on the baby. Gilda answered, "No, I fell on my arm."

He said, "Now, you may have a broken right arm, Gilda, but I think the baby will be fine. You didn't take a tumble down the stairs or anything dreadful, so just rest easy."

Gently examining the small, hard mound on Gilda's

belly, the doctor could detect no trauma. He listened to the steady beat of the baby's heart. He murmured his assurances to Gilda and turned his attention next to her arm. It was indeed broken, so he told her that he would be right back.

He stepped out of the bedroom, where Thomas was leaning against the opposite wall. David looked into the sitting room and saw no one.

Thomas's distraught eyes met the doctor's. David said, "The baby is fine and so is Gilda. I'm going to set her arm, because she's got a little break, nothing awful. Do you understand me?"

Thomas nodded and breathed a deep sigh of relief. Looking toward the sitting room, he said, "Richard took her to his place. You may have to go over there next. She's in a bad way, I'm afraid."

"Go out and get my other bag in the backseat, and I'll get Gilda fixed up in no time."

As Thomas moved to go, David put his hand on his shoulder and said, "It's all over, son. We'll have Richard explain it all to us when we're done here."

Thomas took long strides to the front door, and turning, said, "I can explain it all myself."

Thomas then fetched some water, while David

prepared to put a cast on Gilda's right forearm. He watched her closely for signs of distress but was feeling more and more confident that Gilda and her child would be fine.

Gilda looked at David and asked, "Where is Richard?"

David answered, "Richard took your repentant stalker to his home. Thomas is fetching some water and says he can explain everything, now that he's seen the face of the woman. I rather expected him to attack her and was surprised when he didn't. I think we'll soon know why."

Thomas entered the room, carrying a basin of water. He hurriedly handed it off to the doctor and went to Gilda's side. He stroked her hair, saying over and over, "I should have known, darling. I'm so sorry this happened. Please tell me you are all right."

"I am, Thomas. I'm fine."

The doctor said, "Now, Thomas, as soon as I set her arm, I want you to explain all of this to us. The anxiety is doing Gilda more harm than anything at this point. She broke her arm, protecting the baby. Unless she starts cramping in the next few hours, the baby has come through the ordeal unscathed."

To Gilda, Thomas asked, "Are you really all right, my darling?"

"I think so. More importantly, I think the baby is all right, too." She indicated the place where the baby had just kicked, and Thomas gently placed his hand there to wait for the next one.

The doctor moved his bags to the far side of the bed, so he could do his work, and Thomas carefully sat down beside his wife. He picked up her left hand and kissed it tenderly.

The doctor quickly set her arm, and tears ran down Thomas's cheeks when Gilda winced with pain. Once the pain subsided, he watched the color slowly come back into her face. She looked up at him weakly and smiled.

Looking at her deformed hand, she asked, "How will I do my work now?"

"You won't be working at all for awhile, darling," said Thomas.

The doctor added, "You'll have an eight-week holiday, my dear. In fact, I doubt that you'll return to work at all. It's time you quit."

"But how will I do anything at all for myself?"

Thomas stroked her hair back from her forehead and smiled knowingly, saying, "We'll get by."

Gilda smiled, too, as she remembered how helpless Thomas had been when he had first come to the manor in

January and the embarrassment she had felt, helping him do what he couldn't do for himself.

Then Gilda said, "Tell us everything, Thomas."

As the doctor wrapped the splinted arm in the wet gauze, Thomas said, "The woman is Mrs. Gates, Candace's mother. She escaped the explosion, if you remember, because she had gone to fetch her mother."

※※※※

There was no way for Gilda to take care of herself, so she and Thomas moved into the sewing room at Greystone Manor the following morning. There, Mrs. Wood had prepared an army cot for Thomas beside Gilda's small bed. Edith had offered either her room or the other bedroom, prepared for Jane's coming, but Thomas had kindly refused, saying, "This is temporary; we'll be fine."

He had been excused to come to work an hour later than normal, so he could get Gilda comfortably situated. David had visited Willows Edge early that morning, before Gilda was moved, to make sure there were no reasons for her not to be. Once he'd assure himself that she'd had no cramping or bleeding during the night, David allowed her to walk out of the cottage on her own power.

Priscilla took on the responsibility of being Gilda's

nurse and companion until the afternoon, when Gilda's mother was expected to come.

Although Eleanor was tempted to hover in the sickroom, she determined to set a good example by staying downstairs. Dotty, too, was eager to do things for Gilda, but the airmen's breakfasts had to be served, and with Gilda out of it, there was more to do than ever. Priscilla took care of Gilda's needs and helped out in the kitchen, whenever she could.

David had ordered quiet for Gilda. She'd had a shock, and he didn't want her answering questions all day for those who might decide to descend upon her. He asked Eleanor if they could use the drawing room that evening to explain everything to all the interested parties. She agreed to that and also to spread the word that Gilda was not to be questioned. She was to tell everyone to meet in the drawing room for tea that evening at eight o'clock, where all would be explained.

When the hour arrived, Gilda came downstairs and was situated on the sofa with her right arm propped up. She was still pale from her ordeal, but her mother had helped her bathe and Priscilla had done her hair, so she felt almost presentable.

Others there included her parents, Simon and

Agnes, Sam and Dotty, David and Priscilla, Eleanor, Edith, Richard, and, of course, Thomas. A sign was fastened to the door, explaining to the airmen that the drawing room was off limits for the evening.

Emma and Willy were put to bed at their usual early hour, so Lucas stayed above the carriage house with Emma, and Matty stayed upstairs, keeping watch over Willy.

Dotty brought in a large tray of tea and biscuits, and everyone talked to Gilda briefly, before finding a place to sit. Eleanor helped Dotty pass the tea around, and a relaxed conversation ensued until David thought it time to begin.

He said, "We don't want to keep anyone late this evening, but I knew you all wanted to know all the facts about Gilda's fright last night. Since everyone had to perform their regular responsibilities today, I thought it best that Gilda didn't have to rehearse the events over and over, as each of you had time to listen. As I remind all my patients, talking is tiring."

Everyone nodded, and he continued, "First of all, Gilda is fine, and the baby is fine. Gilda protected her little one by falling on her arm. As for it, she broke her radius, but it wasn't a messy break and will heal perfectly. Gilda, though, will hate the inconvenience of her helplessness for the next few weeks, but she has many volunteers to take care of her, I understand, whenever Thomas is away."

Thomas patted Gilda's left hand, and everyone looked at her lovingly. She was embarrassed by all the attention but also humbled by their concern for her.

"I'm going to let Richard explain everything that happened, since it was he who was the first to figure it out, and also, the first on the scene."

Richard leaned forward in his chair, saying, "I had the mystery solved and was planning to prove my theory that evening by placing a simple telephone call. However, Gilda decided to come home alone, without so much as a telephone call to me, so I was unable to prevent anything."

With a sheepish look, Gilda said weakly, "I had things to do at home. When I couldn't find David, I didn't think to bother anyone else."

"Ah, you didn't even think of me," said Richard feigning rejection.

"Sorry," said Gilda with a smile.

Richard continued, "After both Gilda and Thomas saw the woman last week, it became very clear to all of us that they had a stalker. I cancelled my Christmas plans in hopes of solving the mystery and thought that, since Gilda was staying at the manor, someone should keep an eye on their cottage. I called around to the various inns, as Thomas had done earlier, but learned little more than he did. However, I did learn from the old desk manager at Codgett's Inn that they had a female guest, who stayed there from time to time. He clammed up, though, when I pressed for a more information. I had also talked to the Englewood constable, but no one else had reported seeing anyone suspicious."

Retrieving a piece of paper from his pocket, he said, "On Christmas Eve, I went home and decided to be more methodical in my methods. I thought it made more sense to figure out who might have some reason to bother Thomas and Gilda than to stake out the inn or watch from the hedgerows for a woman I had never seen."

When David laughed, Richard explained, "As David knows, I did try the hedgerow idea, and I woke up stiff, damp, and embarrassed."

Thomas laughed, saying, "You didn't!"

Nodding, Richard said, "I'm afraid I did."

As Richard glanced at his list and put it back in his lapel pocket, the others chuckled quietly at the mental picture he'd given them.

Richard said, "Having become a good friend of Thomas's these past few weeks, I have become privy to some of your greatest trials, but until the day before

Christmas, when David told me about Thomas having been once engaged to a Gates girl, I had heard nothing of it. Weeks before, Thomas had shown me the article of the explosion that had killed the Gates family, but he didn't explain his connection to the family, so when David told me that Thomas had been engaged to a Gates girl, I decided to look at the news report again. On Christmas morning, I let myself into Willows Edge to find it.

"Upon studying the article, nothing really became any clearer, but then, on Christmas night, David further explained that Thomas had been previously engaged to none other than Candace Gates, herself. Then the lights began to go on. I read the article again, looking especially for mention of survivors. When I saw that Mrs. Gates had been absent during the blast to collect her mother for the engagement party, I believed, then, that the stalker was most likely her. I was planning to telephone Codgett's Inn and ask for Mrs. Gates that very evening, but before I could do that, Gilda did the unexpected and came home on her own."

Richard pushed his gray hair back from his brow and admitted, "Let me say, though, I was glad I knew who Gilda's stalker was, before I attacked her from behind and took her to the ground. When, from my window, I saw

Gilda approaching the cottage and Mrs. Gates standing menacingly in the willows, I grabbed my coat. As I approached on a run, I first heard Gilda cry out, and then I heard Mrs. Gates crying her apologies and proclaiming that she hadn't known that Gilda was pregnant."

There was a murmur of reaction from Richard's audience before he continued, "In a calm voice and calling Mrs. Gates by name, I approached her carefully, not entirely certain if she meant Gilda any further harm. She turned her distraught face to me, utterly shocked at what she had done. I helped her to her feet, and she opened the cottage with Gilda's key, so that I could carry her inside. I laid Gilda on the bed and told Mrs. Gates to stay sitting on the settee while I ran to call David. She was sitting there, still sobbing, when I got back, and I honestly knew then that she was no longer dangerous to Gilda or anyone else. I did, however, begin to fear that she might be a danger to herself."

"Good heavens!" said Dotty and Eleanor together. Gilda's mum sat quietly shaking her head, while Edith, Sam, and Simon remained motionless, utterly stunned by the story.

Priscilla had been privy to this information earlier, so she was less emotional than those hearing it for the first time. Quietly, to Richard, she urged, "Please, go on."

He complied, saying, "Once Thomas was home and David had done all he could for Gilda, he came to my cottage to have a look at Mrs. Gates. The shock of the ordeal may not have done her heart any good, but it brought her out of her stupor of grief. She told us she had wanted someone to hold accountable for what had happened to her family. She said she had even needed to blame someone, so she blamed Thomas and the girl who had taken him away from her daughter. She reasoned that if Thomas had married Candace, they likely would not have been at her home the night of the blast, and Candace would still be alive and well today. She admitted that she had become obsessed by Thomas's apparent happiness with the pretty woman who had taken Candace's place. When David and I took her back to the inn yesterday, we both knew she was going to be all right." Richard looked at David for his concurrence.

Nodding, David said, "It was agreed by Thomas and Gilda that no charges of any kind be brought against her."

Everyone in the room sat quietly, mulling the information that they now had in full.

David said teasingly, "I saw Richard enter Willows Edge Christmas morning, and, for a few hours thereafter, considered him a suspect."

That brought a laugh from Richard and prompted him to look intently at Eleanor, who blushed deeply, realizing he knew full well that she, too, had considered him a possible suspect.

That night she wrote, *So a Miss Marple, I'm not, but my intentions were good. When Mr. Fitzgerald looked at me accusingly tonight, I knew he had been fully aware of my distrust of him. I tried to make up for it by filling his teacup and walking him to the door myself when he left.*

*Ruth Davies was buried yesterday, but I haven't yet heard from Jane. I hope she can come soon. I also hope we see Larry Bradford before long. I don't think he's in a dangerous situation, but Edith looked washed out tonight. I must take over the care of Willy tomorrow. Perhaps, I've expected too much of Edith. She's been doing everything, since she got here. I hope she's not getting ill.*

ೊೀೊೀ

As soon as the first breakfast was cleared away the following morning, Edith came into the kitchen with the mop and said to Eleanor, "Mum, what are you doing next?"

Hanging the drying cloths on the wooden rack, Eleanor said, "I'm done for awhile, and so should you be.

You do look tired, Edith. I think I've worked you too hard."

When Eleanor turned to look at her daughter, she saw a pale face, streaked with tears. She exclaimed, "Come to my room. You need to rest."

Edith followed her mother into her little room off the hallway. Her mother told her to lie down, but she rejected that idea and patted the bed beside her, bidding her mum to join her there. Eleanor sat down obediently and waited for her daughter to confide in her.

"Larry called this morning, and he'll be here tonight," said Edith smiling weakly.

"Well, that's good news, isn't it? We'll find a bed for him, just as we've done before on the RAF side. That will pose no problem at all."

Edith looked even more distressed, so Eleanor asked, "Have you had a quarrel?"

"No, Mum, not at all, but I have to tell you something. Larry has been pressing me to tell you since October, but I never had the chance. I didn't want to tell you over the telephone."

Thinking of Marva's rushed spring wedding and naturally alarmed, Eleanor asked, "Edith, are you pregnant?"

"Could you ask me another question, first?"

"I don't know what you mean. You can't be pregnant, are you?"

"Mightn't you ask me first if I'm married?"

"My God, Edith, when did you do that?"

Edith burst into tears and began to sob. After a few moments, she managed to say, "We decided to get married in October, on a whim. We met in London one weekend, and we decided that we didn't want to wait any longer. We just wanted to be together. We were arranging for our lodgings, when Larry suddenly proposed we get married, so we did, just like that. We have been able to be together just once since then. I'm so sorry I didn't tell you."

Eleanor was surprised, but not as surprised as her daughter had supposed. She said, "Edith, I've always known you to be utterly independent. I wish I could have shared your wedding day with you. I truly do, but I'm happy for you." Trying desperately to lighten the moment and get a smile out of Edith, she said, "So, I suppose we shouldn't put Larry in the east wing, after all."

Shaking her head, Edith tried unsuccessfully to smile, and her uncharacteristic tears continued running down her wash-out face. Eleanor was at a loss for words, until she finally thought to ask, "So, are you pregnant?"

Edith's watery, dark eyes looked into her mother's

blue ones and said, "Yes, Mum, I think I am. I'm sick and tired and lonely."

Having said that, Edith broke down in sobs again, and all Eleanor could do was hold her daughter and chant, "There, there, everything is going to be all right. Everything is going to work out. It always does."

As she rocked her daughter gently back and forth, Eleanor thought, "Well, at least I got to put on weddings for Marva and Gilda. One can't be greedy. One can't have everything."

That night, Eleanor wrote, *I am going to be a grandmother again. I missed out on the wedding, but as I sat holding my lovely daughter today, I realized that she hadn't needed me like that since her kitty went missing about twenty years ago. I think I'm learning to accept and appreciate the blessings that life presents, instead of demanding the ones I think I'm entitled to.*

## Chapter Twenty

On the twenty-ninth of December, a delivery came to Willows Edge for Gilda Gardner. When there was no one there to accept the large boxes, they were left with Richard at the nearest cottage. He arranged for David to take them to the manor in his car, as they were far too cumbersome to carry across the field.

That night, Gilda joined the others at the table in the kitchen for an early dinner. With the addition of Edith, Willy, Gilda, and Thomas, the kitchen table had to be pulled into the middle of the big kitchen and extra chairs added to accommodate the group. With only her left hand, Gilda had been afraid that she would be unable to feed herself. But, by the third day, the pain was gone in her right arm, and she found she could use that hand a little, making all the difference. She was so happy to be doing for herself again that she didn't mind the teasing that resulted in her return to the table.

Little Willy seemed to be bothered by the teasing and said, "It's not kind to pick on *othows*." His comment brought a giggle from some at the table, which he didn't like either. His face began to make all the contortions indicating an imminent breakdown.

*At Willows Edge*

Willy had been so easy and happy since his arrival, but Eleanor knew that Willy needed his mum. She said, "Let's ring your mama tonight, Willy. How does that sound?"

Willy ignored his grandmother and leaned down over his plate, as if hiding his face was the equivalent to hiding his whole body. When Thomas saw tears dropping on Willy's plate, he asked, "Who will help me get the big boxes and open them up for Gilda?"

"Me!" cried Willy, making a quick recovery.

"We should eat our food, first, because Mrs. Armstrong cooked it for us, and it would be unkind for us not to eat it."

Looking at Mrs. Armstrong, who he now knew by name, Willy nodded his head and dug into his meal.

Thomas winked at Eleanor, whose relief was expressed by a large sigh.

Before the others got up and the table was cleared, Thomas and Willy carried and slid the boxes into the kitchen beside Gilda. Thomas opened the box marked No. 1, and he allowed Willy to present to Gilda the letter that lay on top.

"Read it, darling," said Thomas.

"*Wead* it, *dawing*," parroted Willy.

With a little help from her husband, Gilda opened the letter and then read it aloud.

*Dear Mrs. Gardner,*

*I hope your arm is healing nicely. I have rung Mr. Fitzgerald's residence twice now to inquire after your health and that of your unborn. I've been very grateful to learn that you have not discovered any additional injuries.*

*My mother has never thrown anything away in her life, and when she heard what happened between us, she allowed me to look through the trunks in her attic. Before she was killed, my daughter made me aware of the gown business that you and Mrs. Priscilla Gardner were starting. Candace didn't approve of a made-over gown, but then she never saw the value in something that had been previously owned. She got that kind of thinking from her father, because I was raised by a woman who thinks it immoral to buy something new when it can somehow be avoided, and she still believes wholeheartedly that as far as quality goes, older is better every time.*

*I wanted to do something for you that might express my deep regret for my actions of the past three months, and I hope the contents of these boxes accomplish that. I send my best wishes to you and yours. Thank you for treating me*

*as you did. I'll be forever grateful.*
*Sincerely,*
*Mrs. Martha Gates*

As gown after glorious gown was pulled from the boxes, squeals of delight came from the Willy, the women, and sometimes, even the men. The contents were a dressmaker's dream come true. There were gowns with exquisite beadwork and materials of great value. They had been stored so carefully that it was hard to tell how old the gowns really were, but they were of the finest quality, and there were many of them. At the bottom of the second box was a bag containing ribbons, beads, and yards and yards of beautiful lace. When Willy held up the lace, everyone applauded him. So delighted to be trusted with such treasures, he danced in a circle to more applause.

It was during all this ruckus, with everyone talking at the same time, that they realized someone was standing in the hall beyond the kitchen doorway. They looked up, and before they could welcome him, their visitor declared, "Damn, it's freezing out there!"

Edith screamed, "Larry!"

The excitement peaked when Eleanor poured out wine for everyone, except Willy, of course, and made a toast, saying cheerfully, "Let's drink a toast to the new Mr. and Mrs. Larry Bradford, married in October without so much as a 'by your leave' from the bride's mother."

A cheer went up and Eleanor asked Thomas to run to the carriage house to see if the Coopers would like to join in the celebration.

That night, Eleanor wrote in her journal, *Larry surprised us by showing up tonight during dinner. Edith was thrilled to see him and glowed with happiness. We asked him to tell us what news he had from the front, and he said the fighting was fierce. Respectfully, we asked about the news of his brother, and he said that Craig was considered missing in action. He had been part of the American 285$^{th}$ Field Artillery Observation Battalion that was captured on the first day of the German offensive. He said there were terrible rumors of a massacre, which he was hoping would prove false.*

*Edith and Larry retired to their room early, and Willy moved into my bed with me. I love having his warm little body close to mine. When I asked him if he needed nappies at night, he was so offended, I thought he might not sleep with me, after all. What a strong-willed little character he is. For that matter, Emma has a strong personality, too. Perhaps God arms each generation with the temperament they need to survive their time on earth.*

*Jane rang tonight and will join us in two days, on the thirty-first. I could hear exhaustion in her voice and knew she was disappointed that Willy was already in bed and sound asleep. I told her he was playing so hard each day that he could barely stay awake after our early dinners. He and Emma do enjoy each other's company, and I've banished all rules I ever had about using the great hall as a playground. The wagon is putting on lots of miles in there.*

*Thomas insisted on sleeping on a foldaway bed in the sewing room, so Jane's room still awaits her. We'll have to move Willy's cot from Edith's room. I'm certainly glad I've been allowed by the quartermaster to send all the bed sheets out to be laundered. I have my limits.*

Gilda, with her pencil held oddly in her right hand because of the cumbersome cast, slowly wrote a few words in her diary that night.

*December 29, 1944*
*Dear Diary,*

*As I write, I am watching Thomas slide his uncomfortable army cot next to my own very comfortable bed in the sewing room at the manor. I have broken my arm, due to a fall. It still hurts a little, but I am enjoying the holiday I'm having, if not all the attention. Thomas and I are staying here until I can do things by myself. Boxes of gowns arrived today from Mrs. Gates, as a gesture of apology. I will relate that story, in full, at a later date.*

*Larry came tonight, much to Edith's delight. We just learned that they got married in October and never told anyone. I thought Mrs. Wood handled the situation beautifully. I want to grow into such a woman, who accepts disappointment and triumph with equal graciousness. Writing makes my arm ache; must stop.*

Early the next day, after helping with the first breakfast, Edith and Larry walked Willy and Spanky to the carriage house to play with Emma. It was Dotty's half-day off, and the Coopers had not joined in the celebration the night before, because Emma was already in bed. They had sent the message that they would look forward to congratulating Edith and Larry the following morning, if they would bring Willy and Spanky to the carriage house to play with Emma.

After leaving an excited Willy with the Coopers, Edith and Larry walked directly back to the manor, where Eleanor was alone in the kitchen. As Edith unwound her new gray scarf from around her neck and slid her coat from her shoulders, she said, "The skies looked especially foreboding today. I think the wireless may have called this one right. We are in for a storm."

Larry quietly hung up their coats on a kitchen hook and moved to the window to observe the sky. "We are in for it, I'm afraid. I feel for those poor soldiers on the continent. With the snow and freezing rain they've had, a person can't help asking whose side God is on."

"I don't think the Germans are too fond of the weather, either, right now," said Edith, joining him at the west window.

"Probably not, but that fog was certainly in their favor a week or so ago."

Returning to her mother, Edith asked, "Is there anything else we should be doing for you here?"

"We are done for a few hours. Thank you for filling in this morning. I hated to deny Dotty her morning off again. I've done that enough times. I'll be sorry to see you two go for more reasons than one."

Larry joined them saying, "Now that it is no longer a secret that we are married, Edith needs to quit working at the farm. I'm finding out what paperwork needs to be accomplished, but I don't think she'll be going back. She isn't feeling well enough to do a man's work in this miserable weather. I'm arranging to have her stay here with you."

"Oh, I'm so pleased, Edith," exclaimed her mother.

"Well, I could help you out here for awhile. If Larry found us a flat in London, I could go be with him there, but the prospects aren't good. He'll probably have to stay in his barracks for awhile yet. With Gilda out of it, you are going to need me," said Edith.

"I do, already. I'll see if I can make it official and get you a paycheck."

Larry said, "I'd rather you didn't. If she's not on the clock, I think she'll take better care of herself."

"I agree. You noticed I didn't announce the baby last night. I thought we should do the announcements one at a time," said Eleanor smiling broadly.

"We'll announce it to the others on New Year's Day," said Larry grinning.

"Larry doesn't want people to think we got married because of the baby. The baby is coming because we got married, not the other way around," said Edith, emphasizing the 'because.'

Eleanor said, "If Jane is here, you might not want to state your position quite like that, if you know what I mean."

Edith had previously told Larry about Willy's mother and her situation, and he nodded his understanding. He said, "Maybe, it doesn't matter what people think."

Smiling at Edith and her mother affectionately, Larry left the room to use the telephone in the library. He was going to get a start on his wife's release from the Woman's Land Army. She would need Dr. Armstrong's confirmation of her pregnancy in order to be released, and before he left in three days, Larry also wanted to make sure they had taken care of any additional red tape and to get Edith the proper "green" ration cards for pregnant women.

Bracing herself for the dreaded answer, Eleanor forced herself to ask Edith, "Will you and Larry go to America as soon as the war is over?"

"That depends on a couple of things," said Edith.

"Such as?" queried her mother, hopefully.

"If we can find something to do to sustain ourselves, Larry has agreed to live here in England until William comes home. Once he's home, I'll feel like I can pursue a new life in America. Until then, I'd never settle in."

"I knew that you and William were close, and I always wondered how you kept that bond with so many years and miles between you."

"He was always so good to me when I was small. His kindness still wraps me in a blanket when I need it. I know he's alive, Mum, because I cannot believe he could have died without me feeling it."

"Oh Edith," said Eleanor in tears, "what a beautiful person you are!"

❧❧❧❧

Since the incident at Willows Edge, Priscilla had been hard at work finding materials to make curtains for Gilda's sitting room. She had brought with her two coordinating pieces of lightweight fabric that would work as far as the size needed, but they would do little for privacy. Hearing this, Eleanor had given her some worn bed sheets for lining the curtains, giving them more weight and opacity.

Priscilla knew the approximate width of the window, which was close enough. She would generously double her estimate and the panels would hang in lovely folds, but she needed an exact measurement for the length. That afternoon, after they'd served and cleaned up after the two o'clock breakfast, she commented on that to Eleanor. She remarked that she may ask David to go, or perhaps even Larry.

Eleanor said, "I haven't been off the estate and perhaps not even outside the manor since Dotty and I attended midnight church service on Christmas Eve. I would like to run get the measurements for you. I need the fresh air, even if it is a little cold."

"It's bitterly cold, Eleanor," cried Priscilla. "What will Dotty say?"

"I'll bundle up with layers of warmth, wear trousers, and I'll even wrap my new scarf around my head," said Eleanor, now determined to get some solitude in the crisp winter air. "I'll see if Mr. Fitzgerald can meet me there. I could trouble Gilda for the key, but I know he has one. I'll call him now."

"Good, I don't want Gilda to know anything about my project."

Bundled against the brisk wind and sneaking out of the manor without Dotty's knowledge, Eleanor set out north and east to cross the main road into Englewood. Eleanor rarely even saw that thoroughfare, unless she was going south to Nuneaton, because, for going into Englewood, she always took the lane past the Morris's cottage, Gilda's childhood home.

Eleanor crossed the field, just as Gilda had done

every day since the harvest. Once Eleanor was out in the open, she realized that the wind was colder than she'd originally thought. She began to regret her determination to go and even thought about turning back, but she knew Mr. Fitzgerald would be waiting for her at Willows Edge.

Pressing on, Eleanor realized that Pricilla had been dead on. It was bitterly, bitingly cold. She actually looked down at her coat to make sure she'd fastened all the buttons, because it felt like the wind was going right through her. Head down, she pressed on until she saw the welcoming green door of Willows Edge. Standing in front of it, watching for her, was Mr. Fitzgerald, who looked as cold as she felt.

"Why didn't you go in, my good man?" exclaimed Eleanor as she approached him.

Opening the door for her, he said, "Oh, I don't know. It didn't feel very gentlemanly to go in before you did. Besides, it's not much warmer in there than it is out here. All they have for heating in the place right now is a single bar heater near the water pipes. I made sure it was on myself, when I saw how cold it was. They don't need the nightmare of frozen pipes."

"They certainly don't," agreed Eleanor. "You are a very good neighbor."

"Why, thank you," teased Richard. "I believe I've moved up in your estimation."

Embarrassed, Eleanor could think of nothing so say, and as she was freezing, she got the window measurement quickly, so she could go home again.

Just as they were leaving the cottage, a frozen rain began to pelt their heads like arrows. Richard pointed to his cottage, and they ran there as fast as Eleanor could manage it.

Once inside the heavy wooden door, Eleanor felt the warmth of the fire draw her to it like a moth. Richard helped her off with her wet coat and pulled his favorite leather chair up close to the fire, so she could get the most benefit from it. Eleanor's feet were cold and wet, so she took off her shoes and dark stockings and held her bare feet up to the golden flames. Trembling with cold, all she said was, "Heaven."

"Have you no wellies?" asked Richard, taking his own off and putting on his shoes.

"It was dry when I left," said Eleanor, trying to slide her chair closer to the fire.

Richard pushed her a few inches closer to the warmth, and then, ducking his head to avoid the low wooden beams, went into the tiny kitchen to start the water for tea. When he came back into the sitting room, Eleanor was shaking uncontrollably. Richard quickly fetched a blanket and a drying towel. He wrapped the blanket around Eleanor's shoulders and tucked it tightly around her. He pulled the foot stool alongside Eleanor, and once seated, held the towel up close to the flames until it was warm. Then, wrapping it around Eleanor's cold wet feet, he began to rub.

Eleanor knew she should be mortified, but she was beyond cold, and the last thing she needed was another bout with pneumonia.

Looking at Richard's kind face with a look of remorse, she said, "Dotty's going to have my head on a platter for this."

Knowing Dotty only a little but aware of her dedication to Mrs. Wood, Richard said nothing and concentrated on getting the blood circulating in Eleanor's cold feet.

The kettle whistled, so Richard got up to bring the tea. When he returned, Eleanor was no longer shivering and the fronts of her trousers legs were nearly dry. She eyed the steaming tea with longing.

Placing the tray on the floor and returning to the foot stool, Richard poured out the tea and gave a steaming cup to Eleanor. She clasped her cold hands around the hot cup and said, "I'm not going to be able to walk home."

"Precisely," agreed Richard, now handing her a biscuit.

"I'll have to call Dotty, right away. She'll be in a state, probably Priscilla, Edith, and Larry, too, if you want the whole truth, but it's Dotty, who's not going to let me hear the end of it."

Richard reached behind him and pulled the telephone set towards him, setting it on the floor at his feet. He asked the operator for the extension he now had memorized and talked to Dotty himself.

He said, "I didn't want you to worry about Mrs. Wood. The freezing rain didn't begin until we were safely inside my cottage. She decided that it would be wise not to walk home in the cold, although she did say the trek over was invigorating. Do you think you could ask Dr. Armstrong to come for her when he arrives?"

Richard listened to Dotty for a moment and then said, "Yes, she knew you would feel that way, so she was wise and is now sitting in front of my fire with a cup of hot tea."

He listened again before saying, "Too true. She probably hasn't gone calling in the afternoon in years. I'm going to show her my stamp collection. Everything all right there?" He nodded Dotty's response to Eleanor and then hung up.

He said, "Dotty thinks perhaps you have gotten smarter after some of your close calls."

"I'm glad I'm so wise," said Eleanor, "or a man I hardly know would have to wrap me in blankets and rub my cold feet with a heated towel. How absurd would that be?"

Richard chuckled at her lively sense of humor and told her a little about the cottage. He added, "Thomas tells me that all the cottages on Gypsy Row have been named, not for their grandeur, of course."

Looking at the low ceiling and the blackened beams, Eleanor said, "I imagine your wife was smitten by it. What's it called?"

"We were never told, and there is no sign or anything. It is just Number 3, Gypsy Row to me and the post. How would a person find out something like that, if one was curious, that is?" asked Richard, his hazel eyes twinkling.

"One would hand the telephone to me," said Eleanor smugly.

She telephoned the bakery, where the baker, Agnes

Morris's employer, knew everything there was to be known about Englewood. Eleanor greeted him and posed her question.

She nodded and asked, "Are you certain?" She nodded her head again, and thanked him very much. She put the telephone gently on its cradle and looked up at Richard with as serious of a face as she could muster. She said, "This cottage has always been known by the name of Two Hoots."

"Two Hoots?" asked Richard incredulously.

"Two Hoots," said Eleanor chuckling.

They laughed together companionably, and occasionally, one of them would say the name of the house, just so they could laugh about it again. Eleanor finally asked, "And how did Mrs. Fitzgerald like your cottage?"

"Oh, she picked it, you know. And I would say she was smitten by its charm, but she was even more smitten with the idea of visiting our grandchildren on the other side of the pond. She and our daughter were always very close, so going there meant everything to her. Once we realized we were stuck there, Myrna was torn between her desire to stay safe in upstate New York, and getting home in the hope of learning the whereabouts of Alec. I understand from Thomas and Gilda that you, too, have a son missing in the Pacific."

Eleanor nodded and said, "We have found William, as you have probably heard. He's in a Japanese prisoner-of-war camp. We've heard from him twice now, which, we have been assured, is very fortunate."

"From what I've heard, too, that is remarkable."

Eleanor said, "When I say we, I include Jane, the mother of my grandson, Willy. She and my son, William, were unable to marry quickly, when Singapore fell, and I can't believe I just told all of that to a relative stranger."

"Not to get Thomas and Gilda in any trouble, but I have known of the story since before Christmas. And you can hardly call me a stranger. You must remember that I have wrapped you in a blanket and rubbed your feet," teased Richard.

"Yes, I suppose you have," said Eleanor with a smile. More seriously, she continued, "William's first letter was unusual looking, and I thought perhaps it was V-mail that the airmen talk about, you know, the microfiche."

"Your airmen have been keeping company with Americans. That's what they call it. We call it Airograph, or something. What did it look like?"

"Well, the writing was so small, but that could have been because there was so little space in which to write. I need to look at it again, which I will, when Jane arrives."

Richard said, "Trying to track down anything at all about Alec, I have learned that some POW camps have their own mail form, allowing space for only a few words. One gentleman in London told me that one camp he'd heard of required all outgoing post to be typed, probably for preventing any codes that the handwriting could conceal. And then, Eleanor, the camp had no typewriter for the men's use."

"How awful! No way of knowing if it's true or not until the war is over, I suppose."

"How did you stand the not knowing, Eleanor?" asked Richard.

"I did it very poorly. It nearly killed me, literally."

Richard said, "Not knowing, I always say, is agonizing. It reminds me of the absolute opposite of a toy catalogue at Christmastime. My American granddaughters mulled over a catalogue for hours in the days leading up to Christmas. The possibilities were endless. Once Christmas was over, the possibilities were narrowed down to one or two things, and I think it was almost a letdown for the children, after carrying around the catalogue of infinite wishes for weeks."

Richard became quiet, so Eleanor said, "Likewise,

but in an opposite way, as you say, not knowing about our missing sons is the same in that any myriad of horrific possibilities may have happened to them. Once we know, it is narrowed down to one fate, but until then, we imagine them in every warlike scenario we can morbidly think of."

"You really do understand, Mrs. Wood," said Richard warmly.

"Please call me Eleanor. I have enough people calling me Mrs. Wood. It suddenly makes me feel very alone, for some reason."

Richard nodded, saying, "Only if you'll call me Richard."

Eleanor agreed.

Richard said sadly, "Terrible trials can make one all alone in a crowd. I'm sorry you have endured, as I have, the agony of a missing son…"

Eleanor interrupted, "Two sons. I had two sons missing until about a year ago when it was confirmed that Andrew had been killed at the Alexandra Barracks Hospital in Singapore. It was a bloodbath. The Japanese attacked the hospital itself, killing patients, killing everyone."

Richard said, "I am so sorry. How devastating!"

"It has been, but I couldn't stay in that hole forever, so I rallied. I'm not sure how I did it, but it had something to do with Gilda coming to the manor, when I got her called up. She was so elated to be doing her bit. Now, I think you should tell me about your son. It will do you good to talk about him."

"Alec was not really a soldier type. He was more of a writer, and I'd say deeply religious in his own way. The things he wrote were like songs. I cannot imagine him surviving a POW camp. I truly cannot. He enlisted in the navy, because he thought he'd feel safer. All I know is that his ship was destined for Singapore, before Singapore fell. They can't account for many of the personnel, yet."

Eleanor shook her head sadly and waited for him to continue.

"Before going to New York, we wrote him a letter, telling him of our plans, and then we sent the Royal Navy a forwarding address of a neighbor and friend in London, in case something should happen to Alec, before we got home. We should have used my brother-in-law instead, but he was in the middle of a move at the time, and it seemed more practical to do it as we did. Our friend's house took a direct hit during the blitz, so any post directed there could have gotten lost in any number of ways. The term 'lost in the mail' takes on all sorts of new meanings during war."

"When you think of all the displaced people, I can

imagine a vast room full of lost letters. News, expressions of love and longing, all going nowhere," said Eleanor, shaking her head sadly.

"That sounds rather poetic, almost like something my son would write."

"Did he have a girl waiting?" asked Eleanor.

"She died in the blitz, as well. It was her father to whom we directed Alec's mail. Good friends of the family."

"My God, war is awful," exclaimed Eleanor. "Since you don't even know if he got your letter saying you were buying this house, you are lost to him, as well!"

"It appears so," said Richard sadly. Changing the subject, Richard asked, "Are you warm?"

"Thanks to you, yes I am."

འ་ཚོའི་ཚོའི་

That night, Eleanor wrote, *As long as I don't come down with a dreadful cold, I may have gotten away with drenching myself in freezing rain today. Mr. Fitzgerald, who I now call by his first name, Richard, helped me pull off the deception.*

*At his cottage, known to us now as Two Hoots, I got dried off and warmed up as quickly as possible. By the time*

*David fetched me, all my clothes were bone dry. I'm glad I wear my hair up instead of curled, or I'd have never gotten away with it. Dotty doesn't miss much around here. Since I'm not good at crime detection, perhaps I should go into crime itself. I'm getting rather adept at deception. In this case, though, deception was my only option. I could not have borne the lecture I'd have gotten if Dotty had found out.*

*Lying here beside Willy has reminded me how much I like sleeping with another person. I forgot how comforting it can be to hear the soft breathing of someone you love. Willy had a great day with Emma and Sam and nearly fell asleep at the table tonight.*

*I have a great desire to talk to Priscilla about her amazing recovery. I must make time for that tomorrow.*

## Chapter Twenty-One

Early on the morning of December thirty-first, Eleanor awoke, not knowing what day of the week it was. It didn't matter, really, because, unless they were given a specific day or two off, they fed airmen seven days a week. Recently, though, what with the massive air attacks on Germany and holiday leaves, the airfield had been particularly quiet.

Finding Dotty in the kitchen, looking quite perturbed, Eleanor asked, "Is something the matter, Dotty?"

"I just now got word from the quartermaster. He was sorry not to let us know ahead of time, but it seems we have no airmen upstairs. So what am I supposed to do with all these eggs?" she said, looking at the bowl.

"How many had we planned for?"

"Less than twenty, but that's a lot of eggs," said Dotty, pointing at the eggs accusingly.

"They won't spoil, Dotty," assured Eleanor. "We'll serve them up tomorrow, instead."

"He said there wouldn't be anybody to feed tomorrow, either," said Dotty, shaking her head.

"Have you looked around?" asked Eleanor cheerfully. "We have plenty of folks to feed. You aren't telling me you don't want another two days off, are you?"

"Heavens no, Mrs. Wood, but had I known, I would have stayed in my warm bed next to my warm man. What a wasted opportunity!" she exclaimed innocently.

Eleanor laughed at the unintended innuendo and said, "I'll put everything away. You go on home as fast as you can and get back into bed. Now hurry, before Sam and Emma wake up. I think today must be Sunday."

"It is indeed, but no church for us. I'm not taking my family out in this weather," said Dotty, quickly putting on her coat and tying her scarf around her head.

"You are off until Tuesday, then, but please do come for dinner tomorrow night. We'll feed the little ones early, have the pantomime, put the children down on my bed, and then we'll have a quiet adult dinner about eight o'clock."

"Are you sure you don't want me to stay and help feed everyone this morning, Mrs. Wood?" asked Dotty, hesitating at the door.

"Go quick, before I change my mind," said Eleanor laughing.

She didn't have to tell her again. Dotty was gone like a shot.

Eleanor made herself some tea and waited for David

to come down to prepare the tea and toast that he and Priscilla ate in their room each morning. He was usually the first among the house guests to show up and helped with the airmen's first breakfast, whenever help was needed.

When Eleanor heard the creaking of the stairs, indicating his imminent arrival, she greeted him warmly and asked, "Is Priscilla going to be here this morning?"

"She certainly is," replied David.

"I thought I'd drop in on her, if I can find someone to watch my sleeping Willy for awhile."

"I suggest you take her breakfast upstairs, and I'll listen to your wireless and be here when Willy awakes."

"That sounds wonderful."

A few minutes later, Eleanor knocked lightly and entered Priscilla's room. She was greeted warmly. She put the tray on the table and said to Priscilla, "I have come to talk, because I am a busybody. I want to know when you got better."

Priscilla chuckled and replied, "After all you've done for us, I suppose I owe it to you to satisfy your curiosity."

"Please do; it cannot be ignored any longer. Hard as I try, I can't seem to help it."

Priscilla pulled the chairs up to the table and invited

Eleanor to join her. Once they were settled and tea was poured out, Priscilla asked, "So you want to know when I made my leap?"

"Precisely. I'm dying to know. Tell me everything," said Eleanor shamelessly.

Priscilla nodded and proceeded to tell the story of Emma's clandestine activities in pursuit of Father Christmas.

Eleanor laughed heartily and asked, "When did this happen?"

"Early in December. So, you see, I had quite a bit of time to sew. In fact, if I'd just had one more day, I would have even finished knitting the baby shawl. I have to say, though, that everyone's reaction at seeing the protruding knitting needles and the ball of yarn roll across the floor was rather priceless."

"I agree. That will be the one thing that everyone will remember for years, a family story to be passed down through the generations."

Eyeing Priscilla, Eleanor asked, "Why didn't you say something sooner?"

Priscilla said, "Actually, I did let on to Gilda a few days ago when she told me that Thomas was flying again. I believed that I was my really old self again, ambitious and full of energy, but I wanted to be certain, so I decided to keep to myself awhile longer and work like there was no tomorrow."

"You know, I thought I heard you humming one day as I walked past the workroom, but I decided that it had to be the sewing machine. You really surprised everyone with all the gifts. And those dresses for the girls are just lovely!"

"And you are wondering how I made the transition from not bearing to lay eyes on Emma to wanting to give her a beautiful Christmas dress," teased Priscilla knowingly.

"Well yes, I really am," said Eleanor sincerely. Cautiously, she added, "I feared those eyes of hers would set you back when you saw them."

"The appearance of Thomas's eyes was nothing compared to the shock of seeing Jeremy's dimples again," said Priscilla emphatically. "She took me completely off my guard. I was rather brusque with her, at first, but then she began saying things that made me laugh so hard, I found I couldn't possibly do anything but love her. It happened that fast. When she left, she turned and matter-of-factly told me that my bedroom was nice, but not as nice as hers, confessing, without confessing, of course, that she had been snooping around in there, too. I tell you, Eleanor, I couldn't stop laughing for hours."

"So that's how it happened," said Eleanor smiling and shaking her head.

"Yes, dear friend, that's when I took the leap. Thank you for the advice and everything else you have done for us!"

"The pleasure has been all mine," said Eleanor, rising to leave.

At the door, she turned and asked, "And what, may I ask, did Emma whisper in your ear on Christmas night?"

Standing up, Priscilla stated, "She thanked me for the dress, and then she said, and I quote, 'By cranky, Mother *Chrisnas,* you made a good job of keeping our secret from Father *Chrisnas*. He gave me everything I ever wanted in my whole life.'"

Eleanor returned to Priscilla to give her a brief embrace and said, "You made a good job of keeping lots of secrets, I'd say, Mother *Christnas*."

ৰ্ক্কৰ্ক্ক

After a very quiet and uneventful New Year's Eve, Eleanor penned, As *previously planned, Willy and I spent a quiet evening sitting by the wireless, playing with his building blocks and awaiting the arrival of his mother. I bribed Willy to have a rare nap this afternoon, so he wouldn't be sound asleep when his mother arrived.*

*Edith insisted that she and Larry fetch Jane from the station, since David did not even know what she looked like. Furthermore, Edith insisted that Jane would be more comfortable being picked up by someone she knew, so David and Priscilla loaned them the car and retired to their own room to bring in the New Year in their own way, so they said.*

*Much for the same reason, I'm sure, Thomas and Gilda announced that they would stay above stairs, too, so as not to overwhelm Jane when she appeared. I'm thinking everyone is just a little too eager to spend the entire evening in their bedrooms, but perhaps, I'm just jealous. I won't have a warm body lying next to mine tonight.*

*Jane finally arrived and looked done in. She was thin and exhausted to the point of being unable to speak. She thanked Edith with a brief hug, and then Edith and Larry disappeared above to the west wing of the first floor (which, from this day forward, I will privately call "The Hall of Marital Bliss)*

*Jane cried when she saw Willy, and he happily accepted the teddy bear she presented to him. He then climbed into her lap and fell asleep, while I warmed the soup. It was gratifying to see mother and son united, at last.*

*We put Willy on my bed while I fed her some soup and bread and ran a hot tub for her in my bathroom. Then I put them to bed upstairs in the children's room, where David had recently moved Willy's cot. The only time Jane smiled a little was when I asked her if the lingering smell of apples in the adjoining room was too much for her. She assured me that it was not, saying, "It's very pleasant and about the first thing in days that does not seem to be too much for me."*

*All New Year's festivities are happening tomorrow evening. Edith has orchestrated it so that those involved will come gradually, over the course of the day, for Jane's sake. Long before dinner time (an early one at half past six) Jane will know all but the Morrises, who will come in time for dinner, bringing the elderly Levanthalls, who came from Shrewsbury today to bring the Smith children their Christmas presents. The Leventhalls are a charming couple, who have decided that the Smith children should have some doting grandparents. The planned event tomorrow night is a pantomime put together by Agnes and Lucas, which will somehow include Willy and Emma.*

*It was Edith's idea to invite everyone, in spite of my*

*previous promises to Jane. I thought it best to keep it intimate, and after seeing the fatigue in Jane's face, I still think so, but Edith said she had a well-thought-through plan for making Jane feel welcome. How does anyone argue with that?*

ಹಿಳಿಹಿಳಿ

The entire household slept later than usual, enjoying the holiday given them by the Royal Air Force. Eleanor was the first to wake, just after dawn, and arrayed in her dressing gown and slippers, she made her way to her kitchen-corner sitting room and settled down with the wireless and a cup of hot tea. She listened to a song by the Glenn Miller Orchestra and then a BBC tribute to his contribution to the war. The public was still stunned by his mysterious disappearance days before.

Sitting there, Eleanor's spirits were lifted when she remembered Jane's promise to bring William's letters. She sat waiting contentedly, happy in the knowledge that her wish to have Jane and Willy at the manor had been granted, at last.

At the sound of light feet on the staircase, Eleanor knew she would soon be joined in the kitchen and wondered who it might be. Dressed and ready for the day,

Jane appeared, smiling in the doorway, with two envelopes in her hand. Eleanor greeted her, "Happy New Year, Jane. Come sit here, while I turn on the heat under the kettle."

When Eleanor was seated again, Jane handed her the letters. She said, "I want you to keep them in your room until I leave. You may want to read them repeatedly, as I have done. Of course, there are but a few words, but they are comforting, that is, if you can keep your mind off the possible explanations of the differences in the handwriting."

"I'm sorry you didn't hear from him again. I'm sorry for all of us."

"Since I've learned that getting two is a real boon, I've quit having such high expectations," said Jane realistically.

"Perhaps, I should just keep one at a time. Then you'll have one to put under your pillow."

"I've got Willy now, and I want you to enjoy them to the fullest. When you put them side by side, you will wonder how I ever mistook the handwriting, even the writing style, of the second letter, but for Willy's sake, I must put those worries aside for now."

Jane's addition of the words "for now" spoke volumes to Eleanor, who reminded herself, once again, that the news contained in the letters was weeks or even months old. Anything could have happened between then and now, but she didn't need to remind Jane of that ominous truth.

Sitting in companionable silence, listening to the quiet music from the wireless, Eleanor remembered her recent conversation with Richard and his exercise of opposites in the phenomenon of the Christmas catalogue and the angst for the missing men. She chided herself for failing to record that in her journal and promised to do so soon.

Her reflections were interrupted by the sounds of many voices in the hall above. She looked down at her dressing gown and slippers and said emphatically to Jane, "I must get dressed!" Her utterance made Jane laugh, and chuckling, too, Eleanor jumped up and darted toward the door. She stopped, turned abruptly, and returned to Jane, who was holding the letters in her outstretched hand.

"How could I forget these?" asked Eleanor, once again dashing for her room. As she closed her bedroom door, she could still hear the ring of Jane's lovely laughter.

"How wonderful," exclaimed Eleanor to her reflection in the dressing table mirror.

As she was about to open the first letter, she decided to wait until she had time to read properly, so she tucked the letters into her drawer for later in the day.

She quickly got dressed and did her hair, so she could cook the eggs that had been prepared the day before. She could hear everyone's loud voices saying, "Happy New Year," to each other and realized that she had deserted Jane, instead of doing the introductions that Jane had been dreading for weeks.

Arriving in the kitchen, she found Edith preparing the eggs and Larry making toast. Priscilla was setting the long table in the dining room, and David was building a fire in the enormous hall fireplace that was open to both the dining room and the great hall. Willy was helping David, Jane was putting the plates in the oven to warm, and Thomas and Gilda had just made their appearance.

Just as Eleanor was going to introduce them to Jane, Edith turned and said, "Thomas, Gilda, meet Willy's mum, Jane."

Eleanor thought the introduction was lacking but then realized that maybe Edith's way was the best way. Jane seemed to be taking everything in stride, and amid the breakfast chaos, she seemed protected from scrutiny. Eleanor greeted everyone, while thinking, "I'm becoming redundant."

Everyone ate and talked, and Eleanor noticed that

Edith was still in her dressing gown. Eleanor thought, "The younger generation seems to be free of the binding rules I lived by. Oh yes, how could I forget? There is a war on."

The breakfast was left out on the table most of the morning. The pile of eggs was kept warm over a flame and a new stack of toast was added from time to time. Edith had made a unilateral decision that the breakfast period should be extended and that luncheon should be eliminated altogether, since an early dinner was being planned that evening.

Just as Eleanor was wondering why she hadn't thought of it herself, she suddenly wished that she had invited Richard to dinner, seeing as everyone else seemed to be coming. She decided to ask Edith about it, since she was apparently in command and now well-acquainted with Jane. Approaching her, Eleanor asked discreetly, "Edith, do you think the addition of Richard tonight would be too much for Jane?"

Edith replied, "Oh, he's been invited, Mum. He's bringing some cooked game. It's all been sorted out."

Just as Eleanor was wondering what to do with herself, she thought of retreating to her room to study William's letters. That idea went by the wayside, though, when Willy took her by the hand and wanted to show her how he was hauling all his wooden blocks around in his wagon. "The letters will keep," thought Eleanor, "but childhood is fleeting."

◈◈◈◈

Whenever anyone new arrived at the manor that day, Edith introduced them to Jane by saying simply, "Meet Willy's mum, Jane." The robust conviviality of the large crown proved more comfortable to Jane than an intimate gathering might have been. Quiet conversations were quite impossible as card tables were set up, fires were attended, food was dealt with, and Willy and Emma pulled the wagon around and around the great hall with accompanying engine sounds.

When Richard came across the field at six o'clock, he carried the cooked game in a covered pot, which he carried in a sling contrived with the use of a bath towel. Doing so enabled him to carry his torch in the other hand, much needed in the dark, starless night. Edith met him at the door, took the pot from him, and carried it to the kitchen to be put in the oven to stay warm until dinner.

Without Edith in the room, Eleanor realized that she should do the introductions, but just as she was about to do so, Richard extended his hand to Jane and said, "You must be Willy's mum, Jane. I'm Richard Fitzgerald, newer to the family than even you, I think."

Jane responded warmly, saying that she was glad to have finally come to Greystone, and a relaxing conversation ensued as Richard described to her Willy's antics when he played the part of the sheep in the nativity play on Christmas Eve.

꿈꿈꿈꿈

That night, Eleanor wrote, *We had a lovely dinner tonight, after enjoying the silliest pantomime I've ever witnessed. The littlest ones played their parts impromptu, as Lucas and Agnes had designed it, and it was more hilarious than any well-practiced play could ever have been. There was plenty of help from the audience, with the occasional, "Look behind you," and "Oh no it isn't." Of course, the children all looked beautiful in their new clothes. The girls were darling in their blue velvet dresses.*

*When it was over, the children, who had been fed earlier, were put on my bed, so we could check on them from time to time. Although it took awhile for them to settle in, after all the excitement, they finally slept like angels.*

*Dinner was quiet, once the children were in bed. Lucas and Matty now considered themselves adults (all things being relative) and their manners were impeccable.*

*Agnes has done wonders with them, and they have done wonders with her. Richard seems to fit in with any crowd, and I think he put Jane more at ease than anyone, alluding to himself as the odd man out, who had crashed a family party.*

*Our meal was reasonably abundant with two choices of meat, several choices of vegetables, and, of course, bread. Apples supplied us with our pie for afters, and contentment filled the atmosphere, as games of cards began and little groups broke off for quiet conversations, moving chairs as needed around the dining room. Any airmen passing through were greeted warmly, given some dried apples by Emma, if they hadn't yet gotten any, and occasionally one lingered by the irresistible fire to visit for awhile.*

*We enjoyed having the Levanthalls here tonight. They were such fun and seemed like part of the family. It was a fine collection of guests, and I'm proud of Edith's efforts. She threw a lovely party.*

*Larry will leave tomorrow. He and Edith announced that she would be staying on at the manor, and everyone cheered when the reason was proudly announced. David and Richard took the car and quickly retrieved another bottle of the good stuff from Richard's cottage for celebrating the happy news.*

*The following day, Jane plans to return to Trubury. She insists there is so much to do, although I can't imagine what it might be. She mentions her need to get back to Mr. Jameson, so I won't interfere. I will miss Willy very much, though. It has been on my mind that she might consider moving here and giving up the house in Trubury. Edith told me how mistreated she has been in that community, and I yearn to interfere, but hesitate to do so. Our dear David has promised Willy that he will personally deliver the wagon to their door at his earliest opportunity.*

*Gilda, although quite handicapped by her broken arm, is managing all right with Thomas's help and insists on moving home to their cottage in a day or two. She'll be on her own part of the time, but Priscilla and Agnes have offered to take in some meals, and that will help.*

*I'm glad the Armstrongs have made no mention of leaving. For one thing, I like my evening meal prepared for me each night, and for another, they are such good friends to us all. I'm happy, also, that Edith will stay on. She looked very tired tonight after all her hard work, but she is happy and coping well with Larry's leaving. I overheard them talking about his putting in a transfer to Nuneaton, where the Americans have taken over Arbury Hall. That would be perfect.*

*I read and reread William's letters and cannot imagine how Jane mistook the second letter as being penned by William. From what I learnt from Richard the other day, his letters aren't from microfiche at all, but rather standard Japanese forms for prisoners. The tiny handwriting allows them to get their quota of words to fit on the page. The second letter is troubling, but I'm not going to worry Jane about it further. I am, though, going to ask her about the smudged writing at the bottom of the page. Maybe she had been able to make it out, before she read it a hundred times and slept with it every night.*

*She wouldn't know this, but the use of the word "whom" in the letter would have been all I would have needed to know that William hadn't written it. He hated that word and the rules that dictated its use. Funny I should remember that now.*

*I am too tired to share Richard's Christmas catalogue metaphor, concerning the feelings of my constant concern for William. I must take time to do that properly, sometime. In a nutshell, it all comes down to the myriad of possibilities in both scenarios. My worries for him are always there in the background, running around in my mind like a mouse in a wheel. Richard's comparison makes perfect sense to me, but I'm afraid if one hadn't experienced what we have, they might not understand at all. Writer's cramp. I'll take this up later.*

*Happy New Year, William, God speed.*

ം൙ം൙

The night before Jane was to go home to Herefordshire, Eleanor collected William's letters from her room to give back to her. She tucked them into the pocket of her cardigan, so she would have them at hand.

Eleanor, Edith and Jane sat together in the kitchen sitting corner that night and listened to the wireless. The others kept to their rooms, so that Eleanor could have the chance to sit uninterrupted with Edith and Jane.

As the wireless played song after song by the Glenn Miller Orchestra, the women talked of mundane things. Eleanor pulled the letters from her pocket, and looked at them longingly for what she thought was the last time. Thinking of the smudged writing at the bottom of the letter, she asked, "Jane, have you ever noticed the little bit of writing at the bottom of the second letter?"

"You mean the letter that wasn't really written by William at all?" asked Jane with eyebrows raised.

Nodding and taking the letter from the envelope,

Eleanor held it up for Jane to see what she was referring to. "Right here," she said. "Have you ever been able to decipher it?"

"It arrived smudged in that way, I believe, but I didn't even notice it until the second or third time I went through it. And then it was still a long time after that, before I finally realized that the letter wasn't written in William's hand at all. Lately, it has bothered me, you know, the smudged writing at the bottom, so our doctor showed it to a friend of his, who put it under magnification. He said it was more than likely a name. Since it turned out not to be written by William at all, I've come to believe it was the signature of the person who really wrote the letter. I should have mentioned that earlier."

"I can't make out anything," said Eleanor, peering closer with the help of her reading glasses. "It is about the right length for a name, I suppose. How intriguing."

"I have a piece of paper on which Dr. Hughes's friend wrote what he believed to have been some of the letters that he could make out the best. For instance, he could tell there was an 'L' because it matched exactly another one, above in the letter. He was convinced that it was the signature of the person who wrote the letter. I've had a little too much to do to delve into it further. Maybe you'd like to study it."

"I admit I am very curious about it."

"I'll leave the second letter and the findings of the gentleman here with you."

"Are you sure you can do without it?"

"I'll keep the one that William wrote. That will be enough for me. The mystery will give you something to think about, and it will only agitate my mind. With Willy around, I don't have time to do anything about it, and as you will see, there is little to go on, anyway."

Eleanor nodded, saying, "I will enjoy playing detective, although it seems I'm not that good at it."

After putting Jane and Willy on the train that afternoon, Eleanor ate little at dinner and retired early. Missing William something terrible, she crawled into her bed and turned on the bedside light. Putting on her reading glasses, she read again the prisoner's letter, and although she could imagine William having those kinds of thoughts, he would have never chosen those particular words to describe them.

Eleanor then turned her attention to the piece of paper on which the doctor's friend had made some notes. She read, *"By comparing what can be seen in the smudged writing with the formation of the letters in the message above, certain letters can be made out with some exactness. This may not be helpful, but I am relatively certain that the last name begins with 'T' or possibly an 'F' and ends with two tall letters that could be a combination of 'b, d, or l'. The first name is just an initial and could be many letters, I suppose, but I would gamble it's an 'A, O, or a Q'.*

Eleanor thought that it was no wonder that Jane had failed to share the findings with her earlier, since there really was nothing at all to go on. Feeling privileged to have the letter and feeling a little silly, Eleanor put it under her pillow, turned off her light, and tried to imagine Willy's little body lying next to hers.

༄༅༄༅

Once the others had left the manor, Gilda decided to make her move home, too. Thomas was granted a morning off to pack up, and David drove the Gardners home to Willows Edge, stopping by the grocer and bakery to get a few essentials.

Driving up to the door, Gilda was so glad to be home, she nearly cried. After thanking David, Thomas hurried to make Gilda comfortable before he left her on her own. When he closed the door behind him, Gilda sighed with contentedness. It felt rather good to be alone.

Although she was frustrated by her inability to do anything worthwhile, she relished the idea of lying on her bed, reading a stack of books she'd borrowed from Eleanor. She had the entire works of Jane Austen and one by each of the Bronte sisters.

Feeling that the Brontes might be a bit too intense for her mood, Gilda opened *Pride and Prejudice* and began to read, "It is a truth universally acknowledged, that a single man in possession of a good fortune, must be in want of a wife."

When she had finished the first chapter, Gilda put down the book and reached for her journal and pen. As much as the cast restricted her ability to write much, she thought it was better than not writing at all.

*January 5, 1945*
*Dear Diary,*

*Thomas and I are, at last, home at Willows Edge. I can write but a few words with his cumbersome cast, but I will say that I am happy and well. Edith surprised us by being, not only married since October, but also expecting a baby. She is staying home at the manor, and I'm glad of it for Mrs. Wood's sake, as Jane and Willy went home yesterday. Jane was here but three days, but I think she was worried about her neighbour, at least that is what she hinted. I'm going to read some books and receive callers like a regular lady. Priscilla promised to come this afternoon to make me tea and a light supper for the four of us. She is bringing the white baby shawl that she gave me for Christmas. She says it no longer has knitting needles poking out of it.*

Feeling sleepy, Gilda closed her eyes for a luxurious nap.

Moments later, Priscilla knocked lightly on the cottage door. As she waited, she thought about how happy she was that Thomas and Gilda felt safe to be at Willows Edge, once again. When no one answered the door, Priscilla used the key she'd been given, and entered silently, carefully closing the door, not wanting to disturb Gilda if she was resting. As she had hoped, she found Gilda sleeping soundly in the bedroom.

There was little heat emanating from the single-barred heater, and Gilda looked chilled lying there on top of the pale-blue counterpane. Priscilla fetched the baby shawl she had finished and placed it over Gilda's lower half and draped Gilda's gray cardigan over the rest of her.

Back in the sitting room, Priscilla went quietly

about hanging the new curtains that she had made in secret. She'd had to use two different prints to have sufficient material to cover the large, single window, so she'd gotten creative, choosing a paisley-patterned material from India for the middle panels and the putting coordinating plaid panels on each end. The pallet of the spicy brown, creamy yellow, and a number of exotic blues looked wonderful in the cottage room with its blackened beams and rustic stone fireplace.

She had lined the panels with the patched sheets donated by Eleanor, and they had just the right weight, thought Priscilla, for shutting out harsh light and insulating against a winter's sharp wind. Using the existing iron curtain rod and rings she had sewn to the top of the curtain panels, she hung them with ease, making sure that they could be slid open and closed with little effort.

Having found another piece of coordinating material, and guessing at the measurements, Priscilla had made a cushioned back and seat-cover for the settee. Then, with the use of all three fabrics and the addition of a contrasting deep-blue remnant she had found at the manor, she'd made two squashy pillows for each end of the settee.

Hurrying now, Priscilla quietly moved the little gate-legged table back into the sitting room from the kitchen and put it in front of the window, where Gilda and Thomas had so liked it before their scare. She covered it first with Gilda's own tablecloth, appreciating the touch of yellow in the mix, and laid the remaining square piece of Indian paisley in the middle. She placed creamy-colored candles in Lucas's homemade wooden candlesticks and arranged them on the exotic table scarf. She stepped back to appreciate the effect.

After moving the ladder-backed chairs to the sitting room, starting the fire already laid in the grate, and opening the curtains partway to let in the setting afternoon sun, Priscilla started the water on the cooker and began preparations for their meal of bacon and vegetables.

Just as she was setting an array of mismatched plates on the table, Gilda walked into the sitting room, holding the baby shawl to her chest. She gasped when she saw the transformation of the sitting room. She knew it was no accident that the golden flames from the stone fireplace and setting sun danced exotically off the warm colors of the curtain panels. The various hues of blue felt as homey as the spicy Indian colors were exciting and foreign. She took in the settee cushion and elegant pillows with delight.

"Oh Priscilla, how wonderful!" cried Gilda, rushing to embrace her kind mother-in-law. "Thank you, oh thank you; it's just lovely!"

"I've never had so much fun," said Priscilla. She then invited Gilda to get comfortable on the settee, while she finished their dinner and waited for the men to arrive.

∽⋆∽⋆

Enfolded in Thomas's strong arms that night, Gilda murmured, "Your mother is so talented, Thomas. Now the sitting room embraces one, instead of looking hard, harsh, and unforgiving."

"My mum always said that textiles were a woman's delight," began Thomas, "and I never fully believed her until this evening."

Gilda said, "She told me this afternoon that there has to be balance between the hard and soft surfaces in a room. Who would have thought?"

"Not I," said Thomas happily. "She hasn't given us too much trouble for keeping her in the dark about our stalker, has she?"

"No, I kept expecting her to chastise us over the last few days, but she's been uncommonly quiet about it. Perhaps she knows we protected her out of concern."

"Or, maybe she's going easy on us, because she's all over David for not telling her," said Thomas, chuckling.

"I think that when she is uncommonly quiet, her creative juices are in overdrive, and an explosion of ideas will soon emerge. She finished the baby's shawl, too," said Gilda, happily remembering the humor surrounding its presentation.

Mention of the shawl shifted Thomas's attention to the excitement of their expected baby, and he asked, "Do think the baby is a boy or a girl?"

"I don't know, and I really don't care. A healthy little body with ten fingers and ten toes is my only request."

Affectionately, Thomas said, "I love you just the way you are, Gilda."

"I know," said Gilda blissfully.

*Chapter Twenty-Two*

A cold January drug on, as the Allies fought fiercely in terrible conditions. Freezing rains and harsh temperatures resulted in trench foot and exposure for the embattled Allies. In spite of it all, the Germans were pushed back, and by mid-January, their lack of fuel finally became evident, when the Germans had to abandon their vehicles and retreat on foot.

News of the Massacre of Malmedy was made known when the Allies finally came upon the murdered Americans of the 285$^{th}$ Field Artillery Observation Battalion. Craig Bradford was found among the dead. Larry was given a short leave, and he joined Edith at Greystone Manor to share his grief. The atmosphere at the manor was overwhelmingly subdued, and even Spanky seemed to be mourning.

Two weeks later, the Red Army liberated the Auschwitz death camp, giving shocking evidence to the world that the rumors, heard as early as 1936, were indeed true. Horrified, and yet unable to turn it off, Eleanor and Edith together listened to the report as it came over the wireless. "**The Red Army has liberated the Nazis' biggest concentration camp at Auschwitz in south-western Poland.**

According to reports, hundreds of thousands of Polish people, as well as Jews from a number of other European countries, have been held prisoner there in appalling conditions and many have been killed in the gas chambers."

Edith and her mother stayed up very late that night, unable to turn off the images now planted in their minds. However difficult, they drank tea and tried to talk of other things. Edith said that Larry had rung and seemed to be coping all right.

Eleanor sighed and said, "The agony of not knowing is over, and that in itself is a blessing."

Edith looked at her mum and said, "Now, if only such agony about William might, one day, end for us."

Her mother replied with a tearful nod and shared this with her diary that night: *Even after dealing with this war for all these years, I am shocked by the acts of horror that the Germans can commit. I understand that the Japanese are equally cruel, if not more so, but I'm unable to dwell on that tonight, as Jane has still not gotten another letter from William.*

*Hundreds of thousands of Americans took part in the latest armoured offensive by the Germans, which most commentaries now agree to have been foolhardy. One has to ask why, and the only solution that ever presents itself is that Hitler is mad. At its beginning, Larry's brother and his comrades were cut down in cold blood, rather than taken as prisoners. From what Larry has been able to learn, the Americans came upon the victims, lying in the snow, where they had fallen some four weeks before. Malmedy was treated as a crime scene, because many of the dead had close-range shots to the head. This wasn't a skirmish; it was an execution. And if that isn't disturbing enough, now, most recently, the Russians have liberated the Auschwitz Death Camp, where suffering of such magnitude took place, it cannot be fully comprehended.*

*As terrible as all of this is, the war will be won, and we are getting closer every day. The airmen speak eagerly of going home, and our work here at the manor, although mundane, continues to be rewarding. Gilda has been officially discharged from her war work but is enjoying her cottage and rest.*

A week later, Eleanor wrote, *Little Emma is here among us, bringing smiles to all who come in contact with her, we are expecting two babies, and I now have Willy in my life.*

*Edith seems to glow with that radiance reserved especially for pregnant women, and she is very happy. I have seen very little of the folks on Gypsy Row, now that Gilda has been released from her war work, but I've heard her arm is healing nicely and her pregnancy continues to go well. I have also heard that Priscilla has done some wonderful things for Gilda's cottage, which, no doubt, makes it that much harder for her to venture out. I should go see for myself. If we could be blessed with a sunny day this week, I believe I will call upon her and perhaps, Mr. Richard Fitzgerald, as well.*

ಞഩಞഩ

Eleanor sneaked out of the manor, without Spanky, to call on Willows Edge. As she approached Gypsy Row, she appreciated the charming thatched roofs and golden sandstone cottages, basking in the afternoon sun. She noticed the smoke coming from the chimneys of both Willows Edge and Two Hoots and recalled the one real difference that she had noticed in the two cottages. Willows Edge had been built with a central chimney, and Two Hoots had an end chimney, but both had high stacks to protect against the chance of a fire, she noted reassuringly.

Looking at Two Hoots and remembering the December day that she had been a guest in Richard's home, Eleanor longed to pop in on him this afternoon, too, but could think of no valid excuse for doing so.

Gilda saw her coming through the wooden gate and welcomed her into her home. Eleanor was enormously impressed with the charming effect the new curtains had on the sitting room, and she also appreciated the cushioned seat of the settee, as she sat down in front of Gilda's fire.

Eleanor had seen the cottage when the Gardners had first found it and said, "You and Thomas have done wonders with this place."

"We have numerous tasks ahead but, at least it is welcoming and clean, now. And since Priscilla worked her magic on this sitting room, I can barely stand to leave it."

"Have you been keeping busy?" asked Eleanor.

"Not really, I don't actually do much at all, but I've read lots of books, and I've been sewing the baby's layette under the tutelage of my dear mother-in-law. "

"You should get the telephone turned on here."

"With Richard next door, it's not really necessary. He keeps a close eye on me. Now, tell me how you have been, and Edith, how is she?"

"Oh, I'm all right, and Edith is, too, since Larry rang with the news that he'll soon be transferred to Nuneaton. He'll join the Americans working out of Arbury Hall."

Eleanor followed Gilda around the little kitchen and helped her put some tea and pie on the table. She said, "You went to lots of trouble today, making pie and all. How did you manage it with your arm still healing?"

"Let's just say I did my best under the circumstances. When I told Richard that you were coming to tea, he recommended I make some pies and send one to him," said Gilda laughing. "He hoped you might deliver it."

"I suppose I could do that," said Eleanor, feeling suddenly nervous. She added casually, "I've wanted to drop by there, but I never seem to get far from the manor."

"He has been busily going through old family memorabilia."

"That's a heart-wrenching exercise when you find yourself all alone," said Eleanor knowingly.

"I suppose that's true," said Gilda.

"Has he learned anything at all about his son?"

"No," said Gilda. "He presses and presses for information, but there is none."

"It's difficult. Jane hasn't had a letter in months, and although she knows she should not expect one every month, she's quite desperate for one now."

"I'm sure she is."

After a lovely hour with Gilda, Eleanor took the pie

for Richard and went through the break in the hedge, where Richard had worn a path to Willows Edge. She climbed the gentle rise, approached the door and knocked.

When Richard answered the door, his appearance shocked her. His hair, which had before been rather long and bohemian-looking, was now downright unkempt. And he seemed a little surprised at seeing her, which she thought was odd, since he had asked Gilda to send the pie with her.

Presenting it, she said, "Your pie, compliments of Gilda."

Without taking it, he said, "Thank you; do come in, Eleanor."

Eleanor stepped into the entry and on into the sitting room. Glasses sat on every surface, and books, magazines, and newspapers covered the floor. Turning toward Richard and finding him very close, Eleanor smelled alcohol on his breath and said, "So, you are putting on a face when you see Gilda and Thomas. They don't know what shape you're in, do they?"

"Well, I hope not," said Richard. "Her mum was a real drinker, once. I'd hate to lose their friendship over my sudden lust for wine, of which I once had a vast supply."

"Why didn't you come talk to me? You know I

would have understood. It was just a year ago that I finally climbed up from a tremendous low point."

"You have your own worries. Come sit by the fire."

"Thank you, I will. I'll put this pie in the kitchen, first."

Eleanor entered the kitchen and was appalled at the sight of it. Dirty glasses sat here and there, and she found only soup bowls in the wash basin to indicate that he'd been eating there at all. Taking off her wrap, she returned slowly to the sitting room and found Richard sitting in the chair she had once sat in. She pulled up the foot stool and stared at the flames.

Richard finally realized that Eleanor was perched on the sitting stool and said, "My apologies, dear woman, I've lost my mind and my manners."

"Stay where you are. I'm perfectly comfortable. You have been alone too much, Richard. You must come to the manor for dinner on the nights you aren't at Willows Edge."

"Oh, I couldn't intrude," said Richard. "You have enough mouths to feed."

"The way your clothes hang off you, Richard, it's apparent you don't eat much, anyway."

"I'm frequently fed next door, you know, and I am

trying. Don't worry, Eleanor, I don't plan to wallow in this low mood forever."

"Well, in my experience, if you stay there too long, you might find it harder getting out."

"I've been going through old pictures and the children's school papers."

"Gilda told me, and I thought then that it wasn't a very good idea."

"I found some things that comfort and torment me, simultaneously," said Richard. He reached for a stack of papers on the floor and first showed Eleanor a drawing done by his daughter, Tess, when she was ten."

Looking at the drawing for a moment, tipping her head to the side and looking again, Eleanor finally said, "She didn't get your artistic abilities, did she?"

Richard laughed aloud and said, "I wondered if you would say she showed great promise. It was a test. I'm glad to find that you are an honest woman."

"So am I," said Eleanor laughing. "What else have you got there?"

"This is a poem written by Alec when he was about twelve, I think," said Richard.

"Will you read it to me?" asked Eleanor tentatively.

"I'd be honored. It is entitled, 'When I'm Alone,'

and goes like this."

In a deep voice and with much feeling, Richard read, *"When I'm alone, I am not really. When in a crowded room, I feel most alone then, missing the connection that I have with an unseen power and the angels of my solitude. I wait patiently, knowing I will find my comfort again, by the mere asking for it and knowing it will come to me in my waking hours and in night's peaceful rest."*

"He was only twelve?" asked Eleanor.

"About that," said Richard. "Can you see how I sometimes almost wish that he's gone home to his maker?"

"I felt the same about William, once, Richard. However, I came to the realization that if he was indeed alive, I owed it to him to stick by him. Does that sound silly?"

"Oh no," replied Richard, "it sounds very brave, indeed."

"Do you have a pair of scissors?" asked Eleanor impulsively.

"I suppose," said Richard, still staring at the writing in his hand.

"How would you like me to cut off a little of your hair and make you look like a successful artist rather than a starving one?"

*Meredith Kennon*

At that, Richard laughed heartily and went in search of the scissors.

❧❧❧❧

That night, Eleanor recorded, *It is the eighteenth of February. Since I have last written, the city of Dresden has been showered with thousands of bombs. It was a city of military importance, but although I had never visited it, I have always known that it was also a cultural masterpiece. It grieves me that it has been nearly flattened, and loss of life must have been extensive. We are winning, but I'll save my cheering until the Germans surrender. We count ourselves extremely fortunate that Thomas was not part of the Bombing of Dresden. He's now involved in implementing the new Dakota aircraft that has recently come to Lindley.*

*Today, I paid a visit to Willows Edge and then Two Hoots. Richard was in a bad way. I don't know how Thomas and Gilda could spend so much time with him and not realise how depressed he is. They are caught up in their own life, and too, for all their wartime experiences, they have never lost a child. One has to experience it, to grasp it fully.*

*I trimmed Richard's hair and went to the kitchen to do the washing up. When I returned to the sitting room,*

*Richard had picked up and had the room looking reasonably presentable, once again. Before leaving, I asked him if he needed help with washing his clothing, but he said it was in hand. It wasn't, but Richard was not prepared to let anyone do that for him. I think he'll get it done, if for no other reason, than to have it accomplished before someone else visits and offers to do it for him.*

*I have invited him to have dinner with us twice a week. He agreed if he could bring something each time, which will give him something to do, besides brood. I must remember to tell Priscilla about his coming, since she is our dinner cook.*

☙◦❧◦

On a brisk morning, late in February, Gilda came excitedly into the manor. She and Thomas were going to London for a month. Thomas was being included in a special meeting, because of his latest promotion to Air Commodore and his extensive war experience, as well as his training on the barrel bombs earlier in the war. They would be gone for a month, leaving almost immediately, and would be staying as guests at the home of one of Thomas's previous commanding officers, who lived north of London by a few miles.

Eleanor's first question was, "Is it safe there?"

Gilda laughed and replied, "Of course, Mrs. Wood. They've had none of the V-1 or V-2 hits there. We will be invited to parties and all sorts of events. I must get Priscilla to help me put together a few things to wear. Do I look terribly pregnant, do you think?"

"No, you don't, but you are, and I'd like you to remember that. What is Thomas thinking of dragging you off to London when you are just weeks from having the baby?"

"I'm not due for two and a half months, and I'm glad I'm not poking out to here," said Gilda holding her hands out in front of her.

"Aren't you worried for your safety?" pressed Eleanor again.

"Thomas's old CO told him that his home has been charmed since the beginning of the war."

"And that's supposed to make me feel better?" asked Mrs. Wood sharply. "What will your parents say? What will Priscilla and David say?"

"They'll be fine with it. Now don't worry, Mrs. Wood. People go to London all the time. I'm looking forward to it. We're going to see if Priscilla and David want to live in the cottage while we are gone. It would be nice having someone there. If they would rather not do it, Richard said he'd keep an eye on the place."

"I wish you weren't so excited to go, but I may as well save my breath. You seem determined."

"I am, Mrs. Wood. I've been indoors for weeks, and I've never really gone anywhere."

"I know, child."

☙❧☙❧

Priscilla and David did agree to stay at Willows Edge, and as worried as everyone was about Thomas's assignment and Gilda's accompanying him, they decided to say no more about it. Richard announced that he was going to his brother-in-law's house for a couple of weeks, which Eleanor thought was a probably a good thing for him, and everyone settled into a quiet pattern.

Edith and Eleanor got into a routine of a very light meal each night, and Priscilla and David joined them once a week. On the rare occasion, Eleanor and Edith walked to Willows Edge for dinner, but even if they walked over early enough to have a little daylight, by the time they went home, it was so dark, David insisted on driving them.

In March, Larry joined Edith at the manor, and they were thrilled to be living together, at last, and set up their quarters upstairs, similar to what had been done for the Armstrongs.

Eleanor was happy for them, but missed Edith's constant company. She missed Gilda, too, and when she thought she'd never hear from her, a letter from London finally arrived.

*The White House, Borough of Torrigan, London*
*March 20, 1945*
*Dear Mrs. Wood,*

*We are having a marvelous time here and have been shown every courtesy, but I'm desperately yearning for home. Thomas promises we will leave within the week.*

*Our hosts have been especially mindful of me in my condition, which is one of the things that we have in common. Marilyn is not very far along and feels awful most of the time. Parties have been kept to a minimum, and for that I'm glad. It only took one or two such events for me to know I would never enjoy the London party scene.*

*I have grown, and my clothes are ill-fitting. I miss my cottage, my garden, my family and friends, but most of all, you. Please give my love to everyone.*
*Affectionately,*
*Gilda*

## At Willows Edge

Many weeks since her last perusal of William's letter and on the eve of Gilda and Thomas's return, Eleanor sat up in bed less than an hour after dozing off. Her heart raced madly, so startled was she by the possibility presented before her.

Reminding herself that one had strange thoughts at night, and that she was no Miss Marple, she calmed herself. Promising herself that she was probably on the wrong track, anyway, she forced herself to lie down and go back to sleep.

The next morning, though, she removed the letter from the drawer. Once again, she read it and the notes made by the doctor's friend to make sure she'd remembered everything correctly. As the possibility grew stronger in her mind, she countered it with, "It couldn't be. It couldn't be."

Eleanor pushed these things to the back of her mind in order to accomplish her daily work. It was going to be a big day. Gilda and Thomas were coming home.

They were expected on the afternoon train, and Priscilla was having an intimate housewarming at the cottage for them. She had invited Gilda's parents, telephoning them from a phone box in the village, but they couldn't come. Agnes had said that Simon had been coughing again, and Matty and Lucas had picked up something at school and had been vomiting for two days. She'd said the last thing Gilda needed was a bout with something like that, and Priscilla had heartily agreed with her. Agnes hung up, saying she would visit Gilda the following day.

Priscilla had invited the Coopers, but Dotty had assured Priscilla that, as much as they appreciated the invitation, she thought they should keep their little bundle of energy at home. She said, "We'll all get together again at the manor very soon, I'm sure. Thank you for inviting us, though."

As for the Bradfords, Larry and Edith, they had made plans long ago for a party in Nuneaton, but Edith promised to visit Gilda very soon. In the end, Richard and Eleanor were the only ones that could come, which rather pleased Priscilla, and she proceeded with her plans. "No sense in overwhelming them," she thought.

On an unusually cold and windy afternoon, David fetched the Gardners from the station and took them directly to Willows Edge. Standing in the open doorway, as they came toward the cottage, Priscilla smiled broadly when she saw how large Gilda had become in her weeks away from home. Once everyone was inside, they greeted each other warmly with hugs and kisses.

Thomas helped Gilda with her coat and returned with David to the vehicle for their bags.

Gilda gravitated to the fireplace. To Priscilla, she said, "Has it been this cold all month?"

"No, we've had some lovely days. March came in like a lamb, so it appears that you've come home in time for the lion's exit."

Gilda nodded and moved to the settee, saying, "I'm unusually tired tonight."

Priscilla said, "Of course you are. We will feed you as soon as Richard and Eleanor get here, and then we'll leave you to rest. It is probably just as well the others couldn't make it tonight."

Gilda replied, "Oh, I hope you won't leave us too early. We've missed everyone terribly."

Thomas and David passed through the sitting room again with the bags, and returning, David looked at his watch and said, "I'll run to Greystone and fetch Eleanor now." He slipped out quietly.

Minutes later, Eleanor was there and greeted Gilda warmly, saying, "My goodness, I'm glad you're back. I've worried about you since the day you left."

## Meredith Kennon

A rapping on the door signified that Richard had arrived. When the door was opened for him, he entered with some cooked rabbit on a platter in one hand and a bottle of wine in the other. After a few minutes of activity, in which too many people were trying to help get dinner on the table, everyone was sitting around the little table in the charming sitting room.

Gilda and Thomas told them all that they had seen and done. Gilda tried to speak as fondly of London as she could, although she couldn't have escaped it quickly enough. She assumed that Priscilla and David missed the bustle of London and chided herself for judging the city in its present state, which wasn't entirely fair.

Priscilla knew her daughter-in-law quite well, by now, and found humor in her feigned excitement of her urban experience. Turning to her son, she asked, "And how did you enjoy the big city?"

Looking up from his plate and directly at his mother, he replied, "I enjoyed it as much as ever, which isn't very much. Gilda and I agreed that judging London now wasn't particularly fair, though. I might as well tell you right away, Mum, that although most of the Gardner property has fared quite well, your corner building for the proposed shop is nothing but rubble. I don't know why we never heard. Perhaps, someone tried reaching you in Surrey. I inquired and found out that no one was in the building when it tumbled."

Everyone looked at Priscilla for signs of distress and saw none. She smiled and said, "Well, we were bound to lose something. There will be other buildings."

Gilda said, "I remembered nothing of London from before. I was pretty young when we moved here, but I thought I might see something that would trigger a memory. It was like being there for the very first time."

"That's understandable," said David. "It might have been different if you'd visited the very street or building you had lived in. A child's world is small."

Everyone nodded and made comments on the tasty meal before them. Conversation was animated at times, followed by relative silence. Thomas talked of meeting some high level people at his meetings, including Air Chief Marshal Sir Arthur Harris, but unable to share more, conversation drifted to the activities at the manor.

Once the dishes were washed up and put away, Eleanor wanted desperately to talk to Richard privately, but she didn't know how to invite herself to his cottage.

Moments later, as if reading her mind, Richard said, "If the rest of you wouldn't mind, I have something I'd like to show Eleanor at the cottage. Could you excuse us for a few moments?"

"Certainly," said Gilda and Thomas together.

To Eleanor, David said, "Pris and I will await your return and drive you back to the manor."

As Richard guided Eleanor through the opening in the hedge and toward his cottage, she said, "I'm glad for this opportunity. I have something to show you."

"I knew you wanted to talk to me by the turn of your countenance."

"Are you teasing me, Mr. Fitzgerald?"

"A little. I did know, though. You looked like you were concentrating deeply. I'm very fond of that look."

Embarrassed now, Eleanor was glad to reach the door of Two Hoots and enter its warmth. She was amazed at the transformation she saw before her and exclaimed, "By the turn of my countenance! It seems that you were the one with a secret!"

The sitting room had been cleaned, and the furniture had been polished. Even the brass tips of the fire guard were gleaming like new. Whereas the cottage had once had a musty smell, it now was fresh and welcoming.

Eleanor declared, "I hope you haven't aired the cottage all day, catching your death."

## At Willows Edge

"I've done everything little by little, most of which I accomplished before I visited the vicar. I deeply contemplated the things you said for several hours after your last visit, and I decided that if you could pick yourself up after your ordeal last winter, I should be able to do it, too. You were my inspiration. I have been busy ever since."

"Well, you certainly have. I'm proud of you, dear man."

"Now, tell me what you've been thinking about so obsessively this evening. Come sit by the fire. I now have two comfortable chairs arranged there. Look, no one has to sit on the foot stool."

Eleanor draped her coat over a little chair, while Richard stirred the fire, added a log, and pushed the chairs a little closer to the blaze. They sat down together in the quiet warmth.

Eleanor looked fondly at Richard, who she could see was indeed feeling much better than the last time she'd seen him. She said cautiously, "At this moment, I'm not sure I should say anything at all. You look so well and happy; why should I risk reminding you of unpleasant things? Of course, if I'm right, that would be entirely another thing, but if I am completely off the mark, as I may well be, I would be doing you no favors at all."

## Meredith Kennon

"Suppose you tell me what you have on your mind. You can't keep it in, anyway," said Richard knowingly.

Eleanor nodded tentatively and then slowly drew an envelope from the pocket of her sweater. She said, "Do you remember when I told you that William had sent a letter written in another's hand?"

"Of course," said Richard, nodding encouragingly. As he did so, a lock of his gray hair fell over his hazel eyes, and he reached to push it back with his long fingers.

Thinking that Richard looked almost vulnerable, Eleanor said tentatively, "Jane left it with me along with a few notes, written by a friend of her doctor's, who put the letter under magnification. At the bottom of the letter, now smudged and unreadable, was what he thought was a signature. When Jane finally realized that the letter was not in William's own hand, she recognized that the smudges below might have significance. Until then, she had not given them any thought. I'll share with you his findings first, and then I'd like to read the letter to you."

Richard rose to turn on the lamp nearest Eleanor, and when she looked unsuccessfully in both pockets for her reading glasses, he found his on the book by his chair and presented them to her.

"Thank you," said Eleanor. "As I said, the

gentleman wrote in his notes that the writing at the bottom edge of the paper was most definitely a signature. He could make out only vaguely what some of the letters might be," said Eleanor, holding the paper beneath the light. She perched the over-sized, dark-rimmed glasses on her nose, as best she could, and read aloud, *"By comparing what can be seen in the smudged writing with the formation of the letters in the message above, certain letters can be made out with some exactness. This may not be helpful, but I am relatively certain that the last name begins with 'T' or possibly an 'F' and ends two tall letters that could be a combination of 'b, d, or l'. The first name is just an initial and could be many letters, I suppose, but I would gamble it's an 'A, O, or a Q'."*

Watching Richard trying to glean any significance, she said, "The letter was written from William's heart, but neither in his words, nor his hand. Whether he was sick, injured, or even absent, we don't know, but the person who wrote this letter must have known William very well and couldn't bear for him to miss an opportunity to write home."

After adjusting the reading glasses once again, Eleanor slowly and carefully read out the contents of the letter. *"Darling Jane, I have faith this letter finds you well, content, and most of all, safe. I pray the skies above you are guarded by angels and yearn for such a place myself. I cherish you and grieve that I have yet to meet our child, conceived in love. I think of you constantly during light of day and dream of you for hours each night. Your lovely face stays in my mind, your sweetness in my heart, unfaded by time. I trust the rest of the family is safe and well, to whom I also send my love, Yours only, William"*

Looking up and without fanfare, Eleanor removed the reading glasses and handed both the glasses and the letter to Richard.

He, in turn, put on the glasses and looked at the letter in his hand. There, in front of him, was the handwriting of none other than his own son, A. Fitzgerald. He looked up at Eleanor and nodded his head slowly and deliberately. In a trembling voice, he said only, "It's Alec's handwriting. I'd have known it anywhere."

Eleanor gasped and said, "That is what I'd hoped."

Reaching deep into his pocket for a handkerchief and taking off his glasses, Richard mopped his tearing eyes and said kindly, "Thank you for breaking this to me so carefully. When did you realize it might have been written by Alec?"

"Last night, in my sleep, the impression came to

me. I sat straight up in my bed, so strong was the revelation. I'd had all the pieces of information, but I'd not thought to put them together. I've never experienced anything like it; it was unworldly. Trying to sleep, I told myself that I was probably wrong, but I really did know it then, Richard. I just knew."

Richard nodded and stared at the fire. He mopped his eyes again, and Eleanor thought she heard a quiet sob escape him.

Touching his arm, she asked gently, "Are you going to be all right?"

"I'm sorry, Eleanor, for all this emoting. Now you know where Alec gets his dramatic tendencies." In an attempt to chuckle, another sob erupted from Richard, and finally, nodding reassuringly, indicating the worst was behind him, he said, "I have no words that could adequately thank you."

Eleanor said, "I'm not the one to thank. Alec's angels had more to do with it than I did. What would be the chances that our sons could end up in the same place and become friends?"

"Well," said Richard, "if both were in Singapore, they could have easily ended up in the same group of prisoners. It stands to reason that Alec should have known about the house in Englewood, because, long before the Fall of Singapore, he should have gotten our letter saying that we had bought the house and were going to the States. Just knowing they had family in the same part of England might have brought them together. It's amazing. I wish he'd had faith enough to send a letter to Two Hoots."

"Sometimes, hoping is too painful. I kept telling myself all day that it couldn't be, but deep in my heart, I knew."

Smiling meekly, Richard asked, "Would it be all right if we keep this information to ourselves for a bit?"

Eleanor nodded her agreement.

"Jane wouldn't need to know immediately?"

"She can wait. She'll be happy for you, but until she receives another letter from William, she won't rest easy, anyway. Besides, I'm not overly eager to confess that I showed you her love letter, although others have seen it by now."

"She's a lovely girl. I enjoyed talking to her."

"You helped her feel less awkward when she was here, Richard. I thank you for that."

He said, "I'd like to offer you something to drink and sit by the fire with you until dawn, but I suppose we should get back to Willows Edge. The Armstrongs will be waiting to take you home."

"Yes, they probably are."

They stood up, and Richard carefully pulled the chairs back a few inches from the fire and turned off the lamp. As he was helping Eleanor on with her coat in the dim light of the dying fire, he impulsively turned her to him and kissed her lips tenderly. He looked into her eyes for permission and kissed her again, and then again.

Holding Eleanor close to him, he whispered, "What a remarkable day."

Closing the door to Two Hoots behind them, Richard said flippantly, "We must do this more often. Do call again."

Eleanor's laugh rang out in the clear night, as they stepped onto the lush new grass in the moonlight. Richard took her hand and made for Willows Edge, from which the glowing lights seemed to shout, "Welcome, welcome, all is well."

## *Epilogue*

The Germans signed an unconditional surrender, and on the morning of May 8, 1945, Gilda got up early to make biscuits for the community celebration for Victory in Europe Day. It was being held that afternoon at Greystone Manor, to which Mrs. Wood had invited the entire village.

Gilda didn't get very far with her preparations, for within minutes of waking, a low, deep cramping required that she sit down. She settled herself somewhat comfortably on the cushions of the settee and waited for the pain to subside. Several minutes later, just as Gilda was going to resume her work in the kitchen, another pain hit her. There was no mistaking it, she thought, their baby was going to be born on VE Day.

As soon as Gilda was able, she went to the bedroom, where Thomas was enjoying a rare lie in.

She calmly asked, "Thomas, can you wake up?"

"Hm?" asked Thomas sleepily.

"I'm in labor, darling," said Gilda, crawling into bed beside him.

"Hm," said Thomas rolling on his side.

Seconds later, in some kind of delayed reaction, Gilda's words penetrated the fog of his mind, and Thomas jumped from the bed and into his trousers in a single leap.

"I'll get David right away," he said.

"I don't think you have to wake him. I just couldn't help waking you," admitted Gilda sheepishly. "It's still early. I'll be at this all day, I'm afraid."

"I'm sending for him. Don't move until I return."

Thomas set off at a run for Richard's cottage to use his telephone. He banged on the door for several minutes before rousing Richard, to whom Thomas gave the assignment of ringing the doctor at the manor.

At the manor, Eleanor had gotten up early, too, and was listening to the wireless, as she worked on some final details for the celebration she was hosting on the grounds that afternoon. She had waited almost six years for this victory, and she didn't intend to miss a single broadcast. She had listened when Germany announced that Hitler was believed dead, and she'd listened, with even greater excitement, to the news that the British had liberated Rangoon, Burma. Her thoughts were interrupted with the ringing of the telephone.

She answered and promised Richard that she would send David to Willows Edge immediately.

David's car was parked on the front drive, and Eleanor walked him to the door in her dressing gown to see him off. She made him promise to have regular updates sent to the manor and was amused when the good doctor raced down the drive with a spray of gravel, such was his concern for his favorite patient.

Returning to the kitchen, Eleanor noticed yesterday's post in a pile on the hall table. Eleanor marveled that she had paid it no mind the day before, but excitement had been running high for days. She flipped through the envelopes, most of which held little interest for her, until she paused at a letter from Mr. Jameson of Trubury, Herefordshire. Alarmed that something may have happened to Jane and Willy, Eleanor raced back into the kitchen, tearing the envelope as she went.

*Number 28, Bramble Avenue, Trubury, Herefordshire*
*May 5, 1945*
*Dear Mrs. Wood,*

*I hope this finds you well and as thrilled as we are to see the end of Hitler's terror. Good news comes from the Far East, too, which has been received here with great excitement. I'm writing you at the risk of angering Jane, but as she has not been able to make any important decisions, of late, I thought we could help her. I don't know whether or not she has informed you, but she and I are intending to lease out our two houses here and move to a new area. We will take a small house together, somewhere, and she will keep house for me until William's return.*

*I have suggested that we find a place near your home, possibly in Englewood or Nuneaton, but she is a little shy of mentioning it to you. Perhaps you might suggest such a thing yourself and pretend you thought of it on your own. I would surely appreciate it. It occurs to me that perhaps you have thought of it, already, but hated to pressure Jane, thus, my timely interference.*
*Yours truly,*
*Mr. Edgar Jameson*

Eleanor sat quietly, grateful that there were no airmen to feed. Having the celebration plans under control, mostly delegated to others by Edith because she had made plans to be gone with Larry today, Eleanor listened to the wireless and reread the letter, glancing at the clock to see if it was too early to place a call to Jane.

She finally decided to get dressed, and as she was leaving the kitchen to do so, the telephone rang. It was Richard saying that Gilda's labor was going well.

Eleanor promised she would stay near the telephone all morning until the day's activities began outside. After that, she said, he'd have to come to the manor with the updates. Richard laughed quietly and promised to ring again when there was news of any kind.

As soon as Eleanor sat down, the telephone rang again. It was Jane. She had received a letter from William the day before, but hadn't been home until late to see it. She said, "He got my letter, Mrs. Wood. He said, in his own handwriting, I might add, that he and his English comrades, Ed and Alec were helping one another endure. He referred to Willy and our future plans, and he sent his love to you and Edith, of course."

"Oh, Jane, that's marvelous news! What are you doing today to celebrate?"

"Not much, really. I've been busy clearing out the attic at the house. I'm leaving Trubury and renting out my house. Mr. Jameson convinced me, for Willy's sake, as well as my own."

Seizing her opportunity, Eleanor asked, "Have you ever thought about moving nearer to Greystone? I would love to be of use to you. I could help with Willy from time to time, you know. If you were close by, it would be wonderful, wouldn't it? Of course, I don't want to pressure you at all."

"I don't feel pressured. It sounds lovely. Mr.

Jameson will be glad to learn of it. I'm going to keep house for him; he's ready to leave here, too."

"Well, you certainly have been busy. How is Willy doing?"

"He's talking nonstop," said Jane, laughing.

"I miss you both," said Eleanor. "Edith would have loved the chance to talk to you, but she is celebrating elsewhere with Larry today. We have some excitement here, too. We are hosting the local celebration at the manor and also expect Gilda's baby to be born today. She's been in labor since early this morning."

"Oh, tell her I'm happy for her. And say hello to Edith and the others. I'll run along; I just wanted you to know about the letter."

"I don't know how I'll get through our festivities today with all this excitement."

Jane said, "I know just how you feel."

"I know you do. Thank you so much for ringing me with the wonderful news."

That afternoon, at Willows Edge, Gilda delivered a healthy baby boy. Richard telephoned the news to the manor, glad that Sam had been in the house to answer it.

Two hours later, relieved that the manor festivities were finally over, Priscilla and Eleanor walked to Willows Edge. They entered to find Richard and Thomas in the sitting room, where they had a quiet celebration already in progress.

As greetings were exchanged, Richard eyed Eleanor closely, knowing her to be bursting with some news or another. He determined that he would use whatever tactics necessary to get it out of her, perhaps later that evening, alone, at his cottage. He smiled mischievously at her, and she nudged him to behave. They had told no one of their budding relationship, and Eleanor wanted it to stay that way, for the time being.

Agnes and Simon Morris had been there and gone, so David allowed Priscilla and Eleanor into the bedroom to see the newborn. He closed the door behind him and joined the men in the sitting room.

Gilda's eyes glistened with pride and joy, for in her arms, wrapped in the white shawl, was a beautiful baby boy. His perfectly shaped head was covered with dark hair, and although he was fast asleep now and showing his eyes to no one, Gilda reported that David had predicted that he had gotten Thomas's eyes. She pointed out that he was perfect, and without disturbing him, Gilda unwrapped him enough to expose his complete sets of fingers and toes.

Simultaneously, the women asked, "May I hold him?"

A burst of laughter woke the infant, and he opened his eyes to treat his devoted onlookers with a display of facial expressions that only a newborn can produce.

Gilda handed the baby to his grandmother, who gazed into his perfect little face and asked, "Have you and Thomas decided on a name?"

"We are calling him Jeremy Simon Gardner. What do you think of it?"

Priscilla tearfully nodded her approval, and Eleanor answered for both, saying, "It's perfect, Gilda, just as he is."

## About the Author

Meredith Kennon (a pseudonym) was born in Aberdeen, South Dakota, and grew up on a farm near there, enjoying all the blessings that such an upbringing affords. She and her husband of forty-one years have six children and many grandchildren. She now lives in a small town in southeastern South Dakota and travels with her husband on consulting assignments around the United States.

She is presently working on *Return to Greystone,* the third in her Greystone Series, which began with *Almost Enough*, followed by *At Willows Edge*.

She welcomes comments from her readers on her Meredith Kennon Facebook page and on her blog, meredithkennon.blogspot.com, which links to sites where her books can be purchased both hardcopy and electronically.

Made in the USA
Charleston, SC
29 September 2010